LARGER
than
LIFE

LARGER *than* LIFE

ALISON KENT

KENSINGTON PUBLISHING CORP.
http://www.kensingtonbooks.com

BRAVA BOOKS are published by

Kensington Publishing Corp.
850 Third Avenue
New York, NY 10022

All Kensington titles, imprints, and distributed lines are available at special quantity discounts for bulk purchases for sales promotion, premiums, fund-raising, educational or institutional use. Special book excerpts or customized printings can also be created to fit specific needs. For details, write or phone the office of the Kensington Special Sales Manager: Kensington Publishing Corp., 850 Third Avenue, New York, NY 10022. Attn. Special Sales Department. Phone: 1-800-221-2647.

ISBN 0-7582-1112-0

First Kensington Trade Paperback Printing: June 2005
10 9 8 7 6 5 4 3 2 1

Printed in the United States of America

To Kate Duffy,
'Nuff said

Acknowledgments

This book, though based in fact, is purely fiction. I've twisted and bent and distorted and warped the inspiration into the end product. Such is the stuff of make-believe.

As always, I can't do a damn thing without Jan Freed holding my hand and vetting every word.

I'd like to thank Jill Shalvis for the emergency early read, Jolie Kramer, too. Jolie, in fact, deserves further recognition. She taught me to pace and to plot. In that regard, Cherry Adair helped as well, though she may not even know it.

To my critters, Emma Gads, Larissa Ione, Lydia Joyce. Thanks bunches!

And special smoochies to my family for putting up with a woman who lives in the closet, rarely cooks, never cleans, seldom listens, but loves you all very very much!

Myra Fleener: *A man your age comes to a place like this, either he's running away from something or he has nowhere else to go.*

Coach Norman Dale: *What I'm doing here has nothing to do with you.*

—*Hoosiers* (1986)

Prologue

"Run, Liberty! Run, run, run!"

She couldn't run because she couldn't see where she was going. Didn't he get that? She couldn't breathe. She couldn't think. He was out of his mind.

"Jase, I can't!" She sobbed, choked, stopped, and wailed, "I can't!"

She spit hair from out of her mouth, spit dirt, swore she spit bugs. It was gross and disgusting, and he was never going to get away with what he'd done anyway, so why did *she* have to run?

Jase came back to where she stood clawing her hair from her face. He grabbed her wrist and jerked her forward, practically breaking her arm. "You better move your ass or I'm going to leave you here, got it?"

She nodded, whimpered, stumbled along behind him. She was wearing her best pair of sandals and she'd spent all afternoon doing her toenails for tonight's date. And now it was all ruined.

Ruined.

Ruined because Jase was stupid and greedy. Stealing money from the printing and office supply store where he worked—what was wrong with him? They paid him more than minimum wage, good enough money to take her out for a salad and Diet Coke anytime she wanted to go.

All he had to do was make the store's deliveries and daily deposits, running some of the money into Carlsbad or El Paso because of the banks being bigger or something like that. Why did he have to be stupid enough to take what wasn't his? Why did she have to—

"Jase!" She tripped, wrenched her wrist from his hand, and went down to the ground in the dark. Dirt clods and rocks the size of Lego pieces dug into her hands and her knees.

She pushed up to a kneeling position, picked the grit from her palms. Tears blurred her eyes and made it impossible to see anything. It was too dark to see anything anyway. The moon was out, but they were in the middle of freakin' nowhere on his father's ranch.

She just *knew* they were lost, and wished at least they were lost on an island with a beach like those people on that show she used to watch before her parents got religion and banned TV from the house. She hated Texas and was never going to forgive either of them for moving her away from California and all of her friends.

Jase skidded to his knees beside her, throwing more dust into the air for her to gag on. She tried not to cough, tried not to cry. She even held back yelling at him for being so dumb since it hadn't done any good so far. But then he pulled her head to his chest and cuddled her close, and she forgot why she was mad.

This was all she wanted, being with a boy who liked her, away from her parents and the stupid way they tried to run her life, even though she knew she was really lucky. A bunch of girls her age at school had been promised by their parents to men old enough to be their fathers.

Men already married to two or three other women. It

made her sick to her stomach to even think about it! Like, who would want to sleep with a guy and get sloppy seconds?

"Liberty, listen." Jase set her away from him, lifted her chin. "I know you're tired and scared, but we're almost there. We've got to be. I just didn't know it would take so long on foot. I'm usually on my ATV."

Yeah. Not to mention he was usually stoned since he used the hunting blind to smoke pot. "They're going to find us anyway."

"Maybe." He sat back, rubbed his hands up and down his thighs, the denim all scratchy and loud in the really quiet wide open spaces. "But maybe we can hide out until this shit blows over."

Dumb. He was dumb, dumb, dumb. And she was dumb to hang out with him.

"It's not going to blow over, Jase. Your boss is going to send Holden Wagner after you, you know that. Holden freakin' Wagner! God! He takes care of all the legal stuff with the businesses in town, and he'll take care of you, too!" She pulled away, curled into a ball on the ground, totally ruining her outfit.

Holden Wagner was a big-shot lawyer in Earnestine Township where she and Jase lived, and one of the most powerful men she'd ever met. Everyone knew him from the church and from around town, Earnestine being such a dinky dot on the map and Holden being the only lawyer and into everybody's business.

A lot of girls at school thought he was hot. Liberty supposed he was. He was only like thirty-five or something, and wore clothes that she'd never seen anywhere but in *People Magazine* or on the People's Choice Awards.

But still! He could turn a molehill of evidence into a big fat mountain and put Jase away forever! Then what would she do? Who would she have to date? How would she ever get away from this dump? She didn't have anyone else on her side!

Jase tried to clear his throat. "Yeah, well, Holden's not really the one I'm worried about."

Liberty heard the break in his voice and grew still. "What do you mean, he's not the one you're worried about? Who else is there?"

"Holden may be all powerful, but even he can't get away with murder. I'm not so sure that's the case with the guys I'm dealing with here. The amount of money I took? It can't be legal, which means they won't be going to the sheriff. They'll be taking care of it themselves."

She sat up slowly, her ears ringing with the word murder. *Murder!* Her heart thudded in her throat until she thought she would never again be able to breathe.

"Jase? What's going on?" Her hands were shaking so badly, she drew up her legs to her chest and tucked her fingers in the pits of her knees. Her voice cracked and she barely managed to whisper, "Tell me what's going on."

Jase sighed, hung his head. Light from the moon made his bleached blond hair look white, the spikes look like tufts of dead grass. The hoop in his ear sparkled. Sweat ran down his cheeks from his temples. "It wasn't only a couple grand like I said."

"What are you talking about?" *Oh my god, oh my god, oh my god!*

"It was a couple *hundred* grand. There's no way it was all the store's money."

She started rocking back and forth where she sat. "You stole two hundred thousand dollars?"

He shoved both hands through his hair, clamped them down on top of his head. "The deposit slip said one thing, but there was an extra two hundred G's in the bag."

"So you just kept it? Not even knowing whose it was?"

She sounded hysterical. Shoot, she *was* hysterical! "What is wrong with you? What were you thinking?"

"I was thinking about us, Lib," he yelled back, really screaming now. His voice echoed in the night. "I was thinking about you. I want us to get out of here. Me off the ranch and away from my dad. You so far away from your parents that they could never force you to marry some old geezer."

He was rocking now, too, and almost crying. "This town is fucked up, Lib. Pastor Straight's hold over everyone is insane. It's like a commune or a cult, and the way the church treats the women is as bad as the Taliban. I'm not going to stay here. I want you to come with me. We only have to hide out a few days, wait for whoever the money belongs to to lose our trail, then we can hitch to Mexico."

Everything he was saying suddenly made so much sense. She'd been so wrong. He wasn't stupid. Not if he could get her out of here. He was smart, and she decided then that she loved him and wanted to be with him forever. "Don't you think they'll look for you in the hunting blind?"

"No, see, that's the beauty of this." He scooted closer, excited now. "My dad tore down the blind two seasons back. He hasn't leased out that plot since and has no idea I put it back up and come out here all the time."

She didn't respond right away, and he went on. "We'll only stay tonight if it makes you feel better. We'll hide out long enough to come up with another plan. That's all we've gotta do, Lib. That's all."

His desperation tugged at her heartstrings like he was playing music just for her. "Okay, okay. But I broke the thong on my shoe and have to go barefoot. I don't know if I can keep up with you."

He got to his feet, brushed dirt from the butt and knees of his jeans. "C'mon. I'll piggyback you."

He was so totally cute sometimes. She shook her head. She could do this. She could. "No, I'll be fine." She pulled off the scarf she'd wrapped around her waist like a belt. "I'll just tie the shoe to my foot—"

"Shh. Listen." He backed a couple of steps away. "Do you hear that?"

She did. A diesel engine grinding hard as the truck it belonged to fought the uneven terrain. She knew the sound well. Eighty percent of Earnestine's population of just under four thousand drove the same.

She finished tying her shoe to her foot, though she didn't know why she bothered. They'd issue her some pair of tacky granny lace-ups in jail, because back in California she'd watched enough cop shows to know she'd be charged as an accessory. Unless she was killed, too, she thought with a big, fat, ugly-sounding sob.

"Stay here," Jase ordered. "Don't move. I'm going to draw them away."

"No, Jase!" Panic rose in her throat and tasted like the bad, cheesy ranch dressing she'd had on her salad at the Dairy Barn.

"I'll lose them and circle back to get you. Just stay put."

He would never find this place again. She'd be lost out here forever. "Wait! I'll come with you!"

But he was already running away. "I love you, Liberty. I love you!"

"Jase, no!" She couldn't even see him anymore. He'd vanished into the darkness. She was alone with dirt and rocks and creepy crawly things. This was all so sucky and so so stupid.

The truck was getting closer. She could hear the gears shifting, hear men shouting. Shaking like mad, she wrapped her arms around her knees and tucked her chin to her chest, praying Jase was as fast dodging tumbleweeds as he was dodging tackles on the football field.

A second later she heard a loud thudding pop. What looked like a bottle rocket arched up and burst in the sky. A flare, she realized, just as she heard the voices yelling.

"There he is!"

"Get the sonofabitch!"

"Go, go, go!"

The driver gunned the truck, drowning out any further words she might've heard. She felt the dampness on her cheeks only when her tears soaked into the knees of her jeans.

The second shot she heard was not from a flare gun. Neither were the three that followed. When she heard Jase scream, her entire body jolted. When she heard laughter and howling, she began to shake uncontrollably.

It wasn't until she heard footsteps behind her that she managed to go blessedly numb.

She lifted her chin, lifted her gaze, watched the figure of a man come toward her like a ghost out of the dark. Once he was near enough for her to see him better, her being numb came in handy. She couldn't react. Not to his camo fatigues. Not to his assault rifle. Not to the knife hanging from his belt halfway down his thigh.

When he reached her, he held out a hand. She gave him her fingers, eerily white against his black skin, and he pulled her to her feet. Then he pointed toward the sky.

"Do you know of the North Star, Miss Mitchell?"

Oh, God, he knew her name. *He knew her name!* It sounded strange when he said it; his accent reminded her of the rapper Sean Paul that Jase was constantly listening to. It was like Jamaican or something . . .

"Miss Mitchell? The North Star?"

She nodded, her teeth chattering as she found the point in the sky. "My folks used to take me and my brother camping when we lived in California. Before they got all into Jesus and we moved here." At least here she'd met Jase. They were like two peas in a pod, both hating Earnestine.

Or at least they had been . . . "What happened to Jase? Where is he? He didn't mean anything bad by taking that money. We just both want to get out of this town—"

"You must do what I say now, Miss Mitchell, and not worry about your Mr. Bremmer. Do you understand?" He took her by the shoulders, turned her to face him. "There is nothing you can do for him now."

She nodded, tears welling in her eyes, wondering if her hair would look as good as his did in dreadlocks, wondering if she would ever see Jase again, wondering where she was going to go because she couldn't go home.

Wondering how anyone could be so nice when he took the bandana from his head and used it to wipe the tears from her cheeks.

"You follow the North Star for an hour and you will come to the county highway. You walk and you do not speak of tonight to anyone. You do not ask questions. You act as if none of what you heard or saw happened. If you do, you may very possibly die. And I may very possibly be the one to kill you. Do you understand?"

She didn't understand anything. "Nothing," she wanted to scream. Instead she asked, "Where am I supposed to go?"

"You are only supposed to walk. That is all that you can do." He placed his hand in the middle of her back and pushed. "Now go. Go before it is too late."

She'd only gone twenty steps when her shoe came off. She was not going to be able to walk like this for an hour and turned back to tell him so, but he was nowhere to be seen.

God, if her parents hadn't gotten all righteous and moved here for the family's spiritual good, she would have dozens of places to go and people to help her. If she actually made it to the highway, maybe she could hitch to El Paso and find a library where she could get on the Internet.

She had to find that website. The one she'd overheard Sherry Petersen whisper about to Teresa Monaghan the day after Sherry's sister went missing and her wedding to Mr. Gaston was canceled.

Sherry swore her sister was with the woman who ran the rescue shelter for girls escaping the arranged marriages in Earnestine. What was it? *What was it?*

All Liberty could remember was something about a barn.

One

One week later

The structure shimmered like a mirage on the horizon.

Waves of heat danced above the hard-packed earth and around the hulking concrete bunker, nondescript, deceptive. A squat bulge like a pregnant belly atop the life teeming below, where the Spectra IT command center monitored the crime syndicate's Western U.S. activity.

And where the syndicate's filthy lucre was sent to begin the process of laundering. Deposits here, wire transfers there. This bank, that bank. Tricky sleights of hand.

Mick Savin dropped his binoculars and squinted against New Mexico's fireball of a sun glaring angrily over the Chihuahuan Desert. He was barely over the Texas border, but the bloody bitch in heat seemed to beat down with twice the number of red-hot hammers she had fifteen miles ago.

He'd left his Range Rover parked just inside the gate off U.S. Highway 62 and had hoofed it the two hours it had taken to get here—here being deep inside the seventy thousand acres of working cattle ranch that served as Spectra's cover.

His own cover, provided by the Smithson Group, the covert spy organization paying him a hell of a hefty salary, was that of a hunter scoping out prime locations for mule deer season. He had his paperwork in order and every reason to be exactly where he was . . . almost.

His leased plot, the one designated in the documents above the Rover's driver's-side visor, was approximately sixteen clicks north. The fact that he'd run across the bunker's location at all was pure dumb luck.

Up until a month ago, he'd been chasing leads gathered in Coahuila, Mexico, by Smithson Group operatives Eli McKenzie and Harry van Zandt. The pair had managed to nail down a nice hard body of evidence before the explosion—the one that had wiped the holding center for Spectra's kidnapping and prostitution ring off the map along with a good chunk of Smithson intel.

All these weeks later, and Mick was still blowing the stench of that fireball out of his nose. The trail he'd most recently been following, the one that had brought him to New Mexico to begin with, was part of the continuing effort to tie up the loose ends of the mission that had kept Eli and Rabbit in Mexico for months.

Three days ago, Mick had been in Carlsbad looking for the missing girl that Stella Banks, Eli's woman, had originally headed south of the border to find, when he'd picked up thirty seconds of a scrambled communication.

In a panic, he'd relayed it to Manhattan and to Tripp Shaughnessey at the communications desk in the SG-5 ops center. Tripp had only been able to narrow the broadcast to an area boxed in roughly by Fort Bliss, Alamogordo, Denver City, and Odessa.

SG-5 had hustled to get Mick in, get him outfitted, and done so quick-like-a-bunny once they'd narrowed down the location of the Spectra IT command center. Mick had taken it from there . . . and ended up here.

He eased from his stomach onto his side and let out two sharp bursts of a whistle. FM, the herd dog mix he'd picked up at the El Paso pound, trotted over on monstrous feet, shoulders rolling, tongue lolling inches from the ground.

The dog had been the final addition to Mick's cover, and so far man and beast had bonded enough that he'd stopped thinking of returning the mutt to his original fate. Then again, he didn't exactly see FM fitting in at SG-5's headquarters in Manhattan.

Hell, as it was, *he* barely fit in in Manhattan. He did a lot better making his way in and out of the Bronx, and figured if he kept the dog, he might get with Hank Smithson about retiring FM to the Smithson Group principal's Saratoga County horse farm.

After all, the mutt had been recruited as an SG-5 operative. Like Mick himself. And like the others—Christian, Tripp, Julian, Kelly John, Eli, and Harry. And, once this mission was done, if it all went down as planned, FM would've earned the doggie retirement.

"C'mere, F."

The dog plopped onto his belly, haunches raised and ready, tail busting a move like nobody's business. Mick couldn't help but grin as he slipped the flash card from his camera into one of several slots cut into the sturdy leather collar ringing FM's solid neck and disappearing into his thick ruff.

"Whew, dude. You are in desperate need of hosing down." The dog's mouth clamped shut, his ears perked as far as floppy triangles could, his bright brown eyes grew sharp. Once Mick had gotten a whiff of more than dog, he took the comeback to heart. "Yeah. You're right. Me, too."

At that, FM started in with the smiling panting thing he did, doing a belly crawl closer as if he couldn't get enough of Mick's love. And since Mick wasn't getting any love anywhere, he let him.

"Yeah, okay, that's enough. It's time to go." He rolled up

into a sitting position and reached for his canteen, poured a good long pull onto a stone that was smooth and bowled in the center. "We've got a bloody long hike back to the truck, so drink up, mate."

FM lumbered to his feet like the old fart he was and lapped up the water. Mick, his bones feeling just as ancient and creaky, did the same, tilting back his head, tilting up the canteen, cooling off with what water he didn't swallow then capping the rest for later.

His eyes were closed and he was using his bandana to mop them free of water when the dog first growled. It was a fierce sound. A terrifying sound. A gut-curdling, ball-shriveling sound that he hadn't heard since recruiting the mutt. He'd be damn well happy not to feel it shiver through his bones again in this lifetime.

Bloody hell. "F, what is your problem?"

And then he heard it, too. He heard it long before he saw it. His ears were clear, his eyes still blinking away the salty sting of sweat and the clean wash of water. An engine. An ATV. Roaring as the driver guided the four-wheel-drive utility vehicle over the rough and rocky landscape.

Make that two drivers gunning two ATVs over the rough and rocky landscape.

He settled his sunglasses back in place, making sure the sports strap around his head was secure, then bent and snagged his backpack and khaki outback hat from the ground. As the dog moved to stand protectively in front of him, he jammed his hat into place.

Reaching to scratch between FM's ears with one hand, he held the strap of his pack with the other, lifting it onto the toe of one boot. His nape tingled in that way it had of telling him he wasn't going to like much of anything about to go down here.

The first ATV pulled up on his left, the second on his right. Both drivers wore ball caps pulled low, reflective lenses,

Wranglers, hiking boots, and snap-front, short-sleeved, Western-cut shirts in hideously ugly plaids. They also wore weapons that didn't fit the theme.

Weapons he'd seen most recently on the streets of Kabul and Baghdad. Spectra thugs, he quickly determined. If not, he was a monkey bone's uncle.

"Howdy, mates." He raised a hand in greeting as they left their rides running and approached on foot. "Hard to believe having navigated my way around the world, but I'm bloody well convinced that I'm lost."

"Mr. Savin?"

Mick nodded, his nape itching and twitching fiercely enough now that he had to resist the urge to scratch at the bugs that weren't really there crawling over his skin. "That would be me."

"We located your vehicle back at the road, but you weren't on your lease." This from the first one's clone.

"Well, I'm damn glad you found us, or me and the mutt might've ended up walking in circles for days."

Clone one nodded. Clone two, being a clone, did the same. Somehow Mick wasn't mollified. The reflective lenses, he decided. He couldn't see their eyes. Couldn't see what was going on in their Spectra-washed brains.

FM wasn't so handicapped. His ruff stood in a fierce ring around his neck. A feral growl rumbled from his body into Mick's where the dog now sat on his foot.

Number one spoke next, while number two returned to his ATV. "We won't let that happen."

"Good deal, eh, dog?" Mick bent, scratched F's ears again, calming the animal as best he could. He needed the dog. He couldn't afford to have him go off on the clone brothers and risk getting himself shot. Not with all the surveillance intel stored in his collar.

In the end, Mick should've been more in tune to his partner's instincts. When the dog growled and lunged forward, he grabbed for his collar and missed seeing the rope. Number one swung the butt of his rifle, caught the mutt in the jaw. FM whimpered and went sprawling.

The rope sailed through the air and cinched Mick's arms tight against his upper body. "What the bloody fuck is going on, mates?" he growled. "I don't remember reading about this particular guided tour in your brochure."

Number two, at the other end of the rope, jerked Mick down to the ground. "What you did read was that trespassers would be shot."

From where he sat, Mick felt a surge of panic burst at the base of his spine and rise. "Trespassers, mate. Not poor lost fucks getting used to the terrain."

A second rope appeared in the hands of number one. Wordlessly, he sauntered over like a man with all the time in the world, a man loving his job, and used one end of the rope to bind Mick's feet.

That done, he tossed the other end to his partner, who gloated like a big bad steer wrestler having thrown his quarry to the dirt—the problem being that Mick didn't much like the impotent comparison.

He cast a quick glance at FM as the dog stirred where he'd crumpled two meters away. The sigh of relief Mick started to breathe was sucked quickly away, however, when the first clone produced a hunting knife and returned. The muscles between Mick's shoulder blades seized, relaxing only marginally once the other man made his intentions known, slicing into Mick's backpack.

He swore under his breath, grimacing as the pack was upended and the contents—camera, satellite phone, binoculars, energy bars—tumbled to the ground. Losing the equipment was a pain in the ass, but the real issue was the pack. He'd secreted away too many tools of his trade in the padded straps and thick leather base.

Clone one tossed away the pack like yesterday's garbage,

squatted to examine the contents. He looped the binoculars around his neck, the camera strap over one shoulder, shoved the phone into a pocket. After a sniff at one of the energy bars, he left those on the ground.

And then he grinned at Mick and pushed up to his feet. "We're going to escort you back to your truck now, Mr. Savin. And hopefully next time you won't be so quick to get yourself lost."

Jesus bloody hell. He grabbed tightly to the taut rope circling his upper body, dug the heels of his boots into the ground. But his palms were already sweating, already slipping. He was unbelievably fucked. "I'm good with walking, mates. Seriously. Just point me the right direction and you won't see me back until opening day."

He watched—impotently—as the two men climbed onto their vehicles, his only saving grace the fact that one man held both ropes, saving him from being ripped apart. He'd simply be dragged to his death instead. The clones revved their engines, laughed like hyenas, revved them again.

He had a switchblade strapped to one calf, his SIG to the other, no time or way to get to either. He wasn't worried about shooting or stabbing himself; the holster and sheath were both secured. But either one would've gone a long way toward stopping this crazy shit before it got started.

Then it was too late. One hard jarring tug, and he was on his way to the great ops center in the sky. He did what he could to stay upright, to use his ass as a snowboard, but at the first awkward jerk of his legs, he went down.

He felt his shoulder go out first, two of his ribs seconds later. A shearing, shredding land mine of fire gutted the upper half of his body. He barely managed to hang onto the rope with one hand, to keep his head off the ground, his chin to his chest.

He shoved his useless fingers into his pants to keep his entire limb from dragging the ground and tearing away, and prayed the terrain would keep the machines from topping out their speed. He failed to take into account the duality of the mean streaks running down the bonehead clones' spines. They knew every bump, rock, and crater and hit them all.

Heat and dust and pain engulfed his hips, his knees, his torso. His spine stretched, threatened to snap. His head bobbed, smacked back. The cowboys up ahead yee-hawed. He thought briefly of FM, briefly of his Smithson Group partners and Hank, briefly of all the women he'd never known.

And then he didn't think of anything anymore.

If not for the dog, she never would have stopped.

She would have kept on driving, lost in thought—she had enough going on in her life to remain indefinitely, permanently mentally adrift—and man and beast would have both ended up as buzzard bait.

But Neva Case had always been a sucker for the underdog—canines included—and so she pulled her gleaming black, dual-axle, crew-cab pickup to the grassy shoulder, shoved open the driver's-side door, and jumped down.

"C'mon, pooch. Let's see what you're all about," she crooned softly, circling around the truck's bed to where the dog, a blue heeler mix—the markings were right, the fur too thick and too long to be pure—struggled to his feet to warn her off.

His growl was feeble, making her doubly glad she'd stopped. "You look a bit on the wobbly side, pooch. How long have you been out here?"

She took a step closer, leaned down and held out a hand to share her scent. His snarl lessened. His bared teeth vanished. He whimpered slightly, and when her next step took her closer, he offered his head to be scratched. She did, checking the tags on his collar, her hand coming away covered in blood.

"Oh, my." She squatted in front of him, let him give her a closer inspection while she carefully examined him, looking for a wound, finding a nasty gash along his lower jaw and a lump the size of half a Ruby Red grapefruit. "I see a visit to Doc Hill in your immediate future, pooch. Maybe he'll know where you belong. Your tags don't even tell me your name."

"FM."

Her head snapped up. Her gaze honed in on the voice, searching the highway's shoulder between the road and the property line. She pushed up to her feet, made her way around the far side of the truck.

A man lay in the scrub brush halfway between the barbed wire fence and her front bumper. His clothes and skin were coated with dust as if he'd been discarded like so much garbage a day or so ago.

No one besides those dumping trash had reason to stop on this long stretch of rural highway between New Mexico and Texas. Trucks pulled stock trailers. Trucks hauled hay bales and feed. Trucks barreled from one one-horse town to another without a single law officer looking their way.

If not for the dog . . . If she hadn't stopped . . . She swallowed to clear away the borrowed trouble weighing heavily in her throat and picked her away slowly through the knee-high brush.

"Oh, dear. Oh, my." He couldn't be more than half alive. "Oh, hell."

One arm lay at an angle in which it was never meant to bend. She winced at that, winced at the streaks of blood on his face and his nearly shaved head. His chest barely rose when he pulled in a breath. In fact, he didn't breathe at all for so long she thought he had died while she'd been standing there staring. His clothes were shredded, the cord of his hat tangled around his neck with his sunglasses' strap.

Moving him could be risky. Leaving him here while she

went for help more so. He was obviously drifting in and out of consciousness; right now, he appeared dead to the world. If not simply dead. She reached down to loosen the constriction beneath his Adam's apple.

His eyes flew open, and she stopped, her fingers on the very hot skin of his throat. He didn't speak, he didn't move, he didn't blink. He just stared, his gaze intense in a way that unnerved her when she considered his condition. It was as if his entire life was flashing before his eyes . . .

Damn him! He had better not die on her now.

"I'm going to load you and your dog into my truck and get you both to a doctor." She went back to work on the uncomfortable binding that couldn't be making it easy for him to breathe. "I'm not sure how smart it is to move you, but I can't leave you here."

He didn't respond except to close his eyes. She was fairly sure the response wasn't one voluntarily made. He was out of it again, which was probably a good thing since there was no way she'd be able to get him into her truck without a lot of undignified manhandling.

She walked back to where she had parked, let down the tailgate, and considered her options along with the boxes of supplies she'd picked up in Carlsbad stacked in the bed. Twine, beads, filament, stones to be polished, charms, crystals, jewelry hardware, and more of the same.

The only thing she could do with any of that would be to accessorize him. She did, however, have a rope, a blanket, and a come-along behind her second seat, as well as two six-foot, one-by-twelve planks she'd picked up for Candy's new workbench. Neva figured those would go a long way toward getting him where he needed to be.

He was a big man, she'd guess a bit over six feet tall, and at the moment at least two hundred pounds of dead weight. This was not going to be easy. Moving him even a little bit would hurt him like hell were he aware of her lugging him around like a feed sack.

From the cab, she grabbed the rope and the blanket and tossed both out the passenger-side door to the ground. The come-along needed to be positioned where she could get the right leverage to muscle him up the plank ramp.

She hopped from the bumper into the bed and fastened the hook and ratchet end to the stake hole on the driver's side nearest the cab. That done, she released the tension on the strap and reeled it out until there was no strap left to reel, finally tossing it to hang over the open tailgate.

Once she'd jumped to the ground, she slid one of the planks out of the bed, leaned it on the tailgate, and wedged it into the shoulder's hard-packed dirt. Dusting her hands together, she then grabbed up the blanket and rope and returned to the man.

He hadn't moved or regained consciousness, and she hoped she wasn't about to do him more harm than good. She could radio Candy, of course, and have her send out Doc Hill. But he'd have to close the clinic and make the trip, and then basically do what Neva was already set up to do.

Besides, waiting for Ed to get here would drive her totally nuts. She had absolutely no tolerance for delay and very little patience these days for anything, especially since the first brick of what she'd thought was her very safe world had recently come huffing and puffing and blowing down around her.

She laid out the rope in a wide zigzag then unfolded the blanket on top, arranging the setup as close to the man as possible before moving to stand at his feet. Taking hold of his ankles, she slowly lifted his hips, sidled over, and lowered him onto the blanket.

He lay awkwardly crossways, and with that arm at the

angle it was, she hesitated on how best to straighten him out. She stared down into his dirty face for a moment, at his dark brows that furrowed even while he was passed out, at the stubble of both beard and hair, at his lips which were dry, cracked, parched. She had a bottle of water in the cab—no, she needed to move him while he remained oblivious.

The dog, FM, sat at the fence line watching, his lolling tongue nudging her to hurry. He needed water, too. The man's mangled arm was fortunately on the far side. Standing on the blanket, she slid one hand beneath his nape and the other beneath his shoulder until she reached his spine.

Squatting to lift with her legs, she hefted his weight up and over and promptly fell flat on her ass. She groaned at the thud, and the rush of air from her lungs. All this time she'd been so proud of her upper body strength. Too bad her balance was shot, but at least he was on the blanket.

It was when she got back to her feet, had swathed him like a mummy and was binding him up, that she saw him watching her again. She stopped, stared, wanting to reassure him without frightening him because the look in his eyes spoke of pure panic. Could she blame him? Unable to move and faced with a wild-looking, freckled, and redheaded Amazon?

She moved nearer his head and, smiling, crouched down. "I'm Neva. I'm getting ready to winch you up into my truck and take you to the doctor."

"The dog?" he croaked out.

"Let me get you some water—"

"The dog?" he demanded again, this time sharply, gruffly, expending so much effort he ended up closing his eyes.

"Him, too. Though he is in better shape than you look to be."

"His collar?"

She frowned, glanced over to where the dog now sat half-crouched, his tail sweeping back and forth. "Still there." Though she knew from checking earlier that the tags showed only vaccine information and a shelter address. Nothing about his current owner.

When she looked back, the man was again unconscious, and so she wasted no time hoisting the end of the rope coiled around his ankles over her shoulder and dragging his heavy body to the truck.

Once there, she lifted his legs onto the slanted plank, wrapped the come-along strap around his ankles, secured the hook, and climbed up into the bed. After ratcheting the slack until the strap drew taut, she tucked into the lever with the full force of her one hundred forty pounds and winched him up one slow quarter at a time.

When his head finally hit the truck bed, her biceps were screaming, her shoulders burning, and sweat ran like the Rio Grande into her eyes. She didn't even bother removing the strap or the rope or the blanket from her living bundle. She simply jumped to the ground and snapped her fingers at the dog. He trotted over, bounded up the ramp, and settled in at his master's side.

Neva slid the plank next to the duo and latched the tailgate. She did make one last circle around the truck to make sure she wasn't leaving anything, forgetting anything, or missing anything belonging to the man. That done, she climbed behind the wheel and collapsed—but only for the thirty seconds she allowed herself to catch her breath.

She had no time to stop and smell roses, lilies, or even manure, and so she turned the key in the ignition and put the rig on the road. And then she reached over and turned off the CB radio before it had a chance to crackle to life. Candy was waiting on the supplies and wouldn't be happy with the delay or with Neva being incommunicado.

But Candy would just have to deal. As long as she'd lived and worked with Neva, as far back as their relationship went, the duality of their backgrounds on which it was based, any upset suffered wouldn't last long, leaving Neva to let that worry go and focus on the one in the here and now.

Because there was something about the added cargo in the bed of the truck that left her itchy and rubbing the backs of her fingers beneath her chin. If she hadn't already been in a precarious position, looking over her shoulder at every pin she heard drop, finding him wouldn't have caused a blip in the circle of her personal radar.

And more than likely a simple explanation existed for the condition of her mummy man. Unfortunately, she couldn't come up with anything that worked in context. Had she found him busted all to hell up in a parking garage or behind a club or in a halfway house in Houston where she'd once lived, that would be one thing. This was another.

He was out of place. One hundred percent out of his element. Staring at the endless road ahead, she thought back to what she had seen. The goatee and mustache that were clipped and shaped, while the rest of his beard was a day's growth waiting to be shaved. The same with his hair; it was just long enough to visibly hint at a dark coffee brown.

No man in Pit Stop wore *GQ*-styled facial hair or purposefully shaved his head. And then there was the tattoo. Not a simple Cupid's arrow piercing a heart or the word *Mom*. No American flag or John Deere logo. This one wore an intricate tribal design, a series of angles and arches, circles and swirls that cupped the base of his skull and his neck.

He also wore combat boots instead of Lucchese's, camouflage fatigues instead of Wranglers. And the sunglasses caught up with a sport strap around his neck were Oakleys and cost two hundred dollars at least. She could see him in Houston's Montrose. In L.A. or Soho. On a Calvin Klein billboard hawking boxer briefs.

She reached over, the sweat running down her spine an uncomfortable tickle, and notched up the blower on the

AC. The man wrapped like King Tut in the bed of her truck was as indigenous as she was to the counties encompassing U.S. Highway 62 between New Mexico and Texas.

And she couldn't help but wonder if the business that brought him here went as far underground as did hers. Or if he posed a more personal threat and was here to put an end to what she'd been doing the last five years.

All she knew for sure was that any man hoping to take her down would have to take her out in order to succeed. And wasn't *that* a comforting thought?

Two

Holden Wagner took a seat in the single visitor's chair occupying the office of County Sheriff Yancey Munroe and settled back to wait. Munroe had sworn he wouldn't be but a minute. A minute which meant nothing, as Holden well knew, in the West Texas way of telling time.

An Ivy League education. An Oxford law degree. And after a rather illustrious career during which he'd made a name defending the religious expression guaranteed by the First Amendment, he'd taken up a new cause—and taken himself off the radar—seven years ago and twenty miles west of the county seat of Pit Stop in a place called Earnestine Township.

Earnestine Township. A community of four thousand, faith-based and inclusive, where polygamist unions and arranged marriages formed two sides of the same coin funding the residents' religious beliefs. Where libel and slander lawsuits filed against militant nonbelievers were instrumental in funding the city's coffers. Where sales and property taxes funded very little at all since the populace believed in austerity, tithing times three, and the church was tax exempt.

He shook his head, breathed deeply, pinched the crease in the knee of his Armani suit pants. Armani in the land of denim, dungarees, and what outsiders considered debauchery. His position as the township's attorney wasn't solely about turning away suspicion of child abuse, welfare fraud, and incest, but was also about guaranteeing the freedom of the religion the population so ardently embraced.

Freedom from naysayers, yes, but from interlopers, too—both in the form of antipolygamist activists, former church members, anxious residents of neighboring communities, and public discontent. To former colleagues, his career move was a long slide down the legal ladder into a murky swill. For Holden, it was a solution, a compromise, a penance—one reminding him who he was. And who he wasn't. What he was. And what he wasn't.

But most of all, what he had—and hadn't—done. And the only thing he could do now.

Sitting in an industrial office, staring at certificates mounted in black document frames, at windows treated with Venetian blinds, at a wood grain rubber waste can overflowing with stained Styrofoam coffee cups, did not reflect on his worth or his abilities. Neither did the fact that he upheld the rights of middle-aged men to take young girls to wife reflect on his proclivities or his moral beliefs.

It did, however, reflect on the resolve and intent that had driven him since the age of eighteen when he'd watched his parents die for their zeal as much as their sins. Coming here today represented a sacrifice allowing him to continue his practice, his success, and most importantly, his life. With all he'd endured, all he'd forfeited, he would not go quietly into any good night.

"Sorry for the delay, Wagner." The sheriff entered the room and closed the door. Holden heard it latch, heard the thud of boots on the speckled linoleum as Munroe rounded the metal desk freshly painted a color more toast than taupe. "Had a bit of an emergency out at the Bremmer place over by Earnestine. Seems Radford's son, Jase—you might know him? He plays football. Halfback? At Earnestine High?—

he's been gone for a week and the old man just snapped to the fact. Thought the boy was staying with friends."

Fighting a choking sensation made Holden doubly glad he'd decided to forgo wearing a tie. "Not a problem, Sheriff."

"Good. Now, what can I do you for?" Yancey Munroe was a tall man of Scandinavian descent, lean but for a stomach that spoke of his love of beer. He was equally fond of his gun.

Holden uncrossed and recrossed his legs, used the delay to regain his composure. "Actually, the Bremmer boy may be tied to the disappearance of my client's daughter, Liberty Mitchell. I understand from talking to her classmates that the two were dating."

After a moment, Munroe sat, his expensive ergonomic chair at odds with the rest of the room's furnishings. "You're here about a missing girl, then."

The obvious. So eloquently and redundantly stated. Hands laced in his lap, Holden met the other man's gaze squarely and refused to release it. "Yes. Liberty Mitchell. A student at Earnestine High reported to have been dating Jase Bremmer."

The sheriff shook his head. "The office hasn't heard a word. Meaning no *report* has been filed. Is that what you're here to do? On behalf of your client?"

"The family isn't yet ready to make this official." Holden's shortness of breath returned. But this time it was about closing in, about the thrill of the hunt. "They're quite sure they know where she is."

"That so?" Munroe sat back, laced his hands behind his head. His khaki uniform was clean and pressed but depressingly dull and faded. "I'm guessing then that your being here means they'd rather not go get her themselves."

"Not when all the evidence points to her being out at the Barn." There. It was out. The reason he was here. The Big

Brown Barn and Nevada Case. Holden wasn't sure whether it was the idea of bringing down the woman or her rumored cause that was responsible for the surge in his pulse.

He saw the lift of the sheriff's brow, the tick in the other man's jaw, knowing his own would have been equally evident had he not worked so long to govern his emotions. One small mannerism gave so much away.

"I see." Munroe slowly sat forward again. He picked up the pencil he'd left on his desk blotter, held tightly to both ends. "What sort of evidence?"

Holden waited for the pencil to snap. "With their parents' permission, the school principal held interviews with several of Liberty's classmates. I was allowed to sit in. She was present during discussions about the Barn's website, and about other girls believed to have disappeared with Ms. Case's help."

"None of that has ever been proven as fact, Wagner," Munroe said, shaking his head. "You know that. Besides, if being present at a discussion is all the evidence you have, you're really stretching. The township's fathers must be getting desperate to put blame for your runaway problem someplace other than where it belongs." He used the pencil to point due west. "On that goddamn travesty you call a church."

"I'm not here to discuss religion, Sheriff," Holden said. Or here to lose his temper. He was too close to his goal of putting an end to the cancer of the Big Brown Barn. "I'm here about Neva Case's possible involvement in the disappearance of Liberty Mitchell."

"Neva Case has never been connected to the girls from Earnestine that go missing. The girl who works for her designing jewelry, that Candy Roman, she's the only one Neva can be connected to that way, and they both came out of Houston." The sheriff's mouth quirked with his mistaken upper hand. "You really can't believe everything you see on those prime-time TV news shows."

"Sheriff, I promise you. I am not here because of anything I've seen on television. Or because of Candy Roman. I've worked for the township long enough to separate fact from fiction," he added, creasing the knee of his slacks again.

"Then you're doing better than most because I can't tell you how many parents have come to this office," Munroe began, counting them with a repetitive bounce of his pencil's eraser against the blotter, "sat right where you're sitting, and begged me to list their daughters officially as missing persons after a thorough search of the Barn turned up nothing.

"Not a strand of hair, a lost button, a barrette, or trash from a favorite candy bar." The pencil stopped. "Now, if you want an unofficial escort while you check out the hearsay bringing you here, I'll be more than happy to meet you out there later this evening after I finish the paperwork on the Jase Bremmer case."

Such an impassioned defensive rebuttal deserved a round of applause, but Holden kept his hands laced in his lap. "Sheriff. I realize the lifestyle practiced by many of the residents of the township leaves a bad taste in the mouths of outsiders. But it leaves an equally bad impression on us when law enforcement does not take our claims seriously. And goes so far as to protect one of its own."

Munroe reached toward the far left corner of his desk and placed his pencil point-down in a mug emblazoned with the likeness of the Pit Stop Pirates mascot. Then he pushed to his feet, his hands flat on his desktop, his body leaning forward to form a silently menacing angle.

His expression, however, when he looked up, was a blank slate. "By one of our own, Wagner, can I take you to mean a law-abiding taxpayer who is innocent of all suspected crimes until proven guilty? Just as residents are in every community that falls under my jurisdiction? Including that of Earnestine Township?"

Too late, Holden realized his mistake. He needed to treat this case as dispassionately as he did the disappearance of any of the girls from Earnestine. It didn't matter that his own existence depended on his plans after finding the missing Liberty Mitchell.

Were that to be discovered in the course of this search, were this case to make the news, were his name to be connected, his past dredged up and into the fray, red flags would be run up poles best left empty for his future's sake.

He got to his feet, as well. "Seven o'clock, then. At Ms. Case's office."

The sheriff straightened, moved one hand to his hip above the butt of his gun. "No need to bother her there. We'll meet at the Barn."

A quick knock sounded on the door before it pushed open. "Yancey, I need to ask—oh, I'm sorry. Kate wasn't at her desk." The woman waved back toward the receptionist's empty chair. "I didn't know you had a guest."

"It's fine, Jeanne," Munroe said, coming out from behind his desk. "Mr. Wagner was just leaving."

"Sheriff. Mrs. Munroe," Holden said, and since the other made no move to do so, showed himself out.

Yancey waited for Wagner to leave before turning to his wife and giving her a quick peck on the cheek. She smelled like fruit and flowers the way she always did after getting her hair done—embracing, as she told him, the onset of middle age, simply adding highlights to the new strands of silver.

Laying her palm to his face, she patted him in that gentle way she did everything. "I didn't mean to run off your guest."

"Holden Wagner's not exactly a guest." A scumbag. A sleaze. A snake oil salesman. A shark. "It was business."

Jeanne turned to gaze at the closed door. "Hmm. Well, I'm not sure if he's what I expected in person."

"I don't know why you would've expected anything," he said, returning to his chair.

"Oh, come on, Yancey. Holden Wagner? Don't tell me having him show up in your office wasn't a surprise." As she sat in the seat Wagner had vacated, Jeanne's smile asked questions Yancey knew he wasn't going to like. "And an intimidating one at that, am I right?"

"No, you're not right." What a load of crap. Intimidation had nothing to do with Yancey's reaction to the other man. "Gimme a break. The man's no better than any of those pervs in Earnestine. He's worse, in fact, helping them get away with that bullshit they call religion. Protected statutory rape, that's what it is."

"The girls aren't forced, Yancey," she said calmly. "And they marry with their parents' permission. You may not like their beliefs or practices, but what they do is perfectly legal."

"Only because of the way pretty boy there twists and ties the law into suits and injunctions and anything else he can. He's a piece of work. The defender of religious freedom, my ass."

"Yancey Munroe." Her smile teased him, the way the brackets around her mouth deepened, the way her lashes fluttered beneath a sliver of bangs, the way her laugh lines crinkled. "Are you jealous?"

"Of what?" he asked with a snort.

"The attention he gets. The fact that he's making the news while making a name. The way he always wins." Jeanne glanced almost wistfully at the closed door. "The way he always looks like he stepped off a big city society page no matter how hot and dusty it is."

"I deserve more credit than that, Jeanne. I don't need a thousand-dollar suit to prove I know the law." What he did need was for a nice cluster bomb to obliterate Earnestine from the map and make his job easier.

"So, why was he here?"

"Business."

"Now, Yancey. You give *me* a little more credit. If Holden Wagner comes all this way to see you in person, it's got to be about one of the girls." She paused. "And the Barn."

Damn Neva Case and her meddling. His life would be a hell of a lot simpler if the Big Brown Barn was exactly what it appeared to the public to be. The business it was registered and licensed and taxed as. A legitimate business. One that designed, crafted, and sold jewelry and other girly bric-a-brac through mail order and the Internet.

Neva did enough business, in fact, that Jonnie Mayer, Pit Stop's postmistress, had taken on part-time help just to process the orders coming in and the packages going out. But Neva's jewelry wasn't the business in question. And Jeanne knew that. His wife was not a dumb woman. And he'd been silent too long.

That became obvious when her blue eyes, which usually sparkled, narrowed harshly. "Don't tell me you're going out there."

"I'm doing my job. That's all. I'm not accusing Neva of anything. A girl's missing, and her family has reason to believe she's hiding out at the Barn."

"Are you going to Judge Ahearn for a warrant?"

Yancey shook his head. "I'm just going to pay Neva a friendly visit."

"When?"

"Later tonight."

Jeanne's mouth narrowed to match her eyes. "Alone?"

"With Wagner."

At that, she slammed her palm down on his desk. "Yancey, you promised me you would not go out there again."

"This is business. It's not about Spencer." And even as he said it, he wondered which of them he was trying hardest to convince.

Jeanne crossed her arms tightly and leaned back, turning her body sideways. "Everything for you is about Spencer. Especially when it comes to the Barn."

"You're exaggerating, Jeanne."

"I am not. I have been married to you for twenty years and have been Spencer's mother for nineteen. The same length of time you've been his father." She pointed at him with one finger, her voice shaking more than her hand. "Don't tell me I'm exaggerating. Not after what went on there with Spencer and Candy."

Candy Roman. Neva's premiere designer. And a big fat thorn in Yancey's side. He was not about to stand back and let that trashy hip-hop piece sink her claws into his only son. Spencer had a football scholarship to Texas Tech. He'd be leaving Pit Stop in less than a month. Yancey intended to see his son had no reason to ever come back except to visit his mother.

"I'm going out there tonight. With Wagner. A courtesy call to see if Neva knows anything about the missing girl. If I happen to run into Candy—"

Jeanne surged to her feet. "You had damn well not happen to, or so help me, Yancey Munroe, you'll be bunking in with your son. And you can explain to him why."

Yancey felt the slam of the office door reverberate in his bones. That woman. His wife. He would not be sleeping in any bed but hers, and she knew that. Taking care of Nevada Case and her Big Brown Barn was the business of law enforcement. Seeing that Candy Roman kept away from his son was the business of Spencer's future.

Jeanne didn't have to like any of it but, quite frankly, none of it was her business at all.

Edward Bronson Hill, DVM, MD, PhD, had moved to Pit Stop, Texas, the same year as Neva, making them both newcomers in a town where old-timers were slow to accept change. Embracing such required a sign. Pigs flying. Hell freezing. Roosters laying. The moon turning blue.

The initial cold stares and colder shoulders had only recently begun to thaw. At least in Doc Hill's case. Everyone out here in ranching country would eventually need a vet, probably more often than they'd need a general practitioner—one who made regular house calls.

And, besides, who could find fault with any man who devoted his life to the honest service of others? Especially one who'd shown up just as the town's only veterinarian had put himself out to pasture.

Neva, an attorney from the big city—aka Sodom or maybe Gomorrah—had been automatically suspect and subjected to a longer probationary period. She expected to retire before fulfilling it. She'd made friends, yes; Jeanne Munroe was one of her best.

But two years ago, when the crew from the weekly national news program had rolled into town and dropped boom mics and spotlights over everyone's head, had started asking questions about the Big Brown Barn for their exposé on Earnestine Township, her progress toward Ed's level of acceptance had skidded to a halt.

The people who chose to live in Pit Stop did so for a reason. They were either running away from something or had nowhere else to go. Whatever the individual case, no one had wanted—or welcomed—the exposure. Including Neva herself. Especially Neva herself.

After backing her truck up to the rear of Ed's clinic, she

cut the engine and climbed from the cab. Before lowering her tailgate, she walked over and hit the big red button next to the clinic's rolling door and waved at the camera above. The motor engaged and the door began to crawl upward.

Seconds later, the doctor appeared feet first in the doorway, his legs clad in denim spattered with, well, Neva didn't want to know what, and his top half garbed in his standard green scrubs. At least his hands looked clean. His face she only gave a quick glance. As well as she knew him, she needed no more.

"I've got a couple of patients here for you." She waved a hand over the truck bed. "Both on their way to being road kill, so I went ahead and broke all the medical rules and moved them to bring them in."

"Now, Nevada," Ed said with a patronizing shake of his head. "What have I told you about emergency protocol?"

"Uh, nothing?" She jerked at the latch, lowered the tailgate. She knew he was teasing. She'd just never liked his idea of a joke. "But *I* have told *you* not to call me Nevada."

Ed winked at her quickly before turning his attention to her human and canine cargoes. At that point, he was stern and all business, and she stood back and watched him work. His hair was military short and a Richard Gere gray, his eyes only a little bit darker.

He was a man in his forty-something prime, fit and fine. And she wished, she really truly wished things between them had worked. They definitely had in bed, and still did when she got the itch, though she hadn't itched in too many months to count, and Ed had noticed.

But out of bed? He asked too many questions. He wanted to know too much. He found reasons she'd never imagined to be jealous. And that more than anything drove her nuts. As often as he'd been there for her, as many times as he'd dropped everything to help her, no matter how much she depended on him to offer medical treatment to the girls at the Barn, she hated to have her loyalties mistrusted.

"Where did you find these two?"

That she could answer. "Just over the state line. On the side of Sixty-two. Coming back from Carlsbad."

Having given both patients a quick once-over, checking whatever he checked in their eyes with his penlight, he headed into the clinic's large animal suite for a gurney, calling back, "Which one did you stop for? The man or the dog?"

Neva wanted to roll her eyes but stood at the truck bed to scratch FM's ears reassuringly. As if she'd actually get it on with a half-dead guy. "What do you want me to do?"

"Get rid of the rope and blanket. Carefully," he called over the rumbling clatter of the gurney wheels crossing the concrete floor.

She hopped into the bed of the truck, her back to the cab as she straddled and squatted above her mummy man, ridding him of his bindings, and now that the immediate urgency had lessened, looking at him more closely.

She pushed the blanket off his shoulders, away from his chest and abdomen, realizing as she did, as her fingers brushed clothing that was torn and the exposed, hair-dusted skin beneath, that she must have been out of her mind to think she could move him. She had, yes, but owed her success in doing so to an obvious adrenaline high.

He seemed much larger now than he'd seemed then. Much, much larger. Much, much . . . more. His chest, his shoulders, his hands and arms and neck were all proportioned in a way that made her feel small. She never felt small. And she hadn't even uncovered his legs.

The instincts telling her for weeks to keep an eye trained over her shoulder now screamed at her to run. That she had no idea what she'd gotten herself into. That he was a man like none she'd ever known. That any threat he posed was a threat to her personally.

And then, just as she was fumbling with the blanket below his waist, he opened his eyes.

"Where am I?" he barely whispered, a raspy, throaty croak of a sound.

"We're at Doc Hill's clinic. He's coming now with a gurney. You're going to be fine." On what she based her encouraging words, she had no clue.

"And if you're not," Ed walked up to say, "you can always hire Nevada here to sue me for malpractice."

"Jesus, Ed. Don't scare him like that." Her gaze traveled from the downed man to the other and back. "And *don't* call me Nevada."

"Not scared," the man beneath her grunted thickly. "Thirsty."

Neva looked up from his glazed and tortured eyes. "Ed? Is water okay? I've got a cooler with bottles behind the truck seat."

Ed nodded, left the gurney near the tailgate, and opened the driver's-side door. He returned with a bottle, handed it off but didn't immediately let go. "Not too much. Slowly. No gulping."

"Okay," she agreed, adding, "I promise," to get him to give her the bottle. When one of his dark gray brows went up and he still held tight, she mouthed back, "Not funny." Jerking it from his hand, she unscrewed the cap as he moved to attend briefly to the dog. "His name is FM."

"Like the radio?" Ed asked, running his hands over the dog's head and body.

"No, mate. Like the bloody fucking mutt he is."

Neva frowned at the man between her legs, unconscionably glad to hear him speak, though wondering at the Aussie vernacular that didn't come with the Aussie accent. She gave him a bit of an encouraging smile. "Tell me. Is that sense of humor supposed to be wicked or warped?"

"Both," he said, and then reminded her what she was supposed to be doing. "Water."

"Oh, hell. Right. Sorry." She moved to kneel at his shoulders, slipped a hand beneath his neck, cupped the base of his skull, and lifted his head, fingers crossed that she wasn't doing him any more damage. Heat seemed to roll from his body—she prayed it was the blanket and the sun and not a spike in temperature—as he formed his lips to drink, pressed them to the bottle.

She watched his mouth work, watched his throat, saw the relief in his eyes before he closed them, and she lowered him again to lay flat. She wanted to clean his face, the dust and dirt in his eyebrows and beard, the lines of sweat streaking his cheeks. She wanted him to feel cool water on his skin, parched by the sun.

She wanted Ed to get him into the clinic and take a look at the damage to his arm and everything else on his body. FM could wait. "Ed? Could we worry about the dog later and get him inside?"

"Mick."

She glanced away from the doctor and down. "Mick? Your name is Mick?"

Eyes still closed, he nodded. "Savin. Mick Savin."

It fit him, as did the timbre of his voice, a rich and resonant bass. "Hi, Mick. This is Ed Hill, who happens to do double duty as our local vet and GP."

Mick gave an eyes-closed and painful-looking nod. "F took a hit to the jaw."

"A hit?" Neva glance at the dog, her back teeth aching. "What, with a car?"

"A boot." He grimaced. "Seems we worked our way onto a piece of property where the owner wasn't kidding when he posted his 'no trespassing' signs."

Dear Lord. Was he serious? Her heart thudded hard. "Someone did this to you for trespassing?"

"It's not as bad as it looks." His lashes fluttered as his

eyes came open. They were a silvery shade of hazel. "Bumps and bruises. Shoulder's dislocated, couple of ribs cracked, but that's about it."

"I'll be the judge of that," the doctor put in. "The dog needs stitches, antibiotics, and fluids. X rays and blood work will tell me more." Ed gave FM a last scratch for good measure, then turned to Mick. "I'll use the blanket to slide you onto the gurney, Mick, so hang on. Neva, you grab his legs."

"Okay." She moved from Mick's head to his feet, pulling away the blanket completely and feeling his gaze following her movements as she exposed the length of his legs. She refused to look up. She didn't want to catch him watching her, or have him catch her studying him. He left her uneasy in a way she didn't like and couldn't describe. She simply wanted to finish her Good Samaritan duty and leave him in Ed's capable hands.

And she was minutes away from doing just that when she discovered the knife and the gun.

The first she was only marginally worried about; she didn't know anyone who didn't carry a knife in the course of their work day even if this one was as illegal to possess as cocaine. But the second . . . Her hand stilled there above his ankle, and her gaze crawled the length of his body to make reluctant contact with his. The shake of his head was almost imperceptible, but the favor he was asking her couldn't have been more clear. Oh, dear. Oh, my.

Oh, hell.

Her heart beat so loudly in her ears it was the only thing she could hear. She looked quickly, briefly in Ed's direction. Then, while he positioned the gurney and snapped a lead onto the dog's collar, Neva slid the handgun from its holster, reached back, and shoved it between two of the boxes destined for Candy's studio.

That done, she pulled Mick's pants leg down around the top of his boot and took hold of both ankles. "Ready when you are, Doc," she lied.

She wasn't sure she would ever be ready for what the man beneath her was all about. In fact, she was quite sure she wasn't prepared in the least.

Three

Her name was Nevada. And if she wasn't sleeping with the good doctor now, she had been. That much had been easy to figure based on the other man's tension as he'd worked with the woman to move Mick into the clinic from the truck.

He'd regained full consciousness earlier in the day to the roar of the ocean in his ears. He'd tried once, twice to open his eyes, finally looking up and straight into the sun. Turning his head then, he'd found himself squinting into a pair of wide brown eyes beneath ears with the tips flopping over.

FM's chin had come up just as Mick realized they were in the bed of a pickup, he was trussed like a Thanksgiving turkey, flames were licking the right half of his torso, and his ass cheeks burned like hell on wheels. Groaning hadn't been so easy. His tongue had been—and still was—the size, feel, and taste of a moldy summer sausage. Yeah. Damn disgusting.

It was after he'd made where he was that he'd remembered the woman. Her truck. Her trussing. She'd done a damn good job getting him off the ground and up that ramp like she had. She obviously wasn't connected to the Spectra thugs who'd tried to dismember him or she wouldn't have hauled his banged-up butt to the doc.

And bloody hell but his banged-up butt ached. Bounced like chum through water behind those ATVs for who knew how far. Another day or two, he'd be a black and blue canvas, one big fat tribal tattoo. Before that happened, however, before local law enforcement started questioning him or the hinky information on the hunting lease, he needed his clothes and his ride, his gun and his dog, and to hit the road.

Adios. Sayonara.

Right. He winced, his shoulder throbbing from the reduction, his midsection pounding and waiting to be taped, his head roaring with the force of a typhoon blowing through. Like he'd be hitting anything but a morphine drip anytime soon. Not good, but not the end of the world. No one—including his fellow SG-5 operatives—would come looking for him until he signaled for help. Which brought to mind thoughts he wasn't too keen on thinking.

If he hadn't been seen, if no one had stopped, he'd have baked to death, a dehydrated, shriveled corpse wearing combat boots and fatigues, no dog tags, no government-issued I.D. That had been the way he'd lived for so long, the very way he'd expected to die, that it shouldn't have been but a bug on his mortality radar. Instead, it was a full-blown attack.

The only reason he could figure was that he owed his survival, his life, his future to the woman. Nevada. The redhead. With the big eyes. The freckles. The great rack. The mouth that reminded him how much he loved women. Especially those who had the wits and the snap this one did. Her resourcefulness impressed him all to hell.

If she'd been scared, she hadn't let on. If she'd been panicked, the same. All that was left to do now was follow her lead . . . though right now the idea of following her anywhere left him dizzy. He was lying on the gurney in a big examining room, and she was pacing around and around like she was trying to spin the cement floor below into butter—or however that kids' story went.

"Hey. You mind doing your laps over there?" He indicated the far side of the room with a lift of his chin. The lights in the ceiling fifteen feet overhead had been dimmed while he waited for the doctor to finish stitching the dog's jaw and get back with the drugs. "My head's spinning, and I'd prefer not to puke up my guts."

She came to stand at his side, and he sensed her fingers on the edge of his stainless steel bed, sensed her stroke the loose folds of his T-shirt. "You're awake, good. Because now you can tell me why the hell you didn't let the doctor move you into one of the smaller rooms and bandage you up. You'd be so much more comfortable there."

Mick did his best to focus on her face, on her eyes which refused to meet or hold his. "Like I told the doc, getting bandaged and comfortable can wait. I need him to fix up the dog."

She laughed, a sound that seemed a bit hysterical. "You need to have Ed fixing up *you*."

"I'm fine." Relatively speaking. And keeping FM in good working condition was more vital than having his own bumps and bruises diagnosed as bruises and bumps. He wasn't going anywhere. The doc would be back soon enough to tape and patch him to death. "The shoulder I needed taken care of. The ribs and the scrapes can be done when he gets back. The rest is all a matter of time and taking it easy."

"Lying on this gurney is hardly taking anything easy." She knocked twice on the shiny surface. "This thing is hard as a rock."

The echo of the ringing metal clanged in his ears. "All the better to be lying on when he hoses me down to get rid of the dirt and the blood."

She looked over at him then, making eye contact at last, even if it was a wary regard. "Hoses you down?"

He nodded, enjoying the show of nerves breaking her voice. A strong competent woman uneasy at the idea of his taking a shower out here in the wide open spaces. "Sure. Like any large animal. The concrete floor. The drain. The showerhead on the retractable hose." He gestured up toward the ceiling. "If it works for a horse, it'll work for me."

For a long moment, she stood still, frowning up at the contraption Mick was pretty sure the doctor used to clean the room after surgery. And so he was watching her when the truth dawned, when she realized he was kidding, doing what he could to break the ice that had frozen between them since he'd handed her his gun.

She crossed her arms, stepped back and lifted a brow, no longer incredulous, aghast, or even marginally amazed—much less intrigued. "Comparing yourself to a horse, are you?"

He did his best to grin. "Only in the most flattering way."

"I see." She let her gaze drift the length of his body. "So, should I get you ready? I could lend Ed a hand and ditch what's left of your clothes."

If he hadn't been halfway concussed, he would've had the presence of mind to say no. Or to insist she get out of her own clothes, as well. But he wasn't thinking straight. He wasn't thinking at all. Not even to fully remember how much trouble accompanied a sexually charged dare.

Besides, having a woman touch him, undress him, even if it was a twisted, kinky nurse and patient fantasy, hit every one of his buttons just then. "Sure," he said, and could tell by the ice age of the next few moments that she'd never expected him to say anything but no.

He wasn't sure what that said about her, whether it meant she was all talk and no action, that her low, throaty, and very hot bark was worse than her bite, or that she simply didn't like men. Could be it meant she was a thinker, slow to respond until she knew the lay of the land.

It was when she moved to his feet, however, when she began unlacing one of his boots, that he realized one thing—how quick she was to thaw. And it was a damn good thing he hurt too much to feel anything else, because what he wanted to feel—what he thought about feeling—would be next to impossible to accomplish in his condition, much less in this time and place.

She had both of his boots unlaced and loosened before she looked up and fully met his gaze. "Do you want to tell me about the gun?"

Uh, no, not really. He really didn't want to talk at all. "What do you want to know?"

"Why you have it." His first boot hit the floor.

"Protection." Simple enough.

"From what? Gangbangers? Drive-bys?" Her fingers were deft and comforting. "That's not a gun you'll find used out here to take down coyotes or rattlesnakes."

Gangbangers and drive-bys. Interesting how those were the first directions her mind traveled. "You're not from around these here parts, now are you, ma'am?"

His second boot joined the first on the floor. She went to pull off his socks, was stopped by the sheathed knife and the empty holster strapped above his ankles. "About as much as you are. Mate."

"Hey, I'm only here for the mule deer." A lame effort at allaying her suspicions, one he followed up with a breath so deep it reminded him of the condition of his ribs.

"Right." She removed both items, tucked them into his boots, and set the lot on the side counter that ran the length of the room. "Mule deer. Afghani rebels. Jackrabbits. Palestinian guerillas."

He sobered slightly and remained unmoving while she rid him of his socks before she moved to his head. Once there, she raised him up enough to slide off the cords of his hat and sunglasses, letting him fall back rather too roughly. And he only winced once and hissed twice when she jarred his shoulder too hard.

"I'm sorry. I didn't mean to—"

"You sure?" She was standing above him now, her face close but not closed. In fact, what he saw was a sort of terror that gave him pause. "Felt like that was the closest you could get to knocking the crap out of me for carrying that gun."

She added the sunglasses and hat to the boots on the counter, came back with a pair of scissors sporting nine-inch blades. "I know that gun. Or at least ones like it. That's not a gun anyone has reason to carry. Unless they're involved in preventing or committing crimes."

She had a history with the sort of weapon he carried, one he wasn't sure he wanted to take the time to pry free. Not when he would be gone from here tomorrow, if not later today. "Then let's say I'm just passing through and leave it at that."

"Fine."

She said it much less gently than she slipped one blade of the scissors into the sleeve covering his bad arm and snipped her way to the neck. She repeated the process on the other side, then moved to his waist and sliced upward from the hem to what remained of the band of fabric at the base of his throat. That done, she peeled his shirt away . . . and blew out a very loud and long breath.

He didn't need a mirror to see what he looked like. Her

expression was mirror enough. "You think that's something, wait till you see the rest."

"Oh, my god, Mick." She brought a hand to her throat. "Has Ed seen this?"

He shook his head. "Not yet, but he'll be back. And I'll live. I'm just bruised and battered and banged to the back of beyond."

Her gaze roamed the canvas of his torso, and he would've liked to think she was admiring the view when he knew if she was admiring anything, it was the palette of colors. Purple and red that would soon enough turn green and blue, and eventually morph into healing yellows and oranges for a complete wreck of a rainbow.

She touched him lightly then, unexpectedly, her fingertips grazing the skin of his abdomen, the one place with very little surface damage. It was an exploratory touch, the contact minimal, nonsexual, lacking in any sort of heat. But there was warmth. Kindness and concern. Caring. The look in her eyes unnerved him. Mick Savin. Unfazed by a monster pair of scissors. Unnerved by a woman's unshed tears.

Focus, Savin, focus. Get up, get moving, get gone.

His mantra, of course, would've worked better if he'd remembered to add the last part. The "get over it" part. But Neva had shaken off her glazed look, abandoned her study of his personal Picasso, and had moved her hands to the fasteners of his pants.

"Uh, Neva?" he began, really wishing she was close enough and he was well enough for him to play with the waves in her hair. He wanted to know what it felt like, what it smelled like. It reminded him of Indian silk. "Why don't we let the doc take it from here?"

"You know my name," she said, her voice soft though she frowned as her fingers paused.

He nodded, the metal surface beneath him growing suddenly cold. "Neva Case. You told me when you saved me from death by overgrown weeds. Besides, I paid attention when you were talking to the doc."

"I wasn't sure you heard everything." She tucked both hands into her jeans pockets. "You were pretty out of it."

He nodded again, overcome with all he needed to say. He tried to blame his reaction on the pain, his exhaustion, near dehydration. He was hard-core, trained for scenarios he'd never even faced. He shouldn't be maudlin or sappy and soft. But in the end he knew it went a lot deeper than any of that. That he'd reached the point where he was beginning to remember the value of being alive.

"Thank you." He cleared his throat. "You saved my life."

She tried to blow it off with a breezy, "All in a day's work."

An explanation which he didn't even dig into his pockets to buy. "You're in the business of saving lives, then?"

"I used to be a defense attorney." She hesitated, seeming to gather her bearings before going forward to say, "It's certainly not comparable to what the doc here does."

She said it so offhandedly that he didn't believe it. The nonchalance was one thing, but then there was the way she crossed her arms more defensively than before, holding in things she didn't want to say, things she didn't want him to know. Things he would have easily found out had his mind been anywhere near clear.

It wasn't, and so he had to let it go. Let her go. He turned to the side, raised up onto his good elbow, holding back the groan rolling out of his throat. "Listen. Whether it's your business or not, I owe you more than I can afford to repay. Can I at least buy you a beer when they spring me?"

She shook her head. "I don't drink." Then she shrugged. "Unless it's coffee. I've never been known to say no to that. Or to chocolate."

"Okay, then." It hurt to smile, but he did. "I'll come bearing chocolate."

"On one condition."

"Which is?"

"You leave with your gun in your hand." She took a quick step in reverse. "And you don't come back."

He'd have no need to, of course. But her insistence ran a lot of flags up a lot of poles. "Am I putting that much of a crimp in your lifestyle?"

"No. And I'd really like to keep it that way."

Having made the ten-mile drive from Ed's clinic to her own place in record time, Neva took the delivery detour that bypassed her house-cum-office, the acreage between here and there, and circled the property to the rear of the Barn. She parked, turned off the truck, and opened the door.

Candy, of course, had been pacing outside instead of working inside while she waited. The denim of her short pleated skirt bared a whole lot of naked mahogany brown leg. It also slapped against her bottom as she spun on the heels of the worn cowboy boots she wore that matched an ivory lace tank that fairly glowed against her dark skin.

"Damn you, Neva. A quick overnight trip, my ass." Five years younger than Neva's twenty-nine, Candy scolded like an urban mother of twelve. Her dark brown eyes narrowed as she shook a finger. "You were supposed to be back here by nine-thirty."

"What time is it?" Neva asked, though she knew perfectly well. She just didn't want to share all the details of the delay.

"It's noon! *Noon!* Argh!" Candy gestured wildly with both hands. "You had better swear to me here and now that you will never again turn off your radio when you know I am waiting for you."

Neva climbed from the cab and slammed the door before Candy climbed in and slammed her around. "I had an emergency."

"All the more reason not to be out of touch." The other woman's boots crunched on the gravel drive as she flounced, and then she lost her pique as curiosity set in. "What sort of emergency?"

"A dog on the road." Not a lie, not a whole truth. But since she had the dog with her . . . She walked to the back of the truck where FM lumbered to his feet and stuck his big head over the side of the bed. "He's a little loopy from having his jaw deadened and sewn back together."

She still could not believe she'd agreed to keep the dog. Especially when that guaranteed she'd be seeing Mick Savin again. Yes, there was the issue of his gun, but that she could've had delivered somehow or left somewhere for him to pick up. Not so the mutt.

Ed had stitched the gash that had split FM's jaw, given Neva antibiotics and instructions for his care—including keeping his wound dry when she bathed him. How nice of him to leave that task to her.

Candy followed and looked over with an imperious lift of brow. "You brought home a dog?"

Neva nodded, scraping back windblown strands of hair. "Doc Hill stitched him up but is short staffed this week with Lindsey vacationing with her parents. I told him we'd see the pooch got his meds and the care he needs until his owner shows up."

Leaning forward, Candy inspected FM's tags, sneezing when he nuzzled up to her cheek. "His tags are from an El Paso pound."

"I know," Neva said.

Candy turned and shoved both hands to her hips. "You rescue an abandoned dog on the side of the road, and you expect anyone to come looking for him, much less claim him?"

Neva wasn't quite ready to share the details of their new acquisition's ownership. Not when she knew so little about Mick Savin and his gun. The two women were partners and friends—a situation that made the decision to remain mum, to keep this secret that might affect them both, one not entirely guilt-free.

So all she said was, "We'll see."

Sighing, Candy pressed her nose to the dog's, sneezed again, and ruffled the fur of his ruff. "You know, a pet would be a great way to teach little Miss Mitchell what's up."

What was up was that Neva had made a huge mistake giving the girl a job when she'd shown up disheveled one morning and asked. "He's only a temporary pet, Candy."

"Trust me. She's only a temporary hire." Candy held up one finger. "But we don't have to share either fact with the little bitch. Er, brat."

Neva moved to the back of the truck and lowered the tailgate, hopped up next to the dog, and shoved forward the boxes of supplies to unload. "She's not working out so well, huh?"

"Unfortunately, no." Candy examined the labels, sorted the boxes accordingly. "Which brings me back to asking you again why you hired her. It's not like we really need the help."

"No, but she obviously did." As Candy left to get the hand truck from the Barn's porch, Neva jumped down, coaxed FM to do the same, and smiled as she thought back to Mick's explanation for the dog's name. Then she sobered. What was a man like Mick Savin doing with a dog?

"You can't take in everyone that needs help," the other woman called, walking back up, her skirt swinging as she pushed the dolly. Once she reached Neva's side, Candy stopped, and together they began stacking the boxes. "What you do is too important. I know that better than anyone."

Neva nodded, started to speak, to tell her friend everything, then found that she couldn't. Candy didn't know that Neva feared she'd taken in too many girls already, that she'd overlooked details, that she'd hit snags that someone outside of the network had pulled, unraveling the five years of work she and Candy had done here.

Three of the missing girls Neva had harbored, whom she'd then sent on their way to safety, to a real life, a normal life, had vanished like so much blue smoke. And she had no idea what had happened. None of her queries had met with success. None of her contacts had panned out.

Once the girls moved into the deeper web of the network, her responsibility for them ended. That didn't mean her conscience ceased to work. Or that she felt nothing for their situation. How could she have failed so miserably, so completely, thinking she was a messiah, that she'd been called . . .

Candy interrupted Neva's musings to go on. "Besides, you can't mislead news crews indefinitely. One of these days, you're going to be found out. *We're* going to be found out. Rumors don't stay rumors when they're really the truth. If Liberty Mitchell discovers that truth, I don't see her keeping her big yap shut."

Knowing she couldn't argue with any of what Candy said, Neva grabbed the last box, balanced it on top of the chest-high stack, and slammed the tailgate shut, dusting off her hands on her thighs. "She doesn't know anything yet, and I don't expect her to be here long. Something's going on with her, but I haven't figured out what."

"She came here because of the rumors, Neva. She thought she'd be getting some kind of free ride to another life."

"Well, as long as that sort of stupid rumor keeps circulating," Neva said, laughing lightly as she crouched face-to-face with FM, "we should be safe. A free ride is the last thing any of the girls truly escaping Earnestine are looking for. They're so grateful to get out of there that they're willing to pay with their lives."

"And they can thank you and the South Texas College of Law that they don't have to."

Candy was right. Neva knew it. But she was still bothered beyond belief at having lost touch with any of the girls after they left her care. And speaking of care . . . "You really think we can trust Liberty with the dog?"

"I'm telling you. Turning the dog over to her is perfect."

"Where is she now?"

Candy nodded toward the front of the Barn and the showroom. "Supposedly Windexing the display cases."

Neva got back to her feet. "Pooch here has a schedule for his medicine, and his stitches can't get wet. Ed included a bottle of shampoo that I'm sure is going to cost me a small fortune."

"He's sending you the bill?"

"Are you kidding? Anything to remind me that I insisted we work better as friends."

Candy snorted. "With friends like that . . . sticking you with a bill instead of writing it off as charity."

"Hey, you know what they say about a man scorned."

"Yeah. That he'll never believe his dick was too small."

Sputtering, Neva headed for the cab and the bag of supplies she'd left there. "Sad, isn't it. They really don't get that size does matter."

"Something Ed, being a vet and all, should understand," Candy teased.

"Here." Neva shoved the bag of dog supplies at Candy, trying not to picture Mick Savin or wonder about his anatomy claims. "Make sure our Miss Liberty follows the instructions."

"Yes, boss," Candy said with a wink, cocking back the

dolly stacked with the boxes and whistling for the dog. "One doggie bath coming up."

Neva watched Candy go, pushing the hand truck of supplies toward the Barn. Beside her, walking slowly, FM worked to shake off the effects of the sedative. Smiling to herself, Neva climbed back into the cab, turned the key, put the truck in gear, and headed for the house.

Candy always put the truth of the matter into perspective. Size did matter. Whether the size of a man's genitalia or the size of the rumors circulating about what went on at the Big Brown Barn. Thankfully, Liberty had shown up begging for a job when there were no other girls in residence. Not that there ever were many.

In fact, Neva often thought the fewer the better. Fewer girls meant less chance for exposure, less chance for the scuttlebutt about the Barn to grow an investigatory head of truth. But fewer girls could also mean contacting her was becoming more difficult. Or that the underground network keeping the word out was falling apart. Those were her biggest fears because they meant that somewhere she'd failed.

She was done with failure, whether court-documented or self-perceived. The girls in Earnestine Township who wanted to escape from a medieval mindset of arranged marriages foisted on them at a very young age for the gain of their parents, or because of warped practices made acceptable by the cloak of religion . . . those girls deserved that chance.

No female of any age should be forced into a man's bed no matter the circumstances. Neva had seen it happen too often. And she'd be damned if she was going to sit back and watch it happen to anyone else. Not when the opportunity to prevent it had dropped like a gift into her lap the day six years ago when she'd been assigned Candy Roman as a client by the court.

A client who'd been incarcerated for the duration of her

murder trial with a sixteen-year-old girl who'd killed her husband and then run from Earnestine.

At the end of the trial, once it had been proven beyond a reasonable doubt that Candy's wounds were defensive, and that her soon-to-be stepfather, recently deceased at her hand, was indeed her rapist, they'd made their way west together.

No matter her charge to provide a competent defense, Neva had had her fill of defending those who knew just enough of the law to get around it. If that made her a bad attorney, it was offset by the good she now did.

The good that she wasn't so sure she was going to be able to continue doing much longer. At least not with a clear conscience until she discovered the break in her network. Discovered, too, the whereabouts of the last three girls who'd taken seriously her claims of sending them away from Earnestine to a better life.

And, she mused rather harshly as her truck hit a rut in the road she needed to have graded and filled, not when Mick Savin scared her, and she wasn't even sure why. Part of it was obviously the gun he carried. But the gun had been in her truck while she'd talked to him in the clinic. Meaning her trepidation had nothing to do with his weapons. It was all about a knife-wielding, gun-toting, dog-owning, tattooed mercenary type showing up out of nowhere and making her think about sex.

Four

"Are you serious?" Standing outside the showroom door, Liberty looked down at the scruffy tan and gray dog sitting almost on top of Candy's boots and stinking up the place really good. "You want me to give him a bath?"

Candy nodded, squatting down in front of him to nuzzle his face, her skirt flapping behind her and dragging the ground, the scooped neck of her top gaping to show off a lace bra that was the kind Liberty wished she made enough money to buy.

But this stupid job wasn't going to pay her enough to buy anything. Especially the education she would need to get a better one. Why had she ever thought running away with Jase made any sense?

"What's his name?" she asked as Candy sneezed and got back to her feet, handing over his leash.

"We don't know. Neva found him on the highway. The vet stitched him up, and now he's yours to take care of until someone shows up to get him."

"Oh, like that will happen in a million years."

"Maybe not, but knowing Doc Hill, he's sending the info to animal clinics in neighboring towns. And he's contacting the pound in El Paso. Now"—she shoved a sack into

Liberty's hands—"his shampoo and his medicine are in here. There's a hose and spigot around the back of the Barn. Just make sure you don't get his stitches wet."

Meaning she couldn't just spray him down from a distance. Ugh. "What about the display cases I'm supposed to be cleaning? I'm not finished with that."

"You can do those later." Candy grabbed the dolly stacked with boxes, tilted it back, and headed around the Barn to the side entrance into her studio, stopping once to glance back when she realized Liberty hadn't moved. "What're you waiting for? A gold-plated invitation? Get going."

Rolling her eyes, Liberty tugged on the leash, glad the dog actually got to his feet and didn't make her drag him around. She was even more glad he didn't growl and attack. She wasn't exactly scared of dogs; she just didn't know anything about them. Her parents had never let her have a pet.

"C'mon, dog." She walked him down the long side of the huge barn that was really more a ruddy red than brown, passing the decorative rock garden and cactus beds as she made her way to the back.

Once there, however, she wasn't sure about tying him up to keep him from running off while she bathed him. He really didn't look like he had a whole lot of energy and looked kinda sad, in fact. Like maybe he was missing his family and hated being alone.

She wasn't too thrilled about being alone herself, but she didn't really miss anyone but Jase. Then again, that wasn't exactly true, she admitted, setting the bag on the empty crate leaning against the barn wall and looping the end of the leash over the spigot before attaching the hose.

She didn't really miss him, but she had been thinking about him a lot since she'd been here. She was afraid something really bad had happened to him and that she might not ever find out what.

But she'd also realized dating him hadn't really been

about loving him. It had been about him understanding how unhappy she was at home and offering her a way out. Now she was just thankful they hadn't ended up stuck in Mexico. What would they have done down there?

It was bad enough that she was being treated like a slave by Neva and Candy. Whoever it was saying this place helped people didn't know what they were talking about. Yeah, they fed her and gave her clothes and a bed. But if she'd wanted a job making minimum wage, she could've gotten one checking groceries at the Safeway in Earnestine.

Of course, it wasn't like she'd told anyone the truth of what had happened. She couldn't. Not when all she could think about was the guy with the dreadlocks telling her he'd kill her if she talked.

Bending to check the dog's stitches, she had to be honest about the fact that if she *were* still in Earnestine, she'd have to be going to church with her parents, and every time she went it seemed like all the men stared at her like a piece of meat. It was just too creepy to deal with.

"Guess we're both on our own," she said to the dog, who really looked weird with the side of his face shaved around the stitches. "Ouch. That must've really hurt, huh?" When his tongue came out and he licked at her face, she laughed. But then she started to cry. She sat down on the concrete pad beside him, wrapped her arms around him, and sobbed into his stinky fur.

She hated being pathetic, but that's how she felt. Like no one was on her side. Like she was stuck in some bad movie or nightmare and any door she opened to find her way out would lead her in a big fat circle right back into the same room. She was never going to get out. Or else she was going to get killed for something she hadn't even done.

That night last week when Jase had said he had something important to tell her, she thought it would be about taking her away—not about running away. And she sure didn't think it would be about him stealing money from people who would kill him if they found out. Now she couldn't help but wonder how many of the bad guys knew she'd been with him that night.

"So tell me, dog. What am I going to do with my life?" She pulled away to look him in the face. He cocked his head to one side. His ears flopped forward. His big brown eyes stared into hers. "You really do need a bath, you know," she said, and he licked her again.

"Okay, okay. You win. We'll just sit here a few more minutes first. See if we can figure out the secrets of the universe. And a good name for you." When he laid his head in her lap, she stroked his back, her heart swelling with the way he wanted to stay close. Like he really needed her. "Something like Freckles. Or Buster."

She wondered if she could keep him if no one showed up, or if his owner never was found. Having an animal of her own, one who loved her, one she could talk to, would make being on her own a lot easier. Two against the world and all that. A girl and her dog. The thought made her smile.

At least until she looked up and into Candy's scowling face. "I don't see any water being used back here."

Liberty sighed, slid out from under Buster, and stood to dust off the seat of the blue jeans they'd found for her to wear. "I'm doing it, okay? I was just making sure he knew I wasn't going to hurt him or anything."

She grabbed the end of the hose, the bottle of shampoo, and turned on the water, drowning out whatever else Candy had to say. Now that she had Buster on her side, Liberty wasn't going to let anyone else get to her.

No matter how much she wished she could go back in time and choose someone besides Jase to help her find a better life.

* * *

Mick slept away the biggest part of the day in the clinic, unsure when he finally woke how much time had passed since his rescue. He wasn't even sure how long he'd lain out on the side of the road before Neva had stopped and hauled him into her truck. A day, he thought, at the most.

One thing he did know was that he needed to fetch FM from wherever the vet was keeping him and get the data from the flash cards in the dog's collar to SG-5's ops center ASAP. The longer it took him to feed his intel back to the Smithson Group, the more money Spectra would launder. And the harder it would become to tie the crime syndicate to any of the funds.

He also knew that for the next few days he'd feel like he'd been beaten to bloody hell. His shoulder and his bum were the worst. The dislocation and reduction left him aching and sore, but he hadn't lost any feeling or the use of his arm. No nerve damage. No broken bones. Amazing, when he should be pushing up daisies considering the ass-over-tits ride that had gotten him here.

Here, looking up into the bright lights of the small room into which Dr. Hill had moved him once Neva had left. The doc hadn't seemed too thrilled to finish up with FM and return to find Neva, along with most of Mick's clothing, gone. Mick hadn't said a word. He'd enjoyed watching the physician stew about the woman he wanted who obviously didn't want him. It upped Mick's intrigue factor about Neva Case.

He levered himself up onto his good elbow then swung his legs over the table's side, hissing as he put more weight on his bruised backside. The sheet covering him settled around his waist. Water, food, clothes, and a plan. He'd take them in whatever order he could get them. Though, he decided wryly as the sheet slid lower in his lap, he'd do good to start with pants.

He'd just fastened the sheet toga style—not particularly

easy with one arm in a sling—when a knock sounded on the door. "Yeah, I'm up. Come in."

Dr. Hill pushed open the door and did just that, Mick's boots in hand along with socks, boxers, jeans, and a white T-shirt. He dropped the load into the room's one-piece black plastic chair, signaling for Mick to hop back onto the very same table from which he'd just managed to make his way down.

"Let's check your vitals again before you go." The doc readied his stethoscope, reached for the blood pressure cuff on the wall at the head of the table. "The clothes might be a tight fit, but they should do you until you can change them out for your own."

"I appreciate it, mate." Mick tried not to cringe and bawl like a baby when he settled down to sit, or when the tape of the bandages pulled hair in all the wrong places. "I'll get them back to you soon as I can."

The doctor didn't respond until he'd finished taking Mick's pulse. "Don't worry about it. It's nothing I can't spare."

Ed was all business now doing his thing, and Mick let him, submitting to the thermometer, the light up his nose, the poking and prodding of what felt like kidneys and liver and spleen, not to mention every bruised rib and patch of scraped skin along the way. He gritted his teeth, sucked back a sharp breath or two, until Jekyll finished his mad torture.

"You're good to go," the other man said, releasing the air from the blood pressure cuff, "but check in with your own doctor for a complete physical when you get home. Which, by the way, better be soon." His level gaze held the unmistakable warning that he didn't like breaking rules or appreciate the insistence that he take shortcuts.

Mick nodded. He would leave, but not to seek more medical treatment. After his last stint in the Middle East, he was well aware that his body could stand more punishment than this and heal. His mental state, now that was another story. The exhaustion was catching up and bloody well serious about taking its toll.

A man could only hunt down and kill so many others before blowing a fuse or two dozen.

"Listen, mate. I don't suppose you could take a lunch break and give me a lift out to see if my ride's where I left it? The cash I had with me might still be stashed away under the hood. I'd like to pay you for your services before I check out of town."

"It's a little late for lunch. In fact, I was just heading home for supper." At Mick's obvious confusion, the doctor added, "You've been sleeping for about six hours. It was ten or so when Neva brought you in this morning. And by the way, she took your dog home with her."

That would've been damn inconvenient except for the fact that she already had his gun. He prayed like hell she hadn't managed to lose F's collar. Or that she hadn't replaced it with something she thought more fashionably chic from out of those boxes she'd been hauling. "Hope she didn't lock him in a kennel. Even if he's too banged up to run, he would hate being cooped up."

"Something he gets from his owner?" the doc asked while washing and drying his hands.

"It might be, sure." Gingerly, Mick climbed down from the table for the second time, dropped the sheet, and reached for the boxers. He stepped into them before speaking again. "What makes you ask?"

The doc turned then and tossed another bundle toward the chair. Tucked inside Mick's hat, his sunglasses, ankle holster, and knife still in its sheath landed on top of the clothes. "That's military gear. Maybe mercenary. Call me psychic, but I'm guessing you and cages don't get along."

Mick stared for a minute, then shook off the déjà vu and reached for the T-shirt, losing the sling long enough to pull the shirt over his head and down, grimacing as the cotton hit raw patches of skin. "If you can just get me to my ride so I can get my dog, you won't have to worry about seeing me or my gear again."

"Just making sure we're on the same page." The doctor hesitated, scrubbing a hand back over his short-cropped silvered hair and finally adding, "Especially when it comes to Nevada Case."

Mick wasn't about to be lured into a pissing match, to make any sort of ominous or menacing impression that would have anyone looking for him once he was gone. So he transferred his things to the table and sat to pull on the socks, to strap on his knife and empty holster, leaving the doc standing taller, looming larger, hovering above.

A tactical move. "I'm not after your woman, mate. I only want my dog."

"She's not my woman," the doctor said, deflating as he did so, emphasizing Mick's suspicion that that particular truth didn't sit well with the other man. "I just want to make sure no more trouble ends up out her way. She's had a rough patch since moving here."

What kind of rough patch? Mick opened and closed his mouth. He abso-bloody-lutely would not ask. "I told you, Doc. I don't plan to do anything more than—"

"—get your dog and go. So you said." This time the doc let a smile through to his face. "How 'bout a plate of meat loaf and mashed potatoes before we hit the road?"

Jeans on, but not without a whole lot of gritting and grinding of teeth, Mick sat again to lace up his boots. He was just about ready to go naked; the clothes he was wearing hurt him that bad. "You cooking?"

"Oh, hell no." The doc laughed. "Patsy Cline does the cooking. And, no. She's not related. She owns the only decent restaurant for miles is all."

Food and water wouldn't hurt now that he had the clothes part taken care of. All that was left was the plan and to pick up his gun and his dog. "Since the last thing I ate was an energy bar, I could go for a plate, sure."

"I'll lock up. Unless you want to use the phone in the office first?" Dr. Hill gestured behind him. "Let anyone looking for you know you're up and around?"

Mick needed to call Hank or the ops center but he wasn't going to do it from this man's phone. The SG-5 emergency locator line was only to be used should an operative need to be lifted from an escalation, or have help brought in.

This situation required neither. As had been the case for so much of his life, he was on his own. He got to his feet slowly, wincing nonetheless. "No one to phone, mate. I'm good to go."

Jeanne Munroe liberally sprinkled Comet powder over her kitchen sink, which she'd already spent ten minutes scrubbing. Cooking and cleaning, the only things that seemed to define her these days, also served as panaceas.

When she couldn't get Yancey to talk. When she couldn't get Yancey to listen. When she couldn't get him to leave well enough alone, she cooked and she cleaned.

Fortunately, she had a growing son perfectly capable of eating her out of house and home and then some. Nothing ever went to waste with Spencer around. About that, at least, she couldn't complain. A good thing since she had plenty of other complaints.

Enough that were she to spread them like a thin Asiago cheese and spinach mixture over phyllo dough and layer them in her hygienic sink, she'd fill it to the brim and need another. Not that she could get phyllo dough in Pit Stop, Texas. Or that anyone living here would even know what it was.

Except, perhaps, for Neva Case.

Ooh, but if Yancey went out there to the Barn and caused more trouble . . . Jeanne rubbed harder at the scoured surface. She swore if he did, this time she was going to carry through with her threat and kick him out of her—their bed—no matter how much she'd miss having him there.

He just couldn't try to run their son's life. Spencer was near enough to being a man to be making his own decisions about the girls he dated. And, quite frankly, she'd never had a problem with her son seeing Candy Roman.

The girl was black, yes, in a town filled with necks of the red variety, or Latino brown. That alone made her unconventional. But she reinforced it with the way she dressed. The way—and colors—she wore her hair. Still, she was a good girl with a real head on her shoulders. She was creative. She was smart and charming, and quite beautiful in a young Whitney Houston or Gladys Knight sort of way.

Plus, she was here without being from here. She knew there was a lot more to the world than what could be found or experienced in Pit Stop. Pit Stop. A P.S. at the end of the road. Spencer could do a lot worse. At least seeing Candy romantically would give him more reason to come home than seeing his fuddy-duddy parents.

Ugh. Jeanne stripped off her rubber gloves. When had she gotten so old, thinking of herself as fuddy-duddy? She was only forty-two. Supposedly in her prime. Then again, she'd canceled her subscriptions to *Redbook*, *Cosmopolitan*, and Oprah's magazine when the stove needed replacing and every penny counted. For all she knew, as out of touch as she was, she was over that dreadfully painful hill and sliding down fast.

From the front of the house came the sound of a truck on the drive, followed a minute later by the screen on the mudroom door banging against the frame. The mesh was already torn, and at this rate they'd be needing to change out the hinges and the springs, too. Then again, Spencer would be off to Lubbock in another month, and no one else ever let the door slam.

"Hey, Mom," her son called as he entered the kitchen. "I wanted to stop and let you know I'm not going to be around tonight for supper."

Jeanne blew her nose into the paper towels she'd used to dry her hands. She sniffed as quietly as she could before turning. "Then I guess it's a good thing I was only planning soup and sandwiches, isn't it?"

"Dad working late?" Spencer grabbed an apple from the fruit bowl on the table and opened the refrigerator door to graze.

Her son. Tall like his father, yet built like the star wide receiver he was. And such a typical teen. Full of life and hormones. Not to mention being a bottomless pit.

"Are you sure you don't want soup and a sandwich now?" she asked, crossing her arms and leaning back against the sink to watch him rummage.

"Nah. Me and Joe and Mike are heading over toward E.T." Earnestine Township. The kids in the area used the acronym as a joke, Earnestine being a place alien to everything they knew. "This kid, Jase Bremmer, who played football over there, him and his girlfriend are both missing. His dad's always been at all our games, so we thought we'd go hang out and make sure he's doing okay."

Jeanne felt a tight gripping pain in her side. What was that Yancey had said earlier? About Holden Wagner searching for a missing girl? This was not anything she wanted Spencer involved in. It was bad enough knowing where Yancey was going tonight. What he was doing. With whom.

"Okay, but why don't I grill all of y'all some burgers? You boys check in with your friend's father, and I'll get everything ready." She glanced up at the wall clock, which resembled a peach. "Say, be back here at seven?"

Spencer closed the refrigerator, bit off another chunk of apple then into the square of cheddar cheese he'd pilfered. "I don't know, Mom. I'm pretty sure there'll be a ton of food at the Bremmers'. And after I drop off the guys, I'll probably head out to see Candy. Dad working late and all, the timing's pretty good."

Jeanne shook her head slowly. "Except the call your dad's seeing to tonight is out at the Barn. And it may have to do with your missing friend's girl."

She didn't know why she was telling Spencer anything. Yancey was good not to bring his work home, to keep what he could of his cases confidential, even when the Pit Stop phone lines would be burning up with the news.

He didn't talk about his work in front of Spencer because he didn't want to give their son the idea that the supposed excitement that went on here was anything when compared to the rest of the world. The world she and Yancey had chosen to leave behind because of what had happened to her. Because of what had truly happened to both of them.

"No way, really? Liberty's out at the Barn? Jase said her parents weren't into that crap about having her get married, just the religious stuff. I wonder if she knows where Jase is. That would be so weird if they both showed up out of nowhere. Anyhow," Spencer said, heading for the door, "I doubt Dad would still be out there by the time I showed up. And if he is, I'll just come home. 'Bye, Mom."

Jeanne couldn't do anything but let him go. He knew as well as she did that the rumors of what went on at the Big Brown Barn were just that. Rumors. Though somehow in Pit Stop, the end of the road where nothing else happened, rumors easily took on the guise of fact.

In this case, it was the gossip, the juice, the scintillating angle of polygamy and underage sex—even if the girls in Earnestine Township were consenting and legally wed. To think some allegedly went to Nevada Case, Esq., for help, an underground secretive help, especially when Neva denied any such thing happening, was too juicy not to slurp up.

Jeanne wasn't buying it.

She knew Neva better than many, and didn't believe it of her one and only friend. Neither did she believe Neva would keep her out of such a critical loop. Not when Jeanne felt she had so little in her life to look forward to, that she might as well drop off the face of the earth.

Candy Roman pushed the safety goggles from her face to the top of her head and swiped her forearm over her brow.

She only minded perspiring while she worked when sweat started running into her eyes, salting up her contacts, stinging and burning until she had to stop work completely, clean the lenses, and let her eyes rest.

She hated stopping work for something so lame as forgetting to wipe away sweat. In fact, she hated stopping at all, even to sleep. The website and catalogue for the Big Brown Barn already listed an expected shipping date of four to six weeks on her most popular jewelry designs.

She did all that she could to cut that to three. Waiting longer than three weeks for anything she'd ordered made her crazy. Receiving items unexpectedly early had her jumping for joy. She figured most of her customers fit the same profile, and so she balanced her workload accordingly.

When there were girls in residence, she kept them busy with straightforward assembly. Beads on filament. Fasteners attached. Tiny crystals sorted into bins by color and clarity. The more intricate pieces she constructed herself, but lately she had been doing it all. The sorting, the assembly, the finishing work.

Neva pitched in when she had time, of course, but the tech side of the business was her baby, dealing with the site's programmers and designers, not to mention sharing the duties of supply and inventory, the catalogue layout and printing, the packing and shipping, the accounting. Then there was her law practice, which these days was run more on the side.

How either of them managed to do all they did . . . Candy blew her bangs off her forehead, twisted side to side on her stool, and stretched her arms to the sky. That was just the way it was. And the way they were. Keeping busy seemed to be how most people managed to stay a step ahead of their demons.

She had enough to keep her running for the rest of her life.

Leaving the goggles on the worktable and shutting down the grinder, Candy made her way to the studio's door for a stretch and a breath of fresh air. The first floor, which had once been home to tack and animals, now served her well both as her design and living space.

The front half was divided between her studio and the shipping center, with a walled-off and seldom visited showroom where her best pieces were displayed. The rear half had been remodeled into an efficiency that more closely resembled a converted warehouse than an apartment—one she would never have been able to afford, much less outfit, in the city. At least not with the life she used to lead.

But thanks to Neva, going back to where she'd come from was a problem Candy wasn't going to have to face. Even if down the road they split their partnership to go separate ways, to pursue their own things, to have lives without holding one another's hands, her resumé was now physical and solid instead of being one or two lines about K-Mart, McDonald's, and J.C. Penney.

Of course, wearing herself out was not going to do her health or creativity any damn bit of good. And though she knew Neva's big heart was in the right place, what with giving the girl a job and Candy an assistant, Liberty Mitchell wasn't working out and really had to go.

Her nails this, her hair that. Her shoes, her jewelry, her lumpy bed, and minimum wage. The girl could not do any sort of honest day's work without mouthing, and quite frankly, Candy wasn't even sure about the honest part figuring in. She hadn't caught the girl lying or stealing, but she plain didn't trust the little brat. And she couldn't even say for sure why.

Climbing up to sit on one of the picnic tables on the patio at the side of the Barn, she braced her boots on the bench, her elbows on her knees, and her chin in the cup of her palms. A short break, a few minutes max, and she'd get back to work.

When at least fifteen later a pair of big male hands came from behind to cover her eyes and wake her up, her gasp was more about pleasure than surprise. "Ooh, your daddy is going to kill you if he finds you here."

"My daddy can go shoot himself in the foot," Spencer Munroe said, pulling her backwards and dropping a yummy upside-down kiss on her lips. "He doesn't have any say in what I do any longer."

He smelled like clean skin and warm sun and the breeze off the desert. He smelled like she liked her pillows to smell. He smelled like the best times she'd had in her life. And he kissed damn good for a white boy. "You don't have to talk big to impress me, baby. You know I'm going to let you into my pants."

"And I can't think of a better place to be," he said, coming around and hopping onto the table beside her. He looped an arm over her shoulders, and she leaned into his strong, solid body and sighed. " 'Course, you sound too tired to be getting kinky."

"I am tired, but I'm all over you and the kink." She

rubbed one hand up and down his thigh, realizing how great her mahogany skin looked against his worn denim. She could probably get close to the same contrast by working in copper and lapis lazuli rather than the turquoise she most often used.

He held her tighter, leaned his head over onto hers, rubbed his cheek up and down. "We'd probably best stick to public displays of affection for now."

"Why's that?" She squeezed his thigh. "You still scared of all my deep dark secrets?"

"Nah. I can't stay long. My dad's supposed to be coming out here later."

Candy rolled her eyes. "Neva's gonna love that."

"Yeah, that's what I was thinking. Seems he thinks there's a girl from E.T. hiding out here."

She pulled away, looked at him from the side, at his thick brown hair on the shaggy side of sexy, at his eyes that were never the same shade of green, shaking her head when he nodded. "Jesus Lord, I am so sick of people thinking this is some sort of sinister halfway house or something. If you're talking about Liberty Mitchell, then yes. She's here. Neva hired her. She's not *hiding* her."

"Huh," Spencer grunted. "Too bad someone didn't let her folks know. Keep the cavalry from being called out."

Candy bit down on the bad stuff she wanted to say. "Well, maybe the little brat might've thought to do that herself and save us from being hassled by the big bad sheriff."

The minute that followed was uncomfortable with Spencer's silence, before he took a breath and said, "Dad's not hassling you, Candy. He's just doing his job."

Candy sighed, leaned forward and away from the cradle of his body. It was hard sometimes to remember where she was and all the reasons why. That Yancey Munroe wasn't out to bust her ass because she fit a profile, because she was in the wrong place at the wrong time.

Because her background and situation and skin color made it hard for law enforcement to believe she wouldn't be involved in trouble.

Because she had been in the past.

She stared out across the dusky yellows and rich summer browns of the horizon, measuring the distance by the fence posts and lines of barbed wire. "I know, baby. I'm just reacting the way I've reacted to cops all my life. What I've been through tends to color my judgment and not in a good way."

Spencer was silent for several minutes, his palm rubbing circles between her shoulder blades. It felt so good to have him touch her without wanting anything, without asking or demanding or forcing. He did that all the time. Made her feel so cherished. Important. Valuable.

And then there was the fact of her back hurting from all the work she'd been doing. The bending and hunching with never enough stretching between. She pushed off the table, moved to the bench to sit between his spread legs. He took the hint and began to use his big hands the way she so loved, massaging her neck and shoulders.

"You know, Candy, you can talk about what happened to bring you out here. It's not like I can't keep my mouth shut. I wouldn't tell any of the guys, and I sure as hell wouldn't tell my parents."

"I know, baby. And you're sweet to care, but you'll be leaving soon and—"

"Damn it, Candy. I'm going to school. I'm not leaving you."

"School." She sighed with envy. "Where the whole world is going to open up to you, and you'll have the pick of any girl on campus, being the big football star that you are. I won't be the exotic fish in the sea anymore. I'll just be that black girl back home."

He spit out a big mouthful of nasty words. "I swear, Candy, you are so full of crap sometimes."

"Does it make you want to hit me, Spencer?" She looked over her shoulder. "Do you ever want to backhand all that crap right out of me?"

His eyes widened beneath his frown. "What the hell are you talking about? Christ, why would I want to hit you?"

"And that, sweet Spencer Munroe, is why I'm so out of my mind over you." She reached up, patted his chest. "Too many men in my past and my mama's past liked to talk with their hands."

"I thought you liked me talking with my hands."

"Oh, baby. I do." She kneeled on the bench between his knees and took his face in her hands. His eyes were like polished jade; his hair almost as dark as her own. His lashes and cheekbones were enough to make a woman cry.

She felt her own tears threaten to fall. "You're one of a kind, baby. And down the road there is going to be some girl who deserves everything you have to offer. But I'm not crazy enough to think that girl is me."

"Why? Because you're five years older? Because you're black?" His nostrils almost flared. "Because I'm a stupid country bumpkin from the middle of nowhere?"

She stared, backed away. "Why the hell would you think something like that?"

"Because you won't tell me what happened to you. Because you're blowing me off. It's like you think I'm good enough to sleep with, but that's all. That I'm not good enough for anything more."

"That's not true, Spencer. Not true at all." She sniffed, tried to find anything she could of her usual composure. "You make me forget my past. You make me think I'm worth something. Being with you this summer has been amazing. But I'm not going to stand in the way of your future. And since we'll never agree on that, we might as well drop it."

"Shit," he said, shaking his head. "I'll drop it for now, but only because my dad just drove up."

Candy turned and followed the direction of his gaze, slicing off a sharp laugh. "And he's not the only one. Check out Holden Wagner's sweet ride. I'd better go find Neva and Liberty and see what's going on."

Five

Holden drove his white BMW 745Li past Neva's combined home and office and up to the front of the Big Brown Barn. He glanced at the Tag Heuer on his wrist. It was precisely the time he'd arranged to meet Sheriff Munroe.

Breaking his own habit of punctuality, Holden decided, would no doubt make some sort of sense. Less disappointment. Less aggravation. More of a feeling of fitting in. The latter, of course, made no difference. He had never expected to fit in. That wasn't why he'd come to this small Texas town.

He'd come here to find a place out of the limelight. To downplay his past, the good along with the bad. Disappointment, aggravation—those he'd learned to live with long ago. So the status quo would remain. He would be on time and no one else would bother.

After leaving Munroe's office this morning, Holden had gone for a drive—as Sunday-after-church as that sounded—instead of going back to work or even heading home. Since he remained on the fringe of church involvement, he found no need to embrace much of the religious doctrine, especially the one espousing austere self-denial.

The township paid him well, and the work he did for the

church supplemented that income nicely. He enjoyed fine things, his clothes and his car, his home and his office—none of which bore any resemblance to the Amish-like plainness found throughout Earnestine.

As comfortable as were the environments in which he lived and worked, however, returning to either space offered an open invitation to visitors. He had too much on his mind to countenance interruptions—his intolerance was a trait he supposed was inherited as much as ingrained.

The same trait had, after all, been the final lapse of faith that had factored into his missionary parents' brutal, bloody end. And their end had been the determining factor in the direction he'd taken his life.

By the time all was said and done, by the time he'd completed his education, by the time he'd reached the pinnacle of his very public career, he'd even convinced himself that they'd been martyrs for the cause of religious freedom, that they had been massacred for their beliefs.

In reality, their deaths had been a testament to their hypocrisy. To the life they'd lived behind the scenes. To the patience and forbearance they'd presented to their audience but never practiced at home.

He had been the only witness to the truth, the only one able to give testimony, but he'd let their good names stand in the end because it had benefited him to do so. Or it had until guilt crept in to steal away all that he had gained.

In the early years, he'd been too frightened to speak, a cowering little boy afraid to say anything at all for fear that he'd use a word incorrectly, one with a meaning he didn't know or didn't understand. His silence had pleased his parents, as had his devotion to his studies.

Yet it had been those very studies that had pricked at his conscience and begun to unravel his safety net of blind denial. Knowledge was like that, a big bright light shining down on the truth.

Unfortunately, not all truth was so liberating. The truth haunting him now, in fact, presented a reversal of fortunes. All these years later, all the steps he'd taken, backtracking and sidestepping to cover his long and winding path, disappearing into the great void and settling into Earnestine Township, and still he'd been discovered.

He was too deeply rooted to tear up all that he'd built here and start over again. And so he'd made a choice. A decision with which he wasn't comfortable, but which offered a logical situational solution.

If all went as planned, he would be losing the personal freedom he'd enjoyed for so very long. Not exactly the goal he'd been working toward, but certainly a choice he preferred over the alternate.

That of losing his life.

At the sound of car wheels on the gravel road that ran past her house to the Barn, Neva leaned forward to look out the window over her kitchen sink. Oh, dear. Oh, my. The microwave timer dinged from the counter beside her. Oh, hell.

She couldn't even sit down to a nice nuked dinner of chicken noodle soup without Holden Wagner ruining it for her the way he ruined so many things for so many people. She couldn't believe she was going to have to deal with him now, after hours. Seemed nothing about his cause could wait.

Twelve hours ago, she'd been in Carlsbad, New Mexico, about to make her way home. Now it was seven o'clock, the end of a long stressful day, one she was more than ready to put to bed. But when Sheriff Munroe's car pulled in several seconds later, following Holden's down the road to the Barn, Neva accepted the fact that neither sleep nor chicken noodle soup were in her immediate future.

She left the kitchen, soup and all, pushed open the back

door of the two-story, white-framed house, and headed out into the lingering heat of the day. The screen squeaked on its hinges and slammed behind her. She loved this house and the huge pecan trees that shaded it. Her own little nutty oasis in the desert. It was too large of a house for one person, but she didn't care.

She loved the room to roam, loved the privacy, loved the stairs when they groaned, the creaks in the hardwood floor. The sounds were her personal security system, alerting her to the wind, to shifts in the temperature, and to anyone who might be stupid enough to sneak upstairs and into her bedroom where she still slept with a Dirty Harry Colt .45.

And until he showed up to claim it, where she'd be sleeping with Mick Savin's SIG Sauer.

With the gravel of the road crunching beneath her boots as she walked down to the Barn, she wondered if she might've done good to bring one of the weapons with her. There was nothing about this visit from either of these men that made her feel the least bit safe—or anything but out of her element.

And then it got worse.

Just as Yancey stepped from his car, Candy stepped from around the side of the Barn holding hands with Spencer Munroe. At the unnecessarily heavy slam of the sheriff's car door, the pair came to a stop. Yancey didn't remove his sunglasses, didn't acknowledge his son. One hand at his hip on the butt of his gun, he headed straight for the showroom, entering through the door Holden had left wide open.

Neva shook her head, groaned, and picked up the pace, the setting sun still cooking the ground, the heat dampening her shirt where it clung between her shoulder blades, where sweat trickled between her breasts. She really, really didn't need this tonight. Especially since the only clue she had as to what was going on here was named Liberty Mitchell.

The last to arrive, Neva reached the Barn after Candy

and Spencer had followed Yancey and Holden inside. What irony, she thought, walking from bright light into dim. The first time the showroom was filled to capacity, not a single one of the visitors was here to buy a thing.

It was in the next moment, however, as her eyes adjusted to the change, that the irony was lost in the face of panic. Two faces, to be exact. One belonged to Candy, her dark eyes wide as they darted from case to case as if accounting for all of her precious babies.

But the other face, the face of Liberty Mitchell, her long dark hair pulled back in a scrunchie that emphasized her suddenly pale skin, her wide brown eyes brimming with tears, her usually smart mouth with lips that now quivered—it was the panic in that face raising hackles along Neva's nape and chilling the moisture coating her skin.

She looked from Liberty, who stood clutching a roll of paper towels and a bottle of Windex with FM resting at her feet, to Candy, to Spencer, to Holden, and finally to Sheriff Yancey Munroe.

"Uh, hi. Does someone want to tell me what's going on here? The showroom is closed." She tapped the sign in the door's window listing the hours of operation. "So unless you're here for a private viewing or with a warrant, I'm going to have to ask you to leave."

Standing on widespread feet, his arms crossed over his chest, Sheriff Munroe spoke first. "Neva, I have to say I'm disappointed. I've defended you for five years against rumors. Rumors that now appear to be true."

Neva wasn't sure if the knot of emotion in her stomach was dread or relief. She'd known this was coming—she'd just never expected to be so lucky. The showdown over Liberty might not be a pleasant cap to the day, but at least there were plenty of witnesses to the truth.

She stepped farther into the room, raised a brow. "I have no idea what you're talking about, Sheriff. Sorry."

"He's obviously referring to the proof standing in front of us." Holden, posed in the center of the room, turned to face her, the creases in his designer slacks sharp enough to cut glass, as was his vindictive tone of voice. "Proof that you do harbor runaways."

Before Neva even formed a response, Candy sputtered, "I don't know where you got your law degree, but even I know that part about innocent until proven guilty. Neva picked up the dog on the side of the road. We don't know if he's a runaway or if he was abandoned there."

Leaning into his elbows propped on one of the display cases, Spencer chuckled. His father glared. Neva used her fingers to cover her smile. Even Liberty regained a bit of the color in her face.

Holden wasn't amused. "Thank you for that, Ms. Roman. But the runaway you and Ms. Case will be prosecuted for harboring is Miss Mitchell."

"Who said she's a runaway?" Spencer asked. "If she was, wouldn't she be hiding somewhere instead of working out in the open?"

"Stay out of this, Spencer." Yancey's voice was low, just this side of threatening, the voice of the law, not that of a father. "It's none of your concern."

"Liberty's a friend," Spencer argued. "That makes it my concern."

"He does raise a good point, Yancey," Neva put in before the Munroe family animosity could escalate. "The only one here talking about runaways is Holden."

Yancey took a long moment to finally remove his sunglasses, hanging them by an earpiece over his shirt collar. He rocked back on his heels and spoke down to the floor as he said, "Then would you care to explain what the girl is doing here? Why you haven't reported her whereabouts to her parents? Why they had to hire an attorney—"

Spencer snorted. "Sounds to me like someone's jumping the gun, hiring an attorney."

This time the sheriff's pointed tone of voice nearly clipped the thread of his temper. "Spencer, I told you to stay out of this."

Spencer pushed away from the display case, taking a long step forward. His fingers flexed as he fought making a fist. "You're talking about a friend of mine, and making accusations about my girlfriend. I have as much right to be here as anyone."

"Spencer, baby." Candy stepped in front of him to soothe. "It's okay—"

Yancey jabbed a finger at Candy. "You shut your mouth." Another finger at his son. "You go outside. I'm not telling you again."

Oh, no. Neva wasn't going to be having any of this. She was sick of powerful men running roughshod. "No, Sheriff. You go outside. Unless you have a warrant, you have no rights here and no reason to be interfering with my employees or how I run my business."

"I'd say based on the evidence, I have every right in the world and the law on my side." Yancey pulled his handcuffs from his belt. "Nevada Case. You are under arrest—"

"Stop it!" Liberty screamed, heads swiveling her way. "Everyone just stop it! You can't arrest her. I didn't run away. I just wanted a job and she gave me one."

Holden moved closer, a buffer between the girl and the sheriff. "You left home without telling your parents where you were going, Liberty. You left everything you own behind. Don't feel that you have to defend Ms. Case."

"I'm not defending her." Liberty stared at the roll of paper towels in her hand. "I only wanted a job. And besides, I lied and told her I was eighteen. I didn't want her checking with my parents about giving me room and board. They won't let me work, and I wanted a job."

"Liberty, they're very worried about you," Holden said.

"Then tell them I'm fine."

"Actually, you'll have to tell them yourself," Neva said, hating that she had to do so. She'd known when she'd offered Liberty the temporary solution that it was just that. Temporary. The girl had needed a place to lick her wounds and get her head together, and Neva never had been able to tell a troubled young woman no. "I can't have you staying here without their permission if you're underage. It's the law, sweetie. I'm sorry."

Liberty's mouth quivered; her eyes grew wide and wet. "But I don't want to go back. I'm afraid to go back."

The sheriff blew out a long breath of impatience, at which Neva rolled her eyes and which Holden ignored. He moved to block Yancey's access to the girl, asking her softly, "Why would you be afraid, Liberty?" She shook her head, her ponytail coming loose, and he prodded again. "Liberty? Why would you be afraid?"

"I can't tell you."

"I don't understand. Why can't you tell me?"

"Because of what happened to Jase!" Liberty dropped to her knees, the dog rising up protectively in front of her as she sobbed. "Because of what happened to Jase."

Neva started forward, her spine trembling with the fading echo of Liberty's cry. Spencer followed. Already there, Candy bent down, took the towels and glass cleaner out of the girl's hands, set both items on the nearest display case.

Holden hovered close, yet it was Yancey who took command of the room. "Spencer, take Miss Roman and the two of you wait outside. Please. Neva, you, too."

Spencer and Candy did as they were told. Neva stayed, shook her head. He was not getting rid of her now. "I'm not going anywhere. The girl needs an advocate, and I'm taking the case."

"Her family has hired me—"

One raised palm and she cut off Holden's rhetoric. "Right. To look after their best interests. I'm only interested in Liberty's."

Yancey looked from Neva to Holden and back. He held her gaze while asking Liberty, "Miss Mitchell. I need to ask you a few questions about Jase Bremmer. Do you want Ms. Case to stay or to go?"

"Please stay," Liberty whispered, nodding fiercely.

"Of course I will." Neva offered a hand, helped the girl to her feet, insisting she focus. "If there's anything I don't want you to respond to, I'll let you know. Otherwise, just answer the sheriff honestly and everything will be fine."

Liberty nodded as Yancey pulled a notebook and pen from his pocket. "Radford called us over this morning and told us that he hasn't seen Jase for a week. When was the last time you saw him?"

"Last Friday night. A week ago," she answered. "We went out."

Yancey nodded. "Did Jase drive? Did he pick you up? Or did you meet him somewhere?"

"I met him at the Dairy Mart. I had a salad." She shrugged, tilted her head to one side. "Jase had a burger. And a Coke. Except he didn't eat much of anything."

The sheriff's pen paused. "He wasn't hungry? He was in a hurry?"

She shook her head. "I think he was nervous. He said he had something he wanted to tell me." Twisting her fingers together at her waist, she cast her gaze down. "I thought he had figured out a way for us to leave Earnestine and be together."

"Then you were running away?"

She glanced nervously at Neva, who gave her the go-ahead with a brief nod. "Not really." She rubbed her hand over FM's head. "It's just that we both hated Earnestine so much and wanted to leave, but it was really just talk. We never made any actual plans."

"Okay." More notes. Another pause. The sheriff looked back up. "So, Jase was nervous. But if not about running away, do you know what it was?"

She avoided his gaze, reached down to tug on one of the dog's ears. "He'd stolen money from the printing and supply store where he worked."

Yancey glanced at Holden, who shook his head. Neva did the same. She hadn't heard anything either—surprising, since that sort of gossip traveled as fast as rumors about the Barn.

The sheriff took it all in, cleared his throat. "This robbery. Did he give you any details? When it happened? What he took?"

Liberty continued to pet and play with FM, continued to look only at the dog. "It wasn't like a robbery with a gun or anything. He didn't hold up a bank. He just took some of the money he was supposed to deposit out of the bag. I don't know when."

"I'll have to check with the store tomorrow." Yancey talked while his pen scratched over the paper. "See if they've noticed they're short."

"They should've noticed," Liberty said with a snort. "He said it was two hundred thousand dollars."

Neva gasped. "What?"

Holden frowned. "That's impossible. The Paisleys own that store. I know them both."

Yancey remained silent, obviously struggling with his own disbelief, finally narrowing his eyes at Liberty. "Are you sure about that—"

"Yes, I'm sure. God!" The teenage drama queen switched

into high gear. "He didn't know where it came from or how it got in the bag. But it had to belong to the guys who came after him later. The ones with the guns."

"Whoa. Wait just a second—"

"I'm telling the truth, Sheriff." She pleaded with him to believe. "We ditched his truck at one of the back gates into his dad's ranch. It's probably still there. He thought someone was following us, so we ran. He wanted to hide in an old hunting blind. He'd put it back up after his dad tore it down and he thought we'd be safe there."

Yancey pondered that for only a moment. "I know where that is. It's a plot he used to lease."

"We never got there," Liberty added, moving closer to Neva, who wrapped an arm around the girl's shoulders and absorbed what she could of her tremors. "I fell down and couldn't run and then my shoe broke. There were all these trucks and lights and men shouting, and Jase ran off. Then I heard gunshots. And Jase screaming."

Neva stroked her hand over the girl's hair. "Oh, sweetie. You must've been so scared. What did you do?"

Liberty sniffed. "This guy, one of the ones after Jase, he told me to walk toward the county road. So I did."

"He let you go?" Holden asked. "Just like that?"

She nodded. "No one else was around. He told me if I told anyone what had happened that he would kill me. That's why I came here." She turned her beseeching gaze to Neva. "I'd heard the rumors and thought I'd be safe here. I'd have to answer too many questions back in Earnestine, and I couldn't. I knew the guy with the dreadlocks was telling the truth." She swallowed hard. "That he'd kill me if I talked."

"Dreadlocks?"

Liberty nodded at Holden's question. "He was black. And had an accent. Like, Jamaican."

The sheriff returned his sunglasses to his face, his notebook and pen to his pocket, and headed for the showroom's door, leaving the three of them with a curt, "Excuse me."

Deciding they could all do with a bit of fresh air, Neva gestured for Holden and Liberty to follow, closing up behind them as the Mitchell family attorney took Liberty under his wing, guiding her around the side of the Barn to the picnic table on the porch.

Neva followed the duo and the dog, passing the sheriff's car in time to hear a snippet of Yancey's radio call, a mention of a development in the Bremmer case, a request for a state crime scene unit to be called in.

As appalled as she was at what Liberty had been through, Neva couldn't help but send up a prayer of thanks that her intuition had kicked in days ago when the girl had arrived at her door. Liberty's cries hadn't resonated with the same desperate distress as those of the girls Neva helped whisk away from Earnestine in the middle of the night.

The teen had been upset, but she hadn't wanted to talk about why she'd come to the Barn. That reluctance had been Neva's first clue that Liberty's plea for a job wasn't about a forced marriage. Taking her in as a boarder and putting her to work had given the situation time to come to a head. An ugly head, yes, but Liberty was safe, and Neva had dodged another bullet aimed at the Big Brown Barn.

She settled onto the bench beside the girl and leaned in close. "Are you okay?"

Liberty nodded. "I didn't know how much that was killing me to keep inside. I mean, I'm scared—"

"Don't be." Holden pushed off from the end of the table on which he'd been leaning and knelt at her side. "You've done nothing wrong. You're not alone in this. And no one is going to get to you. Trust me."

He sounded so warm and sincerely human that even Neva had to consciously stop herself from being sucked in. Toads of his nature didn't have it in them to be so compassionate, but she didn't have time to analyze the reason for the act.

In the next second, Candy walked onto the porch from the studio into which she'd obviously disappeared earlier, Spencer in her wake. She glanced at the group sitting around the table. "Is everything okay?"

Neva gave a small shrug. "I think so. Liberty's been through a bit of an adventure, but the sheriff's on it."

"Does it have to do with Jase being missing?" Spencer asked.

Liberty nodded. "I'm sorry. I don't know what happened to him."

"Shh." Holden. Calming again. "The only thing that matters now is getting you home, and letting your parents see for themselves that you're safe and sound."

"Do you think that's wise?" Neva didn't like how this pat ending to the drama was going Holden's way. She didn't like it at all. "Liberty can stay here as long as her parents give their permission. It's not like we don't have plenty of space. If she's in danger, being away from Earnestine might not be a bad thing."

The sheriff walked up then, interrupting what would more than likely have been Holden's objection. "Miss Mitchell, I may need to ask you more questions later, but in the meantime, I'll drive you home."

So much for her concern, she mused, looking up at the sound of another vehicle arriving unexpectedly. A big black Range Rover with dark-tinted windows spit gravel and rooster tails of dust on its way down the road from the house to the Barn. She wanted to groan; she so did not need anyone else bringing trouble to her doorstep today.

The SUV pulled in beside the sheriff's car, and everyone at the table turned as the driver shut off the engine. The door opened; a pair of black combat boots, unlaced and tongues flapping, hit the ground, drawing Neva's gaze before drawing a startled gasp she wished she'd managed to stifle.

It was too late. Everyone had heard.

"Uh, Neva?" Candy asked as Neva slid from the bench to her feet. "Were you expecting someone?"

All Neva could do was shake her head because Mick Savin had made his way around the open driver's-side door and captivated her attention. He wore his sunglasses, his outback hat, and a white T-shirt beneath the navy blue sling immobilizing his arm. The shirt was bunched over the waist of a pair of worn jeans, the legs of which were bunched over the tops of the boots.

He looked like a man who'd barely managed to dress himself. He moved like a man in pain. She wanted to go to him, prop a shoulder beneath his good one, wrap an arm around his waist, help him get to where he was going as quickly as he could in order to ease the brackets from around his mouth.

What was he doing up and around? No, wait. What the hell was he doing driving? She couldn't imagine being in his condition and wanting to do more than lie still and sleep. He looked like he'd been chewed up and spit out. The sunglasses he wore did nothing to hide the bruises beneath his eyes.

But none of that meant that she wanted him here. And she certainly didn't want witnesses to her reaction to his arrival. She walked out to meet him at the edge of the patio, stopping and crossing her arms over her chest to keep him from coming any closer.

"What are you doing here?" she asked, a question that was much simpler than all the questions behind it, especially the ones demanding she examine why her heart raced so madly at seeing him again.

He cocked his head to the side, and then he smiled—a

smile that made the day that had gone before nothing but a distant memory. God, but she needed help. She was obviously on the verge of losing her mind. She shouldn't have wanted him here, but she'd never been so glad to see anyone in her life.

He reached up with his one good hand, used his index finger to tug the dark lenses away from his eyes. They sparkled, and her pulse jumped, jumped harder at the sound of his voice when he gave her a wink and said, "I hear from the veterinarian back in Pit Stop that you took my dog."

After watching Liberty Mitchell willingly leave with that snake Holden Wagner, who'd sworn not to let anyone get to her, Yancey climbed into his car. He slammed the accelerator to the floor, spun his tires out of Neva's drive onto the main road, and hit the switch for his lights.

Spencer's truck wasn't but a quarter mile ahead, and damn if the boy was going to get home without having his ass handed to him for making fools out of the both of them. The boy had gotten too big for his britches, back-talking in public. Bad enough he had no respect for his father, but to have no respect for the law was an attitude in need of adjustment.

Spencer had slowed for the curve ahead to avoid rolling his truck. His being a careful driver in this case worked in Yancey's favor. He blasted past the boy on the wrong side of the road, braked and spun in front of the truck, forcing the other vehicle onto the shoulder.

Shoving open his door, he climbed out and headed around the back of his car toward the cab of the truck where Spencer sat dazed. He was wearing his seat belt, and the truck hadn't stopped hard enough to do more than jar him.

Still, Yancey had to force back his initial reaction, the clutch of fear to his heart. He'd be a damn poor excuse for a father otherwise. In this case, however, he knew Spencer was fine. And that made doing what he had to do less hard than had the boy been hurt.

He jerked open the truck's driver's-side door and glared. "Do you have some sort of explanation for what went on back there? Because if you do, I'd really like to hear it."

Spencer was slow to turn, and he kept both hands gripped tight to the wheel when he finally did look over and match Yancey's glare. "You mean the way you threw your weight around and made Candy feel like shit?"

Always back to the girl. *Always back to the girl.* "If she's feeling like shit, you can blame yourself. You know I don't want you seeing her. If you did what I said, we wouldn't be having this problem."

"No, Dad. I blame you. You told her to shut up and get the hell out of your sight."

"That's not what I said, and you know it." Yancey took a deep breath. "I told both of you to leave while I conducted an official interview. Don't turn it into a personal vendetta."

"I'm not turning it into anything." Spencer pulled off his ball cap, threw it across the truck's bench seat. "You started it when you decided to butt into my life and tell me who I can date."

"You don't need to be dating anyone. Not seriously." Why was that so hard for the boy to understand? "And not now. You have football coming up. You have your studies. If you need to be getting laid, do it. Just keep it in your pants and out of your head."

"God, I can't believe you. You're sick, man. You're fucking sick."

"Why? Because I want your future to be more than a postscript at the end of the road? You get more involved with that girl than you already are, you won't think of anything or anyone else."

"There's nothing wrong with her!" Spencer jerked off his

seat belt and pushed out of the cab and past his father. And then he turned back and growled. The tailgate rang with metallic fury from the slam of his open palm.

The palm with which he brought down footballs at the end of Hail Mary passes. Yancey cringed. "Spencer, son. Listen to me."

"No, Dad. You listen to me. Candy's the best thing that's ever happened in my life. I'm not going to give her up just because you don't like her."

"This has nothing to do with my feelings for her. It's about my feelings for you. She's the best thing in your life now, yes, but that's because you haven't had a chance to live. Once you're away from here and at school, you'll understand that she's nothing—"

Spencer swung. Yancey barely managed to duck the boy's fist. He stumbled back against his car, off balance, and Spencer shoved past and jumped back into his cab. He put the truck in reverse and spun backwards off the shoulder, grinding gears as he searched for first and gunning the truck down the road when he did.

Well, that didn't go so well, Yancey mused, dragging both hands tiredly down his face. Jeanne would tell him he had the finesse of an elephant herd when what he really had was a love for his son that was too profound and powerful to put into words.

He'd always wondered how different things might have been had the circumstances of Spencer's conception and birth not been what they were. Or if Jeanne hadn't been adamant that they have no more kids. It wasn't being a parent, she'd insisted, but being pregnant again that she wouldn't be able to bear.

A part of Yancey understood, a part of him never would. But it was her body, not his, her decision, and he loved her too much to ever tell her what it would have meant to him to have another child.

What he'd done instead was show her the type of man he was by being the best husband and father he knew how to be. And if a part of him spent years longing for more, well . . . Nothing mattered now but seeing his son never suffered the same sort of regrets of always wondering over might-have-beens.

Six

Liberty hadn't ridden in a car with leather seats since leaving California. She'd forgotten how sweet they smelled, how warm and rich. Unless what she was smelling was Holden Wagner's cologne or aftershave or whatever it was. God, but she felt so stupid at times. No, not stupid. Ignorant of the world.

She'd only been sixteen when she'd been dragged halfway across the country for her spiritual good. She hadn't been old enough to go clubbing or anything yet. Yeah, so she made straight A's in school and had scored over fifteen hundred on her SATs. It didn't matter.

Even with grants and scholarships, her parents would never let her go away to school. Look at what had happened when all she'd done was get a job twenty miles away. Okay, it was more than that, what with the Jase thing and all. But having the sheriff come after her was way embarrassing.

"Your parents will be glad to find out you're okay," Holden said, watching the road and never looking over.

She liked his voice. It was kinder than she'd thought it would be. And she liked the way he sat in the car's seat. The way he slouched back—one wrist on the steering wheel, his hand on the gearshift knob, his knees spread open—was kinda sexy and hot. "I don't know why they thought anything was wrong. They moved us here so I'd be sheltered and safe."

"Well, this time I imagine it's because Jase Bremmer is missing, too."

She didn't want to think about Jase. The gunshots. His screams. The guy with the long dreads sending her away. She knew she was being sort of selfish, but deep down she also knew that Jase had never really loved her, that she had never really loved him. And, yeah. She was pretty freaked out not knowing what had happened to him. Or what would happen to her.

It had been fun to have the fantasy of a future with him away from E.T., but that wasn't ever going to happen. She wasn't ever going to have the life she wanted. Her parents wouldn't let her work, so she didn't have money. They wouldn't let her go to school, which meant no education. She was stuck. Stuck, stuck, stuck. And now she'd never feel safe; she'd always be looking over her shoulder.

"I'm sorry about Jase. I wish I knew what happened or could help the sheriff more. And I probably should've talked to him sooner, but I was just too scared. Getting the job was the only thing I could think of to do. I just felt safe at the Barn with no one but Candy and Neva knowing I was there."

That much was the truth. Plus, she liked Candy's designs. The pieces were mega cool. And in case the Barn really did help some girls, she wasn't going to bust them by saying she'd gone there to escape when the job made more sense.

"Not that it's my place to tell you what to do," Holden advised softly, "but you probably should have let your parents know where you were and what you were doing. That you were okay."

She twisted in her seat enough to face him. "First off, no car. No way to get back without begging a ride and, trust me, no one goes to Earnestine. Second, no phone. We've lived there a year now, and they still haven't had a line installed. It's torture. Maybe now they'll at least get that much done, though I'll still be on foot until I'm eighty."

Holden glanced over. She couldn't see his eyes behind the cool lenses he wore, but she did like the way he smiled. It wasn't fatherly at all. It was more like the smile of a friend. Almost like one from a boy who thought she was cute . . .

Did Holden Wagner think she was cute? Oh, my god, no way! She turned back to stare out the front window at the road ahead. She would just *die* if he thought she was cute, especially since all the girls at school talked about him like he was as yummy as Brad Pitt.

"Liberty, let me ask you something."

"Sure," she said, feeling all bouncy and giddy but forcing herself to sit still and straight. She wasn't so immature that she didn't know what it would mean for a man this powerful to like her, to take her side. If she played things right, he could be her ticket out of town.

"Do you like nice things? You talked about wanting a phone and not having a car. I just wondered if those things mean a lot to you."

She gave a soft huff. "They obviously don't mean too much since I'm existing without them."

He waited a minute—she couldn't even hear the road as they drove, not like in her dad's truck—then said, "Existing. That's an interesting choice of words to describe your life."

"I suppose. But sometimes it seems like that's all I'm doing. Or all I'll ever be able to do." And now that she'd run off, no telling what sort of punishment she was in for. "Are my folks pretty mad?"

"Hmm. Worried, yes. But I'm not sure I'd say mad. More like . . . concerned."

"Concerned about what? That I'll remember how great life was in California before we moved to Earnestine?" She crossed her arms over her chest, flopped back in the cushy seat. "Trust me. I've never forgotten and I never will."

"I think their concern is for your safety and welfare. For your future. That you'll make bad choices."

"Bad choices? You mean the way I'd choose to get an education if they'd let me? That I'd want a career and a life of my own?"

"Concerned about you being able to look out for yourself, care for yourself. Provide for yourself."

It was the way he added that last part, the tone of his voice. The way he paused. Dread skittered over her skin and settled in her belly. She shivered, and even her nipples got hard. "Oh, no. Don't even tell me they're going to do that. That they're going to try to make me get married."

"You don't want to get married?"

"In the future, sure. Once my life isn't such a screwed-up mess, and to a guy I like. One who likes me. Not some old desperate coot wanting babies, or trying to buy eternal life by stocking up on wives." God, this could not be happening. This entire last week, since that night with Jase, everything had gone so wrong.

"Liberty, be honest with me. Weren't you and Jase running away to be together?"

"Yes, okay. We were. But not to get married. We hadn't even talked about where we were going. Just away. Maybe to Mexico," she finally added, thinking about Jase saying they'd make a run for the border.

Holden remained silent for probably five or six miles at least. Or so it seemed to Liberty. Not that she knew anything about the driving distance between Pit Stop and Earnestine. But she did know how to read the mile markers on the road.

And she knew they were going to be back at her parents' house, that they were going to be home a whole lot sooner than she was ready for. "Could you stop the car? Pull over or something?"

"Are you going to be sick?"

More like she didn't want to break down and cry. Not in front of him. She waved her hands. "I just need some air. I'm sorry. I don't mean to act like a baby."

"I don't think you're acting like a baby," he said, easing the sporty luxury car over to the shoulder of the road. "This news would be a shock to anyone who wasn't expecting it."

"That's the thing. I should've expected it. Sooner or later. I mean, why move to Earnestine if they weren't going to do like the natives do?" She shoved open the car door and nearly tumbled out, she was in such a hurry.

She trudged through the ankle-high grass and weeds, all of it brown and stabbing at her legs like sticks, to the fence separating the pasture from the road. It wasn't what she'd always thought of as a pasture. It wasn't green and dotted with spotted dairy cows. It was dry and rocky with tufts of yellowed wheat-looking plants.

Just like she'd tripped over that night when running across Jase's ranch. Tears were wetting her cheeks when she sensed Holden at her side. "Do you know who they want to marry me off to?"

Holden nodded. "Cal Able. He works the hardware store with his father. And right now he only has one wife."

"Oh, like that's supposed to make me feel better." She didn't think she could feel any worse. "I suppose Cal will think it's his duty to beat me if I don't pluck my own chickens, wear sackcloth and ashes, and wipe his feet with my hair."

Holden didn't respond except to rest his hand on her shoulder for a moment and squeeze before walking back to the car. After a few minutes, she followed, surprised to find him leaning against the side and waiting patiently beside her open door.

His arms were crossed over his chest, his legs crossed at the ankles. The setting sun made his hair look like thick corn silk, almost like Brad Pitt's, like all the girls said. His eyes were hidden behind his sunglasses, but he really was pretty cute.

"So, what do I do now?" A stupid question, but she really didn't want to go home. If she did, she'd probably never see the light of day again, much less the iridescent coral nail polish she missed so much.

She supposed she could truly run away, but it was a long way back to California, the only place she knew to go, and she had no money, no transportation, and ending up as a prostitute, living on the streets somewhere between here and there, was a worse end than marrying Cal Able.

Maybe she could get the wedding postponed until after her birthday. September wasn't that far away, and then her parents wouldn't have any say in what she did. And even if she had to get married then, it didn't have to be forever. She could stand it long enough to figure out a way to get a divorce.

The sex and the babies thing though . . . "I don't suppose I could get a prescription for birth control under an assumed name," she said, then cringed when she realized who she was talking to. God, Holden Wagner supported everything that happened in Earnestine. She tried to smile. "I was just kidding, you know."

He didn't rebuke her. He didn't make her feel small. He looked at her straight on, like an equal. "There is one other thing I need to know. If you want me to help you."

Was he kidding? "Help me how?"

"By making your homecoming easier." He smiled a bit. "By coming up with a solution that might sit better with you while still pleasing your parents and the church elders."

God, but he was thinking of everything! She'd tell him her entire pathetic life story if it would help. "Ask away."

"You're almost eighteen, right?"

She nodded, turned to drop onto the edge of her seat. "In September." And then it hit her. "They're going to rush this through, aren't they? Before my birthday?" Before she could get away or make any sort of plans.

"You're a very smart girl, Liberty. A very pretty girl." He looked away, stared off into the distance. "Are you still a virgin?"

She closed her eyes, bowed her head, shook it.

"Then I guess girl is the wrong word, isn't it?"

"And I guess Cal won't buy super tampons as an excuse, will he?"

At that, Holden chuckled. "I like you, Liberty. And if you like me at all, or at least like me better than you do Cal Able, then I think I have a solution to both our problems."

What kind of problem could he possibly have? And why did it depend on her liking him? Unless . . . She swallowed hard. "A solution?"

He dropped down to crouch in front of her, ignoring the way the weeds messed up his pants. "I've been in Earnestine seven years. I belong to the church, but I've been reluctant to embrace a lot of the doctrine. I've been more concerned with upholding the law and the residents' constitutional rights."

She knew all about Holden's position in Earnestine. Everyone did. He was pretty much a legend. "The First Amendment. I know all about it."

"Good. Now, here's the thing. The city fathers, many of whom serve as church elders, believe my arguments would hold more credence, carry more weight, as it were, if I were married."

Liberty's heart began to pound. "And how many wives do they think you need for that credence and weight?"

He laughed then, a sound that was soft and deep at the same time, as if coming up from a place far beneath the surface of the parts of him she'd seen. "As many as possible."

She snorted, turned her head away. "Have fun."

"What they don't understand," he went on to say, "is that there is still a lot of outsider in me. And I only want one woman in my life."

Her heart thundered harder than before. Her chin came up. Her ears continued to ring with the way he spoke the word woman. "Like I said, have fun."

He took off his sunglasses, rested the hand holding them on her knee. His eyes were dark blue and they twinkled like stars, especially when he smiled. "I want you, Liberty. I want you to be my one and only wife."

"Not that it's any of my business, but do you want to tell me what that was about?"

Having lowered himself gingerly to sit in the swing hanging from the porch wrapped around Neva's house, Mick scratched FM's ears and watched the woman pace a trough in the plank floor, arms crossed over her chest, her fury evident. "Seems like an awful lot of drama for one small town."

He'd stood by earlier, leaning what weight he could painlessly manage against the grill of his ride, and studied the group as those huddled around the picnic table left two by two. The sheriff and the jock kid, obviously related. The shark and the girl, a strange pair.

That left Neva talking quietly to the black woman, both exaggerating their gestures and expressions. Friends, for certain. Coworkers, he assumed. Partners, maybe. But there was something else, too. A deeper thread, a connection. One he'd need more time to dig into and find.

And since it had seemed the two were going to be at it awhile, he'd whistled for FM and headed down the road on foot, accepting that the hike would take a hell of a lot out of him, knowing if he stood still any longer he'd seize up like so many bad gears and never be able to move. He was paying for it now, Neva's heavy footsteps jarring his bruises and bones.

The last time he'd seen her, she'd been cutting him out of his clothes. He obviously hadn't made much of an impression since he was now completely invisible. He was surprised that bothered him; it shouldn't have, even though he had definitely noticed her.

And doing so had obviously thrown his self-preservation tactics for a loop. He'd misread the spark in her eyes, the flare of her nostrils, the pulse at the base of her throat. He'd thought it attraction, not a signal of fear; he'd since had to reassess. And now what he wanted to know was what scared her, what about him had set her off.

He couldn't have that happening. Not in his line of work. Not if he expected to be successful, if he expected to remain alive. That was the reason he'd come here, to figure out how he'd managed to give himself away. He couldn't name another woman—woman, hell, another person—who'd scrambled his instincts so completely.

He wanted to know why Nevada Case did.

Still she said nothing, though she'd stopped with the pacing. Now she simply leaned against a porch post and stared out toward the barn that seemed to be the root of her trouble. He wasn't clear on any of that, except for the fact that the barn wasn't a barn. It was some sort of store where a girl who might or might not be a runaway had been working.

That much he'd managed to pick up from eavesdropping on the tail end of the party. Didn't seem to be enough reason to call out the law and a big shot attorney, but then what did he know beyond the best ways for taking out moving objects, dropping other targets where they stood?

"Oh, hey. I brought you something." He leaned back,

stretched out one leg, and stifled a groan to dig into the front pocket of the jeans he wore. He pulled out a small white box tied in a gold ribbon that he tried to smooth out before offering it to her. "Chocolate."

Neva pushed away from the post and walked over, taking it from his hand and turning it over as if searching for suspicious punctures. "You went to Patsy Cline's."

He nodded, watching her study the box, watching, too, the emotions that flittered through her eyes. Wonderment that he'd thought of her while he was out. Wariness that he had. An interesting pair of reactions. "Yeah. For dinner. Ed took me."

At that, she finally looked up. And this time she didn't even try to hide her surprise. "You went to dinner with Ed Hill?"

"Yep. Then he took me out to get my ride. I stopped back by for the fudge later on my own." Mick was pretty clear on how the doctor still felt about the woman. Now, for some abominably stupid reason, he was curious to know her side. "I didn't want to hear anymore about how I needed to stay away from you."

She shook her head slowly, more in response to her own thoughts than anything he'd said. "He likes to watch out for me. He thinks he's a guardian angel or something."

Mick adjusted his weight, cringed at the scrape of denim over patches of raw skin, at the pull of medical tape on others. "Would that something be a man who's still in love with you no matter how many times you've told him it's over?"

Neva gave a soft huff. "He told you that?"

"He didn't have to." But having Neva confirm his suspicions left Mick on a steadier footing. It was his nature to size up his surroundings, his situation, including the personalities involved. "I figured it out before you'd rolled me out of the back of the truck."

"Amazing." She shook her head. "I'm even more transparent than I realized. You should've been too out of it to notice much at all."

He let her think that. "Trust me. The vibes weren't all coming from you. Doc Ed wasn't overjoyed that you were the one who found me."

"Or that I was the one who cut you out of your clothes, no doubt," she added with a smile.

That smile had him wanting to hand her another pair of scissors. "Too bad you stopped before the getting got good."

She waved an encompassing hand. "Is this more of that horse comparison thing? Because, really, that's a visual I can do without."

He laughed, then groaned, placed a hand over his bandaged ribs. "I've got to stop doing that."

She toyed with the ribbon on the box she still hadn't opened. "I'd say it serves you right, but I hate to see anyone hurting."

"Including Ed?" he asked, continuing to pry when he no longer had need. It was her compassion, her concern making him press. He wasn't used to being on the receiving end of either.

She sighed, came over and sat beside him, rocking the swing. "Yes, including Ed. He's a good man, but he has to be in charge of everything in any situation."

Mick waited for the movement of the swing and the accompanying wave of slow-motion hurt to subside. "A real hands-on guy."

She nodded, tilting her head side to side with her list. "He would choose the drinks, the dinner, the movie. What time a date would start. What time it would end."

What bed they would share, she might as well have added. What position he wanted to take her in. Mick found himself grinding his jaw, and this time it wasn't so much about rough fabric on roughed-up skin. "Could be just a case of his work carrying over into his off-hours."

"Could be," she agreed with a shrug. "But a guy's going to get a lot further with me if he doesn't treat me like I've no more mind of my own than an animal."

Small talk. Personal talk. Banter. Getting to know her better was fine and all, but he also wanted to know about the man in the suit and the one with the badge and the gun. He wanted to know what they'd been doing here because of how angry they'd made her.

He inclined his head to indicate the barn. "You did a good job speaking your mind out there earlier."

"Holden Wagner, ugh. Some nerve that bastard has, bringing the sheriff out here. If I had time, or thought it would do any good, I'd sue him for harassment." Her grin was wry as she pointed toward the shingle swinging from the overhang of the porch. "I can do that, you know. I *am* a lawyer."

"I noticed." He'd been doing a lot of sizing her up since he'd sat down, and it would've been hard to miss the shingle. "You have him showing up a lot?"

"It's been awhile, but yes." She hesitated, as if deciding how much to explain—and whether or not he deserved any explanation at all. "A long time ago I helped Candy out of a bad legal situation. And now there's this rumor attached to me that I just can't shake."

He made the next logical leap. "About operating an underground shelter for runaway girls."

Neva sighed, glanced over. "She wasn't a runaway. She arrived a week ago looking for a job, and I gave her one even though I knew she wasn't being completely up front."

"She give the sheriff the same story she gave you?"

"No, because this time she told all of us *why* she showed up last week." Another pause. More teasing of the gold ribbon. "Seems her boyfriend stole money, a lot of money, that he thought belonged to his employer."

Mick's antennae twitched. "Thought?"

She nodded. "For one thing, the amount was too large to have come from the store where he works. Which isn't hard to believe at all. Earnestine Township has one of the lowest per capita incomes in the state. For another, the guys who came after him had guns. The one who threatened Liberty wore dreadlocks and spoke with a patois." She snorted. "Obviously not locals."

Mick's insides clutched. A patois and dreadlocks. There was no way the man was anyone but Ezra Moore, the Spectra IT assassin who more than once had stepped into the Smithson Group's operations. His being here had to mean the money train was stoking up to pull out of New Mexico.

Jesus bloody hell.

"Anyway," Neva went on as Mick weighed his physical condition against the job he had to do and found the scales way off balance, "Liberty's been the one looking after FM since we got home."

At least the dog was still wearing his collar, and the flash cards were now safely tucked away. Mick flexed his fingers into FM's ruff. "Maybe I'd better run the mutt back by Ed's, make sure he's on the mend. Did you see that she gave him his meds?"

"Dear Lord. You're worse than Candy."

"What?" Mick grinned. "Suspicious natures 'r us?"

"Yes, exactly." She leaned her head back, closed her eyes. The setting sun cast a glow on the skin of her neck. "I know why Candy doesn't trust anyone but herself to get things done, but feel free to tell me about *your* lack of faith in your fellow human beings."

He hadn't had faith in anyone for a very long time, but he wasn't about to share the war stories that were the reasons why. Instead he said, "What a way to talk to a guy who brought you Patsy Cline's fudge."

"I'm waiting here," she said, and when he looked over he saw that her eyes were still closed. And that her skin still looked like vanilla ice cream at dusk.

He swallowed and told her the first reasonable lie that came to mind. "Okay. It's like Ed. A case of the day job carrying over into the off-hours."

"What do you do?"

"Now? I'm an engineering project consultant." An easy answer. The same cover every member of SG-5 used. They were all legitimately employed by Smithson Engineering, Hank Smithson's firm.

She opened one eye, peeked over. "And that requires you be suspicious of others?"

This answer was harder, and he shook his head. "Harkens back to the pre-engineering days."

Ones he didn't talk about with anyone. Ones about which only Hank Smithson knew any details. And even then, Hank didn't know the full story. The truth of what it did to a man to spend his days looking at his fellow human beings from the other side of crosshairs.

Neva looked down, cradled the chocolate between her palms as if it were something precious. "And I suppose the knife and the gun have something to do with those days, as well."

"Nope," he lied. "Those are all about the here and now. If you don't believe me, my hunting lease papers are on the visor in the Rover."

"Then it's an interesting scenario we've got here, isn't it?" she mused, putting the swing into motion.

He tried not to groan as they moved. "How so?"

She stopped the swing, opened both eyes, turned her head, and caught him off guard with her bluntness. "You don't exactly buy that I'm not harboring runaways, and I don't buy for a minute that you're here hunting mule deer."

Anything he said, whether to affirm or deny, would only

dig his grave deeper. And because this woman was no fool, he did neither. He simply watched the evening's dying light flicker in her eyes. "I'm not. Season doesn't open until fall."

She glared. "You know what I mean."

He stalled again. "I hear they're good eating."

"Venison? It's great."

"As good as chocolate?" he asked, continuing the change of subject.

"Are you kidding?" She smiled, her freckles dancing when her nose scrunched up in pleasure. "There's nothing as good as chocolate. Especially when we're talking about Patsy Cline's fudge."

He stared at the box she still held because staring into her eyes had become suddenly distracting. "I only bought the one, you know."

"What, you didn't believe the fine print?" She leaned over, pointed to the tiny gold ingredients label. "Single serving size."

This close, she reminded him of honey and sunshine, the coloring of her skin, the fire in her hair, her scent as fresh and natural as all outdoors. "Bloody hell. Read right over that part."

He sensed her smile as she reached for the loose end of the ribbon and pulled. The bow came free, and she lifted off the top of the box. "Mmm. Nothing in the world smells this good. Or melts in your mouth the way this does. It's like pure chocolate butter."

He reached for the box. "In that case, I'd better take it back. It can't be good for your cholesterol."

"No, but right now it's perfect for my emotional well-being. In fact"—she held the box reverently—"I'd say it's just what the doctor ordered."

It really, *really* shouldn't have pleased him so much, her appreciation of his very small gift. "You want to pass me his name then? Because I'm pretty sure my life-threatening injuries were just treated by a vet. And he didn't say a word about chocolate."

Neva laughed, the sound so light and airy he could almost feel the shift in the swing as a great weight lifted from her shoulders. He'd come here to see her smile, to say thank you with the chocolate, to pick up his dog and his gun, to go. He'd done all of that; he should be ready to leave.

But what he had witnessed earlier with the sheriff and the man wearing gray wool Armani had his nape tingling, coming as it had on top of Ed Hill's admonition to stay away because Neva had enough trouble in her life. Then there was her ability to see through Mick's protective cloak. And now the sighting of the man he was sure was Ezra Moore.

Maybe it was no more than paying forward the second chance he'd received from Hank Smithson, but Mick wanted to stick around. Another day at least. To make sure what happened earlier in front of the barn was the end of the story. That tomorrow wouldn't bring a return spate of accusations from which she'd need a defense. After all, the woman had very likely saved his bloody life.

"Ed's not just a vet," he heard her say. "He's also the town's general practitioner."

"Hmm," Mick murmured. "Must just be us horse types he treats in the big room, then. Size being what matters and all."

Neva laughed out loud. "Shut up and open your mouth."

Shut and up and . . . "What?"

"You heard me. Not another word. Just open your mouth."

He waited until she'd pinched off a bite of fudge from the single-serving chunk. And then, realizing she was giving him the very first bite, he did as she'd ordered. He let the chocolate melt on his tongue, ignoring the wide begging eyes above the snout that suddenly appeared in his lap, and wondered if it was the sugar or the company making the candy so sweet.

"Good stuff, huh," she said, and he nodded, his hand coming up to circle her wrist when she offered him more.

He hadn't intended to seduce her any more than to threaten her. It was simply a case of making sure the candy made it to where it was intended to go. But Neva froze, and the wrist in the ring of his fingers trembled. And the porch light was plenty by which to see he needed to release her.

Her eyes . . . The pain, the fear, the panic. He freed her and lowered his hand to his lap, giving her no reason to think he would hurt her, or that he meant anything at all by the touch.

She ended up returning the candy to the box, settling the lid back in place, licking away a chocolate smear from her thumb. The ribbon she wound like a tourniquet around two of her fingers, and he couldn't help but wonder what thoughts were circulating that she wanted to cut off.

He didn't ask, he just shifted forward on the seat, grimacing as he prepared to stand. "You know, it's late, and I've got to get going or I'll never find a place to stay."

She frowned, asked, "What about the dog?"

Mick winked. "He's not the one driving on a black-and-blue bum."

She smiled just enough to let him know the physical contact hadn't left her damaged. "No, I meant you're going to have trouble finding a motel that will take him in without driving half the night."

"I wasn't going to look for a motel." He pushed to his feet, groaned. "I just need a campground. We'll bunk in the Rover." He'd certainly bunked in worse places, he mused, letting FM nuzzle his hand looking for chocolate.

When he glanced down, Neva was shaking her head. "You can't. Not in your condition." She waved a hand. "You can't even get out of the swing without grimacing. There's no way you can climb in and out of the back of an SUV. You can stay here. With me. It's the only thing that makes sense."

But Mick was already cutting her off and walking toward the steps. It looked good for his cause not to agree too quickly. "I don't think that's such a great idea."

"Look, I'm sorry about what just happened." She stood and followed, stopping when he turned. "It's a reflexive thing. It's me, not you."

"Uh-huh." His curiosity, the bane of his existence, could not have been ramped more high. "That's what women always say when it's really the guy."

"Mick, please. I swear it's not." The look she gave him was an apology. "You aren't in any shape to be driving."

He couldn't argue with that.

"And I didn't go to all that trouble pulling you out of one ditch to have you end up in another. Not when I have a perfectly good guest room at the back of the house now that Liberty isn't using it."

He pretended to ponder the matter, then nodded his acceptance of her offer. "Okay, I'll stay. As long as you tell me where you sleep."

She pushed her hair back from her face. He could see her nervous frown. "Upstairs, why?"

He held tightly to the railing on the porch because he wanted more than anything to touch her, to soothe her, to ease the frown away. "I just want to make sure I don't trespass into hostile territory again."

"Good idea, mate." She backed away, opened the front door, gestured him inside. "Considering I still have your gun."

Seven

"Oh no you don't," Jeanne said as her son slammed the back door and made like a tornado from the mudroom through the freshly mopped kitchen. She knew without asking that he and Yancey had butted their two hard heads out at the Barn. "Spencer Walter Munroe, you get back here right now. Whatever happened with you and your father, you are not leaving me in the dark about this."

"There is no *this*, Mom." Spencer finally stopped on the far side of the kitchen, shoved his hands down into the pockets of his jeans, hung his head. "There's only dad running his family with the same force and intimidation tactics he uses on his department."

Jeanne felt her mouth narrowing, her lips pursing. This was not all Yancey's fault; no matter how much she wished it so, Spencer was no longer an innocent boy. "He caught you with Candy."

One brief nod. "Jase's dad wasn't doing so well, so me and the guys didn't stay out there long. I thought I could see Candy for a few minutes before Dad got to the Barn."

"But you timed it all wrong." Another nod from her son, and Jeanne sighed, pulling out a kitchen chair and wishing she could take this load off her heart as easily as she took the one off her feet. Why did everything lately tire her so? "What happened?"

"Nothing that hasn't happened before." He rubbed at his forehead, fretting, looking like the little boy who'd hated waiting for his father to find out he'd been playing with the tools he knew were deemed off-limits. "Dad got all hostile about Candy being worthless."

"He did not!" Exaggeration was one thing, and she understood her son's upset, but she would not have him lying about or misrepresenting his father. "I don't believe that for a minute."

"Might as well have been what he said." Spencer pulled his hands from his pockets, tugged his ball cap low on his forehead, then crossed his arms. "I know it's what he means."

"Oh, Spencer, honey. Your dad likes Candy just fine." A wife lying about her husband was another thing. "He just doesn't want you distracted from football and school. You know that."

"Yeah, well, I'm already distracted." He leaned back against the kitchen counter, antsy and restless, moving to hook the heels of his palms over the faux marble edge. "It looks like something bad may've happened to Jase. Dad was questioning Liberty about what she saw."

Jeanne's stomach clenched. She didn't know either of Spencer's friends personally—few kids from Earnestine stepped outside to make friends—but she was a mother and she knew about heartache. Knew more than many mothers ever would. "Oh, no, Spencer. I'm so sorry."

And then it hit her. Liberty had to be the same girl, the runaway, Yancey suspected Neva of harboring. If he was questioning her, if he had, indeed, located her at the Barn, the implications for Neva . . . "You found this out from your father?"

"Yeah, uh, sorta." He shrugged, rubbed a hand over his eyes. "Liberty's been working for Neva and Candy, doing stuff in the showroom and packing shipments, things like that."

Working for Neva. Wouldn't that mean the girl wasn't a runaway? "And she knew something about what happened to this Jase?"

"I guess she was with him when he disappeared. It sounds bad. I don't know what it was." He rolled his shoulders. "She was pretty upset, and Dad told me and Candy to shut up and get out of the way. I didn't hear what Liberty told him."

"Is that why you're angry with your father?" Jeanne smoothed her hand over the vinyl tablecloth, finding a tear in the fabric. "Spencer, that's part of his job. And I really doubt he told anyone to shut up."

Spencer finally looked over, his expression challenging, his green eyes cold. "He told Candy to shut her mouth. And then he nearly ran me off the road."

"What?" She clenched her hand into a fist, ripping the fabric further.

"Not only that," he went on, his chin coming up, "he jerked me out of my truck and got all up in my face to make sure I knew that she's nothing."

Jeanne felt the sting of tears behind her eyes. This was not the Yancey she knew and loved. Imposing his will as a father was one thing. But he was not a violent man, and nothing their son said would ever change her mind.

"Anyway, me and the guys were talking on the way back from Jase's dad's place." Spencer paused, hedged, bounced one heel nervously. "He's got that huge ranch to run, and it's calving season in a couple of months. With Jase gone, we thought Mr. Bremmer could use some help—"

"Oh, no." Jeanne surged to her feet, fueled by a rush of

dread. "You're not quitting school before you've even started. You're not staying home another year. You have a scholarship, Spencer. Do you know what that means?"

"It means I'm good at playing football." He waited, as if making sure he had her attention. "But I'd really like for once to be good as a person."

Her chest hitched. "You *are* a good person."

"Candy won't talk to me about anything important, tells me she doesn't want to ruin my future. Dad doesn't want me to date Candy, tells me *he* doesn't want me to ruin my future." He gestured wildly with one hand. "Now you don't want me to help Mr. Bremmer because *you* don't want me to ruin my future."

"Spencer, sweetie—"

"Maybe being here now is more important than my future. Have any of you thought about that?" He was pacing now, the width of the small country kitchen and back. "I'm never going to play pro ball. I know that. And I also know without the scholarship I won't be going to a school like Tech. At least not this year. But there are always other years, Mom. There are always other years."

He looked up as Yancey's car lights cut across the kitchen window, then turned and gave her a look that came too close to telling her his decision was made before he bounded up the stairs to his room.

She waited several seconds without breathing, listening to Spencer's footsteps. They matched the hard pounding beat of her own breaking heart. What was she going to do? Allow her son to be a man and make his own decisions? Destroy his life the way she'd destroyed her own? Acting rashly in the heat of the moment, never thinking of the long road ahead?

Behind her, Yancey slammed the door hard enough to crack the lower corner of the insert glass where it had always been loose. "Shit." He pointed toward the door. "That's coming out of Spencer's pocket."

Jeanne lifted her chin, prepared to play peacemaker when she wished for once she could simply drop this weight on her husband's shoulders. She was so tired of this friction. She so wanted to be absolved of the need to erase it. "Don't be silly. It's been loose forever, and that was an accident."

He jerked out his chair from beneath the table and dropped into it, knees spread, elbows on his uniformed thighs, and stared at the floor. "How the hell we managed to raise a boy who doesn't know the meaning of obedience or respect or responsibility is beyond me."

"He most certainly understands all of those. And you know it." She returned to her own chair, sat facing her husband. "You also know that you butted heads with your own father more than a few times in your life."

Yancey looked up, lifted one brow. "Hopefully when Spencer is my age, he'll have the same twenty-twenty hindsight I do and admit that I was right."

"About Candy?"

"About everything."

Jeanne couldn't help but smile. "So all these years later, you're finally going to admit Clive Munroe wasn't out of his mind to keep you from moving to Nashville to sing for your supper?"

Snorting, Yancey rolled his eyes. "I would've figured that out on my own."

"Just like Spencer will eventually figure out where his relationship with Candy fits."

"We don't have time for him to be jacking around with that girl." He brought his fist down on the table. "You know as well as I do he's not thinking with the right head."

Jeanne refused to speak about sex and her son. "Actually, Candy may not be the problem with his thinking."

"Whaddaya mean?"

"It's about your missing Jase Bremmer. Spencer and his buddies are seriously thinking about postponing school for a year to work the Bremmer ranch for the boy's father."

Yancey's nostrils flared. "Oh no he's not."

She nodded. "Oh yes he is. He wants to be more than a good football player. He wants to be a good person."

"What kind of nonsense is that?"

Jeanne reached for her husband's hands, so large, so callused, his nails always so jagged, and stroked her thumbs over his palms, keeping her gaze cast down as she spoke. "Is this our fault, Yancey? By moving here? Is it my fault for running away?"

He immediately softened. "Oh, honey, no." He leaned forward in his chair, wrapped her in his arms and pulled her almost into his lap. "Why would you say something like that? Why would you think something like that?"

"Because we might have given him a better life if we'd stayed in Dallas," she said, burying her face in the comforting crook of his neck.

"There's not a thing wrong with the life we've given that boy. We've been the best parents we could be." Yancey paused, stiffened. "Unless I haven't been the father he deserved."

This time, Jeanne was the one to pull away. She took Yancey's face in her hands and cradled his cheeks. "You've been a perfect father. Spencer couldn't have been brought up to be the man he is by anyone else. And don't you ever tell yourself anything different."

There was no way Neva was going to be able to fall asleep. Absolutely no way. She didn't know what he wanted, didn't know why he was here. She didn't know what she'd been thinking inviting him to stay.

It didn't matter that she still had his gun tucked safely away with hers. A gun wouldn't protect her. Not when what she was feeling was more about exposure, of her feelings, of her past, of the present, which had turned into the biggest mess she'd ever been in in her life.

When she claimed not to harbor girls from Earnestine these days, she was telling the truth. When she denied knowing what had become of the ones who had gone missing, the truth she told was more painful. She should've known. She should've been able to follow them, to map their journey from the moment they left her care until they reached the end of their journey.

She feared the leak in her network was going to put her out of business. And that Mick Savin was a part of that. That he was law enforcement, looking for evidence in order to charge her with harboring runaway minors on multiple occasions, resulting in multiple counts and multiple convictions. She didn't consider herself a martyr by any means, and she had no desire to become one by going to prison.

Rolling out from between her sheets, she tiptoed to her bedroom door. Her room was above the guest room, and the last thing she wanted to do was wake her guest. In the past, a warm bath had often cured her insomnia.

Tonight she had a feeling she was going to have to add a mug of hot chocolate milk and a handful of whatever drowsiness-inducing, over-the-counter meds she could find in the house. And even then she doubted any sleep she managed would be worth the effort of closing her eyes.

Since Liberty Mitchell had shown up at the Barn a week ago, Neva hadn't been sleeping much at all. She'd been waiting for the other shoe to fall, for the girl's real story to unfold. Looking at herself now in the oval mirror hanging above the bathroom's pedestal sink, she knew a bath wasn't going to get her anywhere but wet. There was too much going on in her eyes and the dark circles beneath.

In her white tank top, white gym socks, and baggy gray sleeping shorts, she padded her whisper-soft way downstairs and into the kitchen, only pausing at the first floor hallway long enough to listen for sounds coming from the guest room. She heard none, which made a whole lot of sense when she turned the corner and found Mick bent over in front of the refrigerator's open door.

Oh, my, but the man had a fantastic ass, leaning over the way he was, his back stretched in such a way that defined every one of his muscles not covered by white medical tape. She crossed her arms, propped a shoulder on the doorjamb. "Patsy's not going to like knowing her potatoes don't stick."

She gave him credit. He didn't jump. He straightened slowly, a hand to his bare but bandaged middle and turned. "I was looking for juice or a soda. Though a sandwich did cross my mind. I've got this metabolism thing going on."

"Uh-huh." She couldn't see his face. He stood in the dark, backlit by the light from inside of the fridge. But she could see that he had on shorts that, when she flipped on the overhead light, were almost a match to hers.

He seemed to realize it at about the same time, glancing from the pair she wore down at his own. Then he met her gaze with a grin.

"Don't even say it," she said, pushing away from the doorway and into the room.

"Hey, I like a woman who shares my taste in things," he said, and she simply repeated, "Uh-huh," because until she got a better handle on her hormonal bearings, she wasn't sure what else to say.

Men weren't supposed to be beautiful the way this one was, standing in her kitchen in nothing but shorts that covered his, uh, attributes but did nothing to conceal them. He might as well have been naked, and for the first time in many, many moons, the idea of being alone with a naked man had her sizzling with an awareness that went deeper than her skin.

She'd undressed him halfway at Ed's clinic, but his bare

body then, laid out flat on his back, was nothing compared to his bare body now. Yes, the black-and-blue bruises were all still there, the bandages in the way, but knowing to expect them allowed her to overlook them.

To see past them to his lean waist and tightly cut abs, to his biceps and pecs that bulged so nicely, to the line of his shoulders, a broad testament to the fact that he was a man twice her size, one she couldn't believe that she wanted to get her hands on—especially when she thought back to the way she'd frozen at his touch.

But it was more than that: a fear that she would forget the threat of who he might be in favor of how easily he had stepped up when she'd needed someone on her side. And so she waved him toward the table and told him, "Go. Sit."

It took her less than five minutes to make him a sandwich, to pour them both a glass of milk, cut them both a slice of sour cream coffee cake, and to join him.

"I hate being unable to sleep," she said, once she'd settled into the chair across from the one he'd chosen at the kitchen's square table.

"I can still hit the road. I don't want my being here to keep you awake." He wrapped his big hands around the sandwich and bit in.

"It's not you," she said, amending her statement when he raised a disbelieving brow while he chewed. "Okay. It's not *only* you."

He swallowed, took a drink of milk. "Honesty is always the best policy."

"So says the mule deer hunter," she quipped, and he laughed. The sound was a rich echo of pleasure, one she enjoyed too much. She didn't need to associate good times with this man she still didn't know and still didn't trust completely.

"Why can't you sleep? Besides the distraction of me?" He palmed the sandwich again, distracting her further. "It's not like you didn't have enough going on today to exhaust an iron man."

"I don't know about that." She rolled her aching shoulders. "Though I've got to think swimming a couple of miles would be a close match to hauling you into the bed of my truck. Metabolism or not, you are no lightweight."

"I've been meaning to ask about that."

"About what?"

"Where you got those muscles."

She sputtered her milk. "Please. Don't make me laugh. If I had muscles, I wouldn't be aching like I've been hauling freight one-handed."

He hissed back a breath. "That bad, huh?"

"It's nothing like what you're suffering, but yeah. I'm not in the world's best shape."

"Guess that depends on the judge." He paused, added, "I'd say your shape's a pretty damn good one."

"As long as this isn't leading back to that horse-size thing, I'll take that as a compliment."

"I meant it as one. Not many women could've managed that feat." He'd been talking about the shape of her muscles not, as she'd thought, her tits and her ass.

Didn't *she* want to crawl under the table and hide? "Well, it's not like I hefted you over my shoulder or anything. It was just your basic cable and pulley engineering."

"Clever. And effective. And deserving of a proper thanks."

The cake in her mouth seemed suddenly dry and tasteless as her nerves began to stir. "You thanked me. You brought me chocolate."

He reached for his napkin, wiped his mouth. "Which you didn't eat."

"Yet." She took a drink of milk. "I will."

"Besides, it was a single-serving size. It only covers one thank-you."

"Is that how it works?" She was nervous. Why was she nervous?

He nodded. "I still owe you for the use of the guest room. And now for the food. And I never did thank you for taking in the dog."

"Look. You don't need to repay me for every little thing. And I certainly don't need any more chocolate."

"What about sleep?"

"Sure, but unless you've got a pill—"

"I've got something better."

"I'm not sleeping with you."

He laughed, a sharp desperate sound. "What I was going to offer isn't *that* good."

No. She wasn't going there. Not even mentally. She narrowed her gaze. "What then? Hypnosis? Bad sitcom reruns? Shakespeare?"

Another laugh, and more of that blossoming warmth in her belly. Why hadn't she at least put on her bathrobe or a bra? "Just sit still. And trust me."

Right. Trust the man who'd told her he was here for the mule deer. "I'll sit still, but that's all. And only until you give me reason to move."

He got up, dragged his chair around and positioned it behind hers. "I'm not going to give you reason to do anything but fall asleep."

Something she wouldn't be doing until she got to bed behind her locked door. "Just to clue you in, I'm not the type to fall asleep just anywhere. Not on a plane, never in a moving car. I even have trouble in hotel rooms."

"That's gotta be hell on your love life," he said, sitting and settling his palms on her shoulders, his thumbs at the base of her neck.

"I was talking about falling asleep. Not . . . other things." And dear Lord, but his thumbs felt good, rubbing pressure circles against her nape right where she most needed to be rubbed.

"I've slept in planes, trains, and automobiles," he said, and she smiled. "I've also slept in a Turkish mosque, a Russian freighter, on the ground in the Australian Outback, and underground in a Tuscan winery."

"A Turkish mosque?"

"Yeah. Don't mention that to anyone. I probably shouldn't have been there."

Funny man. Amazing hands. She was halfway asleep already. "In Turkey? Or in the mosque?"

He hesitated a moment then seemed to chuckle under his breath. "Both, now that you mention it."

Her head lolled forward as he massaged the tendons at the base of her skull. She closed her eyes. "If that's putting too much stress on your shoulder—"

"No worries, mate," he said, and she groaned.

"You don't have an accent. Did you pick up the vernacular while sleeping under the outback moon?"

"Actually, it was on the Russian freighter. I spent a bit of time there chained in the cargo hold with two blokes from Melbourne."

"What?" She tried to turn; he wouldn't let her, but held her head still while he worked his knuckles and fingertips along the slope to her shoulders. "Chained? You mean like a prisoner?"

"You could say. But being chained didn't make me the enemy."

The gun. The knife. "I guess these were your pre-engineering days?"

"About thirty of them, yeah."

"What were you hunting then? Sables? Minks? KGB informants?"

"Bad guys," he said, and left it at that.

She wasn't about to drop it that easily, no matter the fabulous magic of his hands. She shifted to the side, tucking one leg beneath her, and turned in the padded red seat. His gaze, when she met it, was indecipherable, though he did lift a brow.

He'd curled his hands around the padded top of her aluminum frame and red Naugahyde diner-style chair. She placed one of her hands atop his and shook her head slowly, thinking, wondering. "Who are you, Mick Savin? And don't give me that mule deer bullshit."

"What makes you so skeptical, Nevada Case?" he responded, hooking her fingers with his.

"Because I've been lied to by too many people in my life." She narrowed her gaze and her mouth. "And *don't* call me Nevada."

He didn't say anything in response. He didn't release her gaze or her hand. In fact, he seemed to tighten both holds. It was the only explanation for why she couldn't break away, because she wanted to break way. Of course she did; why wouldn't she?

"Then I'm not going to lie to you," he finally admitted. "I'm here on a hunt. And there are some men out there who don't want me to find what I'm looking for."

She didn't know why he'd told her that any more than she knew why she believed him. But she did. And she found herself twining her fingers tighter with his. "What are you looking for?"

"The truth?"

She nodded, unable this time to find her voice.

He smiled softly. "I can't tell you."

"Is that a lie by omission?"

"The lie is only in the lack of details. The truth is that I don't want you to get hurt."

"By you? Or by the men who caught you trespassing?"

"Both," he answered honestly, and she cringed.

"Am I putting myself in danger by having you here?"

"The truth?" he asked again.

And again, she nodded.

"I'm not a very nice man."

She looked down to where their hands were joined, said, "I guess that depends on the judge."

He said nothing, and she feared looking up. Not because he frightened her; he no longer did. And the only thing that had changed was the response of her intuition to the truth he'd told. He wasn't here for her. That much she trusted to be true.

What she didn't trust was the warmth of his skin, the secure hold of his fingers, his claim of not being a very nice man. But more than anything, she didn't trust what she was feeling. And she didn't like at all not trusting that about herself.

In the end, however, she was helpless against the pull of his gaze, and raised her eyes to meet his. The way he looked at her, the way he stared into her eyes searching for . . . she didn't know.

And so she asked, the ache in her chest subduing her voice, "What are you looking for?"

"I think I'm trying to decide if you mean it," he said.

"I don't make a habit of saying what I don't mean."

"What have I done that you would give me that benefit of a doubt?"

"You forget that I'm used to being lied to." Dear Lord, but her chest was aching, her heart hurting. "And I don't see anything but truth in your eyes."

"Even if it's a half truth?"

"If that's all you're able to tell . . ." She shrugged, looked back at their joined hands, admitting to herself that it wasn't so strange that they both had secrets. What was new here was that they both recognized—and respected—the same in the other.

"Neva?"

At his whisper of her name, she once again found her gaze drawn to his.

"If I could tell you more, I would."

"It doesn't matter." All that mattered was that she wanted to smile for absolutely no reason.

"It matters to me." He pulled one hand from beneath hers, reached up and drew the backs of his fingers along her hairline. "I've been involved in a lot of things no one could ever prove I knew a bloody thing about. Like I said, I'm not a very nice man. But that doesn't mean I'm an unfeeling ass."

"Ass." She paused, continued to fight the smile. "Is this that horse-size thing again, because—"

He cut her off with a kiss. He cupped the back of her head, pulled her forward, and kissed her. For a minute, it didn't even occur to her to close her eyes. She watched his lashes flutter, felt the press of his tongue to the seam of her lips. She didn't give it another thought. She simply opened her mouth.

He tasted like the sandwich she'd made him, like she wanted him when she shouldn't, like a little bit more would never be enough, like he was hers. Hardly fair that he'd give her that after telling her that he wasn't a very nice man. She'd known her share of those, yet none of them had come close to offering her this.

His tongue slid over hers, tangled with hers, boldly stroked in and out of her mouth. She gripped his fingers tighter and slanted her head, giving him back the same. Oh, how she wanted this. How right it felt, he felt. How perfectly he kissed. How perfectly he fit. How soft were his lips. How strong his tongue.

Never in her life had she felt the pull of a man from a contact that was so simple while being so goddamn complex. And then he was gone. He abandoned her mouth, nuzzled his nose to hers, his breath warm as he sighed and said, "Go to bed, Neva. I'll clean up here."

His offer was so sweetly made and so welcome that she accepted. She left the kitchen, took his kiss with her to bed, and slept like she was somebody's baby.

Eight

There wasn't a doubt in Mick's mind that the boy involved with Liberty Mitchell had run into a spate of bad luck at the hands of Spectra IT. He wasn't sure he could do anything toward finding Jase Bremmer without giving himself away. But he knew exactly who to call.

He cleaned up the kitchen as promised. It wasn't hard, it didn't take long, and it shouldn't have, considering he knew what he was doing. After all, he'd spent plenty of time on kitchen detail, working his way around the world so as not to appear he was living on Uncle Sam's dime. Taxpayers wouldn't like the idea that they financed murder along with Medicare.

The undeniable thing of it was that there were individuals in need of elimination, and the government called on men trained at their expense by their military to perform these tasks for the greater good. Somewhere along the line, however, what was good for the goose, the gander, and the world as a whole ended up turning the man into a monster.

That's where Mick had been, growing horns and fangs, claws and scales, when Hank Smithson had found him and saved him from an abominably ugly fate that would've been worse than death. Since then, Mick had leaned on the SG-5 team anytime he felt himself sinking into that same bloody pit, drowning, dying, losing everything that had once made him human, that reminded him there was a value to life.

At the moment, however, his imperative need to get to Hank or to one of his partners wasn't about the muck rising up and threatening to suck him back down. Right now what he needed was to relay what he suspected about Spectra's money train pulling out, and to do so without sharing information on what he'd been through, where he was staying, or the woman who'd so selflessly taken him in.

He didn't have time to examine why keeping Neva's existence to himself was so vital. He only knew that it was. Knew that since meeting her, since knowing her, since spending the night on her porch talking about fudge, since kissing her sweet coffee-cake-flavored mouth, the muck hadn't stirred once beneath his feet. He felt warm and safe and cared for, none of which he understood, all of which he was enjoying way too bloody much for his own bloody good.

After a stop in the guest room for his blue jeans and boots and to pop another pill, and a half second taken to listen for her footsteps in the room above, he headed out the back door of Neva's kitchen and around the side of the house where earlier he'd parked his Rover next to her truck. FM, who'd been dozing under the vehicle's front fender, got to his feet, shook off loose fur and dust, and the rest of his sleep.

"We're not going anywhere, dog," Mick said in a low voice, using the bright light of the full moon to navigate by. "So don't be smiling and tripping over yourself like you think we are." FM's only response was to smile wider, trip over himself even more, at which Mick couldn't help but grin and murmur, "Stupid mutt."

After digging into his pocket for his key fob, he hit the remote lock, opened the rear cargo door, and pulled back a square of carpet—a square custom-fitted to cover the panel hiding his electronically secured storage space. He punched the code into the miniature keypad, and the lock released with a soft vacuum whoosh.

Losing his satellite phone to the Spectra goons had been a pain in the ass, though not the end of the world. The equipment inside the Rover's compartment would also put him in contact with the ops center. Unfortunately, he mused, locking the hinges of the panel to view the monitor on the underside, he was a whole lot better at talking than typing.

He unfolded the keyboard, boosted one hip up to sit on the edge of the cargo area, grimacing as he jarred his very sore bones. Once he'd booted up the battery-powered computer, positioned the antenna, and made contact with the satellite, he pulled up a prompt screen and typed the command that would connect him to the only place in the world he ever thought of as home.

This time of night he expected Christian Bane to be manning the communications desk. One of the Smithson Group operatives always did, providing a necessary pipeline for those in the field. But it wasn't Christian that responded. It was Harry van Zandt.

>Rabbit here.
>Savin checking in.
>You good?
>Yep.
>Coming home?
>Not yet. Indisposed.

That much was true enough. He was still aching like he'd lost his best friend along with half of his body hair. He glanced back at Rabbit's response, white letters on a black screen.

>Want reinforcements?
>No. Satellite surveillance.
>Coordinates?

Mick typed in the location of the Spectra bunker. He needed an eye and an ear up above to finish gathering the intel he'd started pulling down in New Mexico while he concentrated on the Spectra connection to the duo of Bremmer and Mitchell and the stolen two hundred thou.

>Done. What else?
>Upload. Ready?
>Go.

Mick plugged the first flash card from FM's collar into the USB reader and typed the command that would send the data to Rabbit. Cards two and three followed, and then he stored away all three.

>That's it.
>Got it. Anything more?
>A lead on the ground. Possible sighting. Ezra Moore.
>Christ. Dude gets around.

Mick gave a wry shake of his head. He and Harry had run into the Spectra assassin in Mexico. Julian Samms had taken on Moore in Miami. And Kelly John Beach's clash with the man had gone down in Manhattan.

Everything on Moore's sheet said he should be hurting and hindering the Smithson Group's efforts to annihilate Spectra IT. Weirdly enough, he wasn't. And now he'd released Liberty Mitchell . . .

>Mick? You there?
>Yeah. What's the deal with Moore?

>A mystery. Another day.
>Check in tomorrow, mate.
>Right. Rabbit out.

Mick signed off and shut down the machine, then secured the equipment in its compartment before locking up. FM, on full alert, sat at the corner of the Rover's rear bumper. Mick reached down and scratched the dog's ears. "I told you, dog. No rides tonight."

Now that he'd touched base with Rabbit, the only thing on tonight's schedule was sleep. That and trying to make sense of what he was feeling for Neva. Groaning, he pushed out of the Rover to his feet, realizing he hadn't even known her a full twenty-four hours.

He wanted to blame some of what was going on with him, the anomaly of an instant attraction he hadn't jumped to gratify, on the drugs. That excuse didn't work since he hadn't taken but half the dosage prescribed, or been on the meds any real length of time.

And since the drugs weren't the cause, he was at a loss. He couldn't even remember the last woman he'd wanted the way he wanted Neva, yet had done no more than talk to. Or kiss. That kiss had left him hurting. The way it had reached out, grabbed him by the throat and squeezed, cut off his breath, seized him like the wrong end of a vise.

He reached up for the cargo hatch, used his good arm to pull it down, and quietly latched it. He wanted to know what made Neva tick, why a woman with her intelligence, her snap and her wit was hiding out in Bumfuck.

He didn't care what half-truths she told him. The full truth was obvious. She was running from something. He recognized the kindred spirit. And because he was soul-sick weary of ball-and-chain secrets, he suspected that she was, too. Coincidence . . . or fate? What if somehow, some improbable way, they each held the key to setting the other free?

* * *

"I want to know everything," Candy said the next morning at the breakfast table while she and Neva drank coffee as they did every day at dawn. "And I mean everything. Do not leave out a single gory detail."

"No gore involved, Candy, my sweet," Neva teased as the other woman rolled her big dark eyes. A half second after walking through the back door, Candy had drilled Neva about Mick's Range Rover, still parked outside. "Unless you count the mess I almost made with the fudge."

"Don't tell me." Candy collapsed back, her chair legs scraping the floor. "He brought you Patsy Cline's. I can't believe it. Ed never even brought you Patsy Cline's."

Neva set cream, sugar, mugs, and a fresh-brewed, filled-to-the-brim carafe on the table, then added a plate of toasted bagels. "That's because Ed didn't want to tempt me with anything that might not be good for me."

Candy took over and poured. "And he wonders why you broke things off. Lord save us from clueless men. Good thing they're not all like that."

"Yeah? Since when?"

"Don't smirk at me, girl. Just yesterday you rescued one from the side of the road and he's already fulfilling all your heart's desires."

Not exactly, Neva wanted to say. She liked the way Mick Savin looked, just not the way he looked at her. And then there was the way his fingers had felt on her wrist, the way his mouth had felt on hers. She hadn't liked that at all. The way her pulse had pounded. The way her skin had been warmed by his. The way he'd pushed her hair away from her face as if wanting to see her better.

She'd have preferred none of that had happened. That he'd done what he said he was going to do, gather his things and go. And damn but if she hadn't become an expert at lying to herself because she'd loved every last bit of last night. "It was a thank-you. That's all. For hauling him out of the ditch to the doctor."

"Honey, I'm not buying it. And I've got enough cash that I could if anything about it was real." Candy rambled on, looking at her coffee while she doctored it up. "I was there last night when he drove up like some badass Lone Ranger. His arm might be in a sling, and he might be walking like a duck, but that man is like no man I've ever seen before. And when he climbed down from his ride"—she shook her head, clicked her tongue—"you could see Holden and Yancey trembling in their boots."

Oh, yes. A moment worth reliving. Neva had done so at least two dozen times. "Holden doesn't wear boots, Candy. What have you been smoking?"

Candy pointed over her shoulder towards the hall. "Obviously not the good stuff because for the life of me, I can't figure why you had that sexy thing spend the night in your guest room with no one but you in the house. You don't even know the man."

"He wasn't in any shape to drive. Like you said, he can barely walk." Though she wouldn't have compared his hobble to a duck's, the "sexy thing" tag fit. Boy, did it fit, Neva thought, and sighed.

"He could've bunked in the Barn."

"With you?"

"No, Neva. Upstairs. In one of the dorm rooms."

Neva narrowed her eyes. "No one knows about the dorm rooms, Candy. You know that. Having a stranger staying there hardly makes sense."

"Yeah, but still. You should've had me come up and sleep on the sofa. Make sure that locked door of yours stayed locked." Cradling her mug in both hands, Candy raised a questioning brow. "Though with all the lady's protesting, I'm beginning to wonder if your guest was the only one sleeping in the guest room."

"Yes. He was. Unless you count the dog."

At Mick's voice, Neva cringed, glared at Candy, then turned. This morning he wore a black T-shirt and loose khaki fatigues. That was it. His bare feet made her smile. "Good morning. Did we wake you?"

He shook his head. "The dog did. He needed out. Plus, I thought I smelled coffee."

Candy got to her feet. "There. Sit." She pointed to her empty chair. "I'll pour you a cup. Black, right?"

Mick was still rubbing at his eyes. "How'd you know?"

"You look like a man who likes it black."

Neva buried her face in her hands, peeking at Mick from between spread fingers, and taking hold of her coffee again at his grin. "You'll have to excuse Candy. As the token black woman in town, she takes her role seriously. Thinks it's her duty to embarrass us ignorant pasty types."

"Only the ugly ones," Candy said amiably, setting Mick's coffee in front of him. "*You*, I was flirting with."

Mick's deep laugh rumbled straight through Neva, more effective at waking her up than the caffeine. From the appreciative gleam in Candy's eyes, she wasn't immune to the jolting thrill, either.

Neva glared up at her best friend. "Don't you have work to do?"

Candy blinked, then returned the carafe to the burner. "Sure I do. We both do. But all work and no play makes for one cranky bitch." On her way out of the kitchen, she paused at the doorway with a final word for Mick. "Think you can do something about that, mate?"

I'll kill her, Neva thought, her face heating.

Once Candy was gone, Mick glanced over. "I don't want to keep you from your work." He jerked a thumb back over his shoulder. "I've got plenty of daylight and time to find a motel or campground. Say the word and I'll hit the road."

If he'd said one word about playing, she would've booted

him out on his ass. But his expression was carefully blank. And she didn't want him to go. She'd examine why later. "You could do that. Or you could stay in bed and catch up on the rest your body needs."

"I won't be in your way?"

"As long as you stay out of my office, I don't see how you could be. Unless . . ." She sipped at her coffee.

He sipped at his. "Unless what?"

She threaded the fingers of one hand back through her hair, pushing it away from her forehead. "If you felt up to it, I could use a hand finishing up the packing and shipping Liberty never got done. They're small boxes, nothing you'd have to lift."

"Sure. Sounds like the perfect job for the walking wounded. Pay off a bit of this room and board."

She frowned. "Mick, I don't expect payment in return for a kindness."

Mick set his mug down on the table, left his hands there, his fingers spread wide. "All the places I've been, all the people I've known, I don't think I've ever run into anyone as kind as you are, Neva Case."

Dear Lord. That was not how she wanted him to see her. Not at all. "Don't make me out to be a saint just because I let you kiss me. I'm anything but."

"What are you then? A rescuer of road kill and runaways?" He looked up, the light in his eyes stopping her before she could answer. "By the way. I was there for that kiss. You were the one kissing me."

"She wasn't a runaway. Just a confused young girl. But yes. I do have a soft spot for anyone suffering misfortune." She waited . . . waited . . . went for it. "Even men who don't understand the subtleties of a kiss."

He almost choked. "You thought that kiss was subtle?"

"That's not what I said." Oh, but he was good. "I said there were subtleties involved."

"Seemed pretty straightforward to me."

"Of course it would. You're a man."

That had him frowning. "It's not the terminal condition you're making it out to be."

"See? Subtleties." He might be good, but she was better. "I happen to love men. Men make the world go round."

Mick shook his head, huffed. "That's because trying to figure out women keeps us spinning. Some of us keep doing it from the grave."

"Ha." She sat back, crossed her arms. "If anything has you spinning, it's all the exaggerating you do."

His head bobbed as he thought, and the tattoo on the back of his neck drew her gaze. "I guess the only way to settle this is to go back to the beginning."

Uh-oh. "The beginning?"

He looked over, his eyes found hers. "I'm just going to have to kiss you again."

She looked at him for a long moment, wanting what he offered but knowing that taking it wouldn't come easy. It was daylight, and she wasn't feeling tired and out of sorts and vulnerable the way she had been last night.

And so she hedged. "I'm pretty sure the beginning is where I found you on the side of the road. Are you sure you want to go back that far?"

He considered what she'd said. "A compromise, then?"

"Does that mean you have something in mind? Something that doesn't involve another kiss?" she hurried to add.

"Halfway between here and there."

"The Barn."

He shrugged. "You can put me to work and tell me the story of how you ended up out here."

Presumptuous, wasn't he? "Who said I didn't start out out here?"

"Your neck. It's too white."

"I work indoors."

"Yeah. But Ed told me." He drained his coffee. "Now you can tell me the rest while you pretend you can't wait to kiss me again."

The man was an incorrigible flirt. He was also way too perceptive. She wanted to kiss him more than she wanted to breathe. But she wouldn't. Last night hadn't been real. She wouldn't let it be real. If she could kiss him, touch him, hold him, even sleep with him and do so without involving her emotions, she would.

In a heartbeat. A nanosecond. The blink of an eye.

But he wasn't Ed Hill, a man to whom her only attraction was what he'd been able to do to her body and her ability to totally detach. Mick Savin was more.

The proof lay in that middle-of-the-night slip of her control. Being this close to him, thinking about his mouth, the way he kissed, the way he tasted . . . She needed distance now, and needed it in a very bad way.

"What I want and what's going to happen are two different things. So I'll tell you what." She gathered the coffee mugs and the carafe. "I'll clean up in here while you get dressed and see to your dog."

"That's it?" He looked crushed that she'd put an end to their banter.

And so she smiled. "We'll see what happens when we get down to the Barn."

Thirty minutes later, FM sniffing every square inch of grass along the way, Mick walked beside Neva from the house to the barn. Since he'd arrived last night near dusk to be caught up in her drama with the sheriff and the shark, he hadn't spent much time checking out the place.

Judging by the drive in and what fence line he could see, he figured her property to be about ten acres, most of it nothing but yellowed grassland. Her house, two-story, white frame, with a storybook cottage appeal, sat in a clustered copse of pecan trees.

She had flower beds with hardy summer blooms but no grass or yard to speak of. Less upkeep, he supposed, not taming the land into something it wasn't meant to be, blending into her surroundings, hiding out in plain sight. Yeah. That was what it was.

He'd slipped his arm into the sling for the walk to the barn and made sure to walk with Neva on that side. Bound up like he was, he couldn't accidentally touch her. Even so, she still kept her arms crossed protectively in front of her body. He could've sworn she'd enjoyed their kiss as much as he had. Now he wanted to swear that she didn't like herself for liking it. Or just swear because that was the case.

She stayed silent as they walked, and he didn't press for conversation, letting her set the pace of their steps. The barn sat straight ahead. It was twice the size of her house, if not three times as big, and looked like it had been plucked out of a Pennsylvania Dutch pasture and dropped into place.

It had a shingled roof that sloped on a deep curve and was as tall as the structure's first floor. The small parking lot out front was the same gravel as the drive; the sidewalk down the one side he could see was concrete. He wondered if she actually had visitors stop in to shop. As off any beaten path as she was, he didn't see how that was likely.

Neva led him around the far side where the picnic tables sat on the covered patio. "The showroom's in the front, but we can access it through a door in the studio."

"Is that where you're going to put me to work?"

"No. That's where Candy works." Neva stopped, pulled open the windowed door leading inside. "The shipping center is at the rear."

He stepped into the big room that wasn't as spacious as the exterior had led him to believe. He pointed to the back wall. "What's on the other side?"

"Candy's apartment." Neva followed him in and let the door close behind her. "It's about twelve hundred square feet."

Making the two-story barn around five thousand. "What's upstairs?"

"Just . . . stuff." She fluttered a hand. "Storage. Typical attic junk."

An awful big attic for junk, he wanted to say, but stopped when a blowtorch fired off at the front of the room. Neva headed the opposite way, around shelves stacked high with bins of supplies, stools tucked up beneath worktables, unused machine stands, and spools of cord, filament, and chain, to the corner of the room.

The corner of the room had a computer workstation against one wall, a numbered cubbyhole system on the other, both separated from the larger room by a counter set up for the packing and shipping he'd been drafted to do. The stack of unassembled mailing boxes was his first clue.

"Welcome to the nerve center of the Big Brown Barn," Neva said, waving one arm with a flourish.

He could see the log-in screen for the e-commerce website on her monitor. "Nice digs."

"We like it. Suits our purpose with the added benefit of tons of personal space." She glanced around as if trying to see what he would see.

All he saw was what she claimed the place to be. At least when he wasn't looking at her, her thick rust-colored hair, the freckles on her cream-colored skin, her body, which was tight and solid and stirred his to life. His throat ached just enough to rough up his voice. "What *is* your purpose?"

She made her way to the computer station. "I told you. We sell jewelry. Candy's original designs."

He let out a low whistle, not that he knew dick about what he was saying. "Must be working with a hell of a markup. Unless you've got private backers helping to keep this place afloat."

"Actually," she began, and bristled, "we do quite well. Candy's designs are sold in a handful of exclusive galleries across the country. Plus, she does a lot of work on commission. So, no. We don't need patrons backing us. In the past, maybe. But not anymore."

Mick decided to back off, to ask later about how they'd started—and why here of all places. "And you do all the grunt work."

"This summer I have, yeah." She tucked her hands into her jeans pockets. "Except last week with Liberty here. During the school year and especially at the holiday season, I always have one or two kids from the high school working for me."

He supposed it wouldn't be easy for her to hide runaways with part-time help in and out. "What about your law practice?"

"All I do these days are wills, real estate deals, and the occasional breeding contract."

"Legal disbursement of semen." He shook his head. "Sort of takes the fun out of the concept of being a stud."

She laughed, and he swore she blushed, but then she just as quickly sobered. There were so many things he could say, none of which he did. He just leaned back against the shipping counter and let the storm of tension spin. It wasn't a gentle storm, it was fierce and powerful, sucking them in and pulling the air from the room.

He saw it in the rapid rise and fall of her chest, felt it in his own. Breathing that should've come easy took effort, as did staying put. He wanted to hook his good arm around her neck, haul her into his body, snap his fingers and rid them both of their clothes. He wanted to learn her scent, to taste her, to teach her what he liked.

He wanted to do things to her that shocked him, and he saw the mirror of that need in her eyes. He ached with it.

He burned. He watched the same fire creep over her skin and color her, unnerve her, reveal all that she was feeling—none of which he was certain she wanted him to know.

And so he searched for his voice, found it, put an end to the flash fire, reducing it to embers with a question. "Why don't you show me what you need done."

"Sure. Okay." Clearing her throat, she walked toward the counter and slapped down the stack of papers she pulled from the workstation's heavy duty printer. "Let me show you how to work these invoices. The shipping labels are on the bottom of each page and are self-adhesive."

"Hmm. Sounds challenging." And not half as fun as what he'd been thinking.

"If Liberty can do it, you can do it."

"Obviously she couldn't, or it would've been done."

Neva pursed her lips. "Let's just say she suffered a lack of motivation."

"Or maybe fear for her life?"

And then she sighed. "I'm sure that was a large part of her distraction. Hindsight and all, I could've been easier on her."

He waited to see if she offered up anything more. When she didn't, he went on. "Hopefully her leaving this job undone wasn't because you didn't show her where and how to pull the items to be shipped."

"Ack, sorry." She grabbed the top invoice and gestured for him to follow her to the wall of cubbyholes. "The item numbers on the invoices correspond to the label beneath each cubby. The pieces have already been placed inside a jewelry box, but open it to make sure you've got a match to the picture printed on the invoice."

She found the item she needed and lifted the top from the box to reveal several colored crystals strung on clear filament and framing a teardrop of hammered silver. "See? Same piece. We're good to go."

"Nice." He fingered the crystals. "Do you photograph the items for the website?"

She shook her head. "Candy shoots them as she's done. We have a program that sizes them automatically and uploads the files. Our tech then makes them live on the site. He's in El Paso."

"Can't get good help in Pit Stop?"

"For ranching, sure. But not for graphics work." She settled the lid back on the box and handed it to him. "Easy enough?"

"I think I can handle it."

"It's not as exciting as hunting mule deer, but it'll keep you busy. And out of trouble," she added, her eyes sparkling.

"Hey," he said, removing his sling. "I'm not the one the sheriff's interested in."

"That's only because I didn't find you on his side of the state line."

The woman didn't give an inch. He wasn't going to get anywhere, find out anything, learn any more about her than he already had. Not at this rate. Under these conditions. "You going to hang around here and supervise?"

She twisted her mouth, screwed it to one side. "I'm trying to decide if it's safe to leave."

"No pockets. No backpack." He turned in a circle. "I'll even let you hang onto the sling if it makes you feel better. 'Course, I could always sneak the pricey pieces out in my pants."

"You sure you have room down there?" she asked, her chin lifting. "Being that you're the size of a horse and all?"

And at that, he laughed. It was either that or admit to feeling offended. "You really don't trust people much, do you? Or maybe it's just me."

"No." She scrunched up her freckled nose. "I mean, it's not you. Not you, specifically. Just . . . men in general that I don't trust easily."

Men in general. As in plural. His blood froze at the implications, and his thoughts about the local doctor were no longer so charitable.

"Look," she began. "Forget I said anything."

"Neva—"

"I'm going to check in with Candy. I'll be back in a few." Whirling around, she headed past the counter and back the way they'd originally come.

For several long minutes, Mick stood still and stared, helpless to do anything more. He was a trained field operative. Bloody hell, he was an assassin—or he had been before coming to work for SG-5. He was valued for his cool head under all conditions. But nothing had prepared him for this fierce wave of protectiveness.

He wanted to track down every bloody bastard who'd ever hurt Neva and break their necks with his bare hands. The strength of his wrath shocked him. Blind anger led to making mistakes.

And too many mistakes would get him killed.

Nine

In his Calvin Klein pajama bottoms, matching robe, and house shoes, Holden stood staring out his kitchen window into his backyard's tropical garden. Beside him on the black marble counter, the coffeemaker brewed. He enjoyed sleeping in on Saturday mornings, but couldn't name a time when he'd ever slept past ten A.M. the way he had today.

He blamed his exhaustion on yesterday's trying events and the immense relief of disaster averted. Had Liberty left the Barn with Sheriff Munroe and returned to her parents' home, Holden would have had to scramble for a backup plan. Right now, he had none. So far he'd had no need.

Things were continuing to go smoothly his way. Liberty was upstairs in his guest bedroom still sleeping, or so he supposed. He'd slept downstairs on the sofa in his study in order to avoid any hint of impropriety. He didn't want to frighten her and have her run off again before he'd tied her to him legally as his wife.

That would happen later today. He'd already put out a call to Judge Ahearn. The judge had agreed to meet Holden at the courthouse in the county seat of Pit Stop at four P.M. Holden rarely had need to exercise the power his position provided. In this case, in the matter of saving his own life, there had been no hesitation at all.

Judge Ahearn would have his clerk draw up the marriage license, would waive the waiting period, and simply replace Cal Able's name with Holden's on the parental consent form the Mitchells had already filed. Hardly aboveboard, but Holden was willing to take the risk.

The Mitchells would be hard-pressed to prove any wrongdoing on behalf of the judge or Holden himself. They were two of the county's most highly respected citizens, while the Mitchells had only lived in the township a year, and their arrival from California and the life they'd lived there was still considered suspect by most.

The coffeemaker finished gurgling and Holden reached into the cupboard for a cup. He wondered if Liberty enjoyed coffee in the mornings, before remembering her age and family situation. The Mitchells were almost rabid in their religious zeal and had no doubt banned caffeine from their home along with television and all things secular.

Still, coming from California as a worldly teen, Holden couldn't imagine Liberty hadn't sampled the menu at Starbucks. He'd have to look into ordering her an espresso machine along with all the other things he'd made note of. The one thing he'd learned about his bride-to-be was that money could indeed buy her happiness.

Last night after he'd proposed, he'd driven her out to see the property where he was building his dream house. He'd walked her through the plot, explaining where he planned to locate the media room with its personal home theater system and computer network. She loved movies, she'd told him.

The lack of entertainment options in Earnestine was one of the two things she missed most about living in California. The other was the beach. At that, he'd pointed out where he'd staked off a section of the property for a wave pool.

Her eyes had sparkled and her smile had grown more animated than he'd seen it all night.

He felt that the tour had gone well, a feeling capped off by her appreciation of the simple gold necklace he'd given her last night and her eventual agreement to the elopement he'd planned for today. She'd seen what he could offer her now, what he could offer her in the future. And with the choice being between him and Cal Able, well . . . there was no real choice, was there?

He picked up his coffee and sipped, reaching for the stack of yesterday's mail he'd dropped on the kitchen bar but had yet found time to sort. He'd shower and dress, then wake Liberty and take her shopping for something to wear to their wedding. If they got on the road soon, they should have time to make it to El Paso and back before they were scheduled to meet Judge Ahearn.

Once the marriage was a fait accompli, they'd visit the Mitchell home and share the joyful news. At least news *he* would consider joyful. Much as he was feeling now. It was almost over. It was almost done. By tonight he would hold the upper hand.

He was feeling so confident that when he ran across it in the stack of mail, the hand-printed envelope failed to cause the same blip to his pulse as the others. The ones that had been arriving monthly for the past year.

Without opening the envelope, he knew what the note inside would say. The threats the writer would make to expose Holden's past. There would be no demands, no offers to negotiate. There would only be small-minded attempts to unnerve him, unbalance him. He was done with both.

He carried the envelope with him to the bathroom off his study, closing the door behind him and standing in front of the mirror while staring down. He'd never had the penmanship analyzed. Instead, he'd begun looking into the backgrounds of those around him who might bear him ill will, have a grudge to settle, feel the need to turn the tables for a grievance mistakenly held.

He'd also looked into church members on the fringe, which had led him straight to the Mitchells. He no longer believed they had moved their family to Earnestine Township for the salvation of their children's souls. He believed, instead, that they had come here for him.

They'd been in San Francisco, he'd discovered, when his parents had died. Liberty's mother had even been a member of the high school class that had graduated the year ahead of his. The couple had been in all the right places at all the right times to know what had happened in the church sanctuary that day. To know about the knife, the murders. To know the secrets Holden still kept.

He looked into the mirror, shocked at his ashen face, at the mustache of sweat covering his upper lip. And then he remembered the girl upstairs. If her parents actually believed him capable of killing, then having Liberty out of their control and under his made her more than a pawn.

It made her his plum, his wild card, the surest guarantee he could possibly hope for that they would never breathe a word of what they suspected he'd done.

He dropped the unopened envelope into the white bag lining the wicker trash can, and then shed his clothes and stepped into the shower stall. He had a wedding to prepare for; that was the only thing on his mind.

At least until he reached for the controls to turn on the water and swore he heard his car start up outside.

Liberty never thought she'd be so thankful as she was now that her best girlfriend in California, Jill Kramer, had taught her to drive a stick. She'd made it from the driveway to the street, from reverse into first, without squealing tires or grinding gears. Now she prayed she could get out of Earnestine without anyone seeing her in Holden's car.

Thankfully it was Saturday. Most everyone in the township was home studying up on their Scriptures, ironing their church clothes, getting all the grub together for tomorrow's big Sunday evening supper on the grounds. No, thanks. She'd had enough green bean casserole and marshmallow Jell-O salad for one lifetime.

Thankfully, too, Holden didn't live anywhere near the church or township offices. In fact, he lived on one of the back streets closest to the city limits. After seeing his place, it wasn't hard to figure out why. She knew he wasn't a big part of the religious scene in town, but wondered if he had any guilt over the way he spent the money the church and the township paid him.

Especially when they were paying him to preserve their way of life—one he didn't even have a stake in. The plans he'd shared with her last night, describing his new house—no, *their* new house—definitely had her drooling. But being married to a man who needed her to make himself look good to a church he didn't even believe in was not her idea of a good time.

"Hypocrite," she muttered under her breath, the car's RPMs up high enough now that she needed to shift into third. She wasn't about to drive fast; she didn't even have a license. And she was really glad the windows were tinted as dark as they were; her chances of being noticed were pretty slim. All she had to do was figure out where to go and what to do once she got there. Oh, and how to get rid of the car.

God, she could not *believe* she was in so much trouble! All of it her own fault for being stupid enough to trust Holden the way she'd trusted Jase. There had never been any hope she'd make her eighteenth birthday and still be single. She saw that now.

She also knew the decision that had saved her was saying yes when Holden suggested she spend the night at his house and they visit her parents later as husband and wife. Make it a dual surprise, he'd said. Her safe return, and the best match she could possibly make.

She'd agreed, but only because it gave her time to wiggle her way out of this jam. Had she gone straight home, she would never have escaped the eternal hell of being married to Cal Able. Her parents would not have let her out of their sight. She couldn't imagine what objection they might have to her marrying Holden Wagner, but she hadn't been willing to take that chance.

So she'd closed herself up in his guest room, trying not to sleep though she eventually had, then listening this morning, waiting for him to shower or cook breakfast, or anything that would keep him distracted and busy while she slipped out of the upstairs window, down the sloped rooftop, then onto the top of the tall cedar fence.

She had horrible scratches and slivers in both of her elbows and a scrape on her cheek, burning now from the tears running over the raw skin. She could hardly see to drive. She was so nervous, her hands shook on the wheel, her foot kept slipping off the accelerator. And she was almost out of gas. There was really only one place she could go.

She only hoped this time Neva believed that she was truly on the run for her life.

The morning for Neva hadn't gone particularly well. She'd accomplished a lot of work with Mick's help, true. But it had been a test of her mental agility trying to focus in order to process new orders, pay bills, respond intelligently to her programmer's e-mails—and do it all with Mick Savin less than ten feet away.

Even knowing that Candy was working at the far end of the room hadn't been enough of a deterrent for Neva to keep her mind on her work. Her mind had been on Mick. Only Mick. Solely Mick. He was getting to her.

And she was letting him—a fact that made the slip in her

armor worse than had he simply loosened the chinks on his own, worked his way in, charmed her, seduced her. But, no. She saw something in him that made her want to help him destroy everything she'd built. Judging by the way her mind couldn't let him go, she was doing a hell of a job.

She'd come back to the house thirty minutes ago to make lunch. She and Jeanne Munroe laughed at how they both seemed to make more sense out of the chaos in their lives when up to their elbows in food. Unfortunately for Neva, Jeanne was a much better cook. All Neva knew how to do was make sandwiches, soup, meals out of the freezer or boxes, and breakfast.

Which was why when Mick and Candy walked into the kitchen moments later, it was to the scent of maple syrup, pancakes, and bacon. "Ooh, girl. Mmm, mmm, mmm." Candy smacked her lips. "I don't know how you manage to get sugar into every meal, but I love you for it."

"Lucky for you, missy, your thighs are much more forgiving than mine." Neva turned to look at Candy. Or started to. Except when looking over her shoulder, she instead caught Mick's eye. It hadn't been but half an hour since she'd seen him, so it made no sense that she'd missed him so much. "How 'bout you, Mick? Do you mind being served sugar three times a day?"

"As long as I'm being served, I'm good with sugar, steak, baked potatoes, pork chops, mashed potatoes, lobster, au gratin potatoes—"

Neva cut him off with a laugh. "Okay, okay. I'll make a trip into town and stock up on meat and potatoes."

Candy's gaze drifted from one to the other. "Does that mean you're going to be staying with us awhile, Mick? Neva doesn't stock up for just anyone."

Neva stared down at the pancake browning on the griddle and waited to hear Mick's reply. She knew he had no real reason to stay, and all the reasons she wanted him to were selfish, not to mention a risk to her cause. Still, she found herself holding her breath, her hand tightly squeezing the handle of the pancake turner.

Mick slowly crossed to the kitchen table, pulled out a chair, and sat. "I was thinking I might head out of here soon. Later today. The hospitality's much appreciated, but I need to get out of the way and back to work."

"What do you do?" Candy asked.

"He's an engineering project consultant," Neva answered before Mick could draw a breath to speak. She didn't want Candy to think she'd taken Mick in without knowing anything about him, but she also didn't want to hear how easily he lied.

"Right," he said behind her. "I've been on vacation this week. Checking out a hunting lease in New Mexico."

"Meaning you'll be back this fall when the season opens."

Funny. Neva hadn't thought about that. "You'll have to drive down and say hello."

"Sure. I'll do that."

But Neva knew that he never would, and was certain Candy knew it, too. It was the polite talk of strangers eating breakfast for lunch. And it wasn't productive to think anything about Mick being here would ever be anything more.

She slid the pancake onto a stack of five others, added the bacon, and carried the platter along with a pitcher of warm syrup to the table. "Eat up. I wouldn't want it said I sent an injured man away hungry."

While Mick and Candy served themselves, Neva returned to the stove and poured out two more circles of batter. She needed space, time, separation, whatever to get hold of the ridiculous emotions insisting she knew him enough to trust him when there were a thousand unanswered questions she couldn't ask. He would expect tit for tat, which she wasn't sure she could give. Other lives depended on her discretion.

Thankfully, Candy saved her from doing just that. "So, Mick, where are you headed? Where do you come from?"

Yes! Neva watched the edges of the batter begin to bubble and blessed her girlfriend's nosiness.

"I work in Manhattan," he said, and she looked back in time to see him lift his glass of orange juice and drink. "But I grew up in New Orleans."

"You have family there?" Candy prodded.

Mick shook his head. "I was an only child. My parents were already in their forties when I was born. They've both been gone now for several years."

"I'm sorry," Candy said, echoing Neva's thoughts as she flipped the pancakes before turning to face the table.

"Don't be." Mick dug back into his food, frowned down into his plate. "They were great together. A long and happy life. And they died together. A freak auto accident. I doubt either would've survived long without the other around. It was for the best." A shadow of sadness softened his gaze.

Neva's heart melted. "It couldn't have been easy for you, though. Being left all alone like that. And so suddenly."

"I was in the army then," he said, shaking his head. "I never had a chance to be alone."

Yet he worked alone, existed alone. If she hadn't picked him up on the side of the road, he would have died there alone. As far as she knew, he hadn't contacted anyone since. And then it hit her. When he told her the truth, she trusted him. When he lied, she didn't believe a word he said.

He was more of a loner than she was. And she couldn't help but wonder how close they were to being kindred spirits—even though their reasons for their solitary ways of life could not have been further apart.

She'd turned off the fire beneath the griddle and started toward the table with the last of the food when she heard the crunch of gravel beneath tires outside on her drive. Glancing out the window, she shook her head, wondering when she'd been entered in the running for Miss Popularity and why hadn't she been told.

"It's Ed," she said to the room as she set the pancakes on the table and headed back to the stove to cook more. She stirred the batter, poured two circles onto the griddle that hadn't yet had time to cool. When he knocked on the screen door seconds later, she called out, "Come in. Have a pancake."

"Love one," the doctor said, stepping into the room and coming to a stop once he saw it wasn't just the two of them eating. His expression clearly broadcast his displeasure at his find. "I thought I'd stop by and make sure Mick made it out to pick up the dog."

Neva snorted to herself. Yeah. More like he'd come to make sure neither Mick or the dog were anywhere around. The idea of another man paying her the least bit of attention was too much for the doctor to deal with. If she didn't rely on Ed for so many things . . .

"I did just that, mate," Mick said, reaching for another strip of bacon. "But Neva wouldn't let me leave."

"Is that so?" Ed took the empty plate Neva held out, his gaze asking too many questions.

She waved him toward the table for four; she didn't need him hovering. "You should know better than anyone that Mick was in no shape to drive. In fact, I was surprised to find you'd released him."

Ed pulled out a chair from beneath the table. The one across from Mick where Neva had planned to sit. "The man insisted. Against my advice, I might add."

"Now, Ed," Candy teased. "You treated the man in a veterinary clinic. What do you expect?"

"I've been beat up worse than this in my life, mate." Mick sat back away from the table, stared at the other man. "I know my limits."

"Most patients think they do." Ed pulled off the glasses he used to drive, slid them into his shirt pocket. "Most patients are wrong."

Neva rolled her eyes. As much as she loved men—and she did, she truly did—this was one thing she hated. This macho posturing, this need for one-upmanship. So it caught her pleasantly off guard, pancake turner poised above the griddle, when Mick spoke.

"And this time I was. I needed the extra night. It did me good."

Smiling down as she did, Neva stacked the two pancakes, lifted them with the turner, and carried them over. "See? No worries, mate. We're all good here," she said, sliding the food onto Ed's plate. She caught Mick's gaze, took his touché of a wink to heart, then sat in the only empty chair to eat the last piece of bacon, having lost most of her appetite.

"What're your plans now, Mick?" Ed asked, pouring syrup before cutting into the food with his fork. "If you're still not up to traveling, I'll check you into the clinic. Do the full workup of tests you need to have done."

"No need. I'll be heading out soon." Mick looked over at Neva; staring down at the half strip of bacon on her plate, she felt the heat of his gaze, remembered the heat of his mouth, didn't want him to go. "Now that Neva's used me and abused me, my work here is done."

Neva groaned, buried her face in her hands.

Candy laughed out loud.

Ed angled his fork across his plate and sat back. "Oh, really? That sounds like a story worth hearing."

"Trust me." Neva grimaced to herself. "It's not."

"Why don't you tell me anyway?" Ed insisted, bracing his forearms on the table with an air of expectation.

"Mick packed up a few boxes I needed to get shipped out. Nothing salacious at all," she said, and was just getting ready to toss both of them out on their ear when she heard a second car come barreling down the drive. "When did I become Grand Central Station?"

She started to get up, but Candy beat her to it, carrying her dishes to the sink. "Jesus Lord up above. It's the man with the white BMW."

At Neva's side, Mick stiffened. "I'm assuming you weren't expecting him."

Shaking her head, she stacked the empty plates, leaving only Ed's behind as she cleared the rest from the table. "That man has darkened my door for the last time. I can whip out my law degree and play rough the same as he can."

She and Candy stood side by side, staring out the kitchen window as Holden Wagner's luxury car came to a jerky stop inches from the bumper of her truck. Neva cringed, then frowned. Something here wasn't right. The car door flew open then. Liberty Mitchell jumped out and ran toward the back door.

Candy was there pushing open the screen before Neva even thought about it. Liberty rushed up the stairs and almost tripped and tumbled to the floor before Neva moved and caught her. "Liberty, what are you doing here?" She wrapped an arm around the girl's shoulders and helped her to a chair. "And what in the world are you doing driving Holden's car?"

"Neva, please. You have to help me." She reached up, pushed wild strands of dark hair from her face. "Really. I'll tell you everything. I promise I won't lie or keep anything secret. I can't go back. I just can't."

"Shh. Calm down, sweetie." Neva cast a quick glance at Ed, who was frowning with concern. "Liberty, what's wrong? Are you injured? Has someone hurt you?"

Liberty shook her head, shuddered where she sat, her hands gripping her arms tightly as she held herself together. "My parents." She stopped, shook harder. "They've set it up for me to marry a guy at the church who works at the hardware store. I can't. I won't. He's got one wife already. So Holden decided I should marry him instead."

"Bloody hell," Mick murmured, scooting his chair back from the table.

Ed was there now, kneeling in front of the girl. "Liberty, take a breath. One deep breath. Good," he added when she did. "Are you hurt at all?" She shook her head. "Has anyone touched you inappropriately?" Again, a negative answer. He gave Neva a sharp nod.

Candy moved to sit in the chair Ed had vacated. Neva looked to her for advice, but the other woman's wide-eyed bewilderment and resulting shrug wasn't a bit of help. Ed being here wasn't a problem. He'd often done physical exams on the girls who came to the Barn, and was as involved with Neva's network as was Candy.

But having Mick here . . . Neva had never felt so conflicted. She trusted him even while questioning whether she was basing that confidence on a false sense of who she wanted him to be. But she had to deal with the problem at hand, to get Liberty settled, to do something with Holden's car before the sheriff started pounding on her door.

At the moment, facing down Mick Savin seemed the lesser of two evils, and so she forged ahead. "Liberty, you need to slow down and start at the beginning. Tell us what happened after you left with Holden yesterday."

"Wait." Ed got to his feet, stared down at Neva. "Is this the time or the place?"

And Neva couldn't help it. She looked over at Mick. His eyes glittered dangerously, a silvery gray beneath a frown that would have intimidated her had she not spent the last eighteen hours absorbing all she could of him.

"I can go. I can stay." He paused, a delay that allowed her to take a deep breath, to focus. And then he said the only thing that she'd ever wanted him to say. The thing she needed to hear more than anything else. "I can help."

It was the right decision to bring him in. She knew it was. She reluctantly dragged her gaze from his. "Candy, can you and Ed get rid of the car? Mick doesn't know the area and doesn't need to be driving."

"Sure," Candy said, already on her feet. "Lib, did you leave the keys inside?"

Liberty nodded. "I'm sorry. I probably ruined the car. I suck at driving."

Ed dropped a hand to the teen's shoulder and squeezed. "Forget about the car. We'll take care of it. You let Neva take care of you."

Ed and Candy left the kitchen, and moments later both the BMW and Ed's truck headed down the drive. Neva offered Liberty a hand, helped the teen to her feet and toward the door, then looked back at Mick.

He pushed out of his chair when he realized she was waiting, lifted a brow along with one corner of his mouth as if he realized the gig was up. "Where are we going?"

Neva returned his look. "Where do you think?"

"Then what?"

"Then we make her disappear."

Ten

Walking behind the two women on the way from Neva's house to the barn, Mick remained silent as Liberty Mitchell told her story. It was a story that should've been hard to believe. A charismatic leader herding his congregation of lemmings toward the edge of a religious cliff, assuring them the rapture of spiritual enlightenment once they took that Olympic-sized leap of faith and went down.

The healthier they left the church financially, the more enlightened their afterlife. The more wives the men took with them, the more rapture bestowed on all parties to the marriages. Thing was, it wasn't hard to believe at all when one looked at the legacies left by Jim Jones, David Koresh, or Marshall Applewhite and the Heaven's Gate cult.

Mick added Pastor Straight from this so-called church in Earnestine Township to the list. Bringing innocent girls into the mix and using them as pawns. Bloody bunch of perverted bastards made him sick. And he couldn't figure why the hell the lawyer protecting this sex racket dressed like he worked on Wall Street and drove a car that could put the girl he proposed to marry through a year or more of a good state school.

Something was very fucking wrong with this picture.

Mick started to interrupt the conversation ahead and ferret out what he could about Wagner, but both Neva's and Liberty's voices had lowered, shutting him out. He dropped back a bit to let them have the private time. FM dropped back, as well. It wasn't a problem. He wasn't here to get involved. He was only here should Neva need help.

That was it. That was all. He wasn't here because he couldn't bring himself to leave when she was in danger. He wasn't here because walking away meant never seeing her again. He wasn't here because leaving seemed so very wrong. On all counts. Every way he turned. Oh, yeah. Bloody well screwed he was, wasn't he? And he would have to deal with it. But later, once he saw for himself the truth of what went on at Neva's Big Brown Barn.

They'd reached the side patio and the door she'd ushered him through when she'd put him to work this morning. Leaving the dog outside, Mick followed behind Liberty as Neva led them both through the structure's first floor maze to the same corner where earlier he'd packed boxes for shipping. Once there, she headed for the wall of cubbyholes, hesitated as she made some sort of decision, then turned around and faced him.

"Wait here a second, sweetie," she said to Liberty before taking hold of his good arm and guiding him several steps back into the labyrinth so that they stood out of Liberty's sight and earshot between shelves of supplies. "Look." Neva stopped, twisted her hands together at her waist.

He looked. At her show of nerves. At the way her freckles stood out on her pale skin. At the way she held her chin high even as it threatened to quiver. He wasn't about to move until he found out what was wrong. Seeing her this terrified when she was one of the strongest women he'd had the pleasure to know had him on edge, had his nape tingling, his gut drawing up tight like a red rubber ball.

"I shouldn't be doing this, involving you," she was saying. "My instinct tells me it's okay. That I can trust you. But I'm running into a wall here. Keeping my mouth shut has been a part of my self-preservation for so long that I'm not sure I can get past it."

He understood. He had expected no less. "I'm not here to bust your operation. I know you've wondered."

"I have," she admitted. "You told me you'd done some things in your life that no one could prove. Well"— she paused, shrugged—"so have I. You may not have come here for me, but you're here now. And if you're law enforcement I expect you to do your job. You can't be who you are and not."

He reached out, toyed with the open collar of the plain purple shirt she wore tucked into blue jeans. It wasn't the way he wanted to touch her, but it was all he would let himself do. "I'm not law enforcement or military. I'm not a mercenary. I don't do what I do for money.

"I'm not even a private investigator," he added for good measure, certain each of those options had at some point crossed her mind. "I told you before, I'm no saint. I'm also no stranger to working outside of the law. I've been known to cross lines that I shouldn't."

"Like trespassing?" she asked, her voice shaking though she did at least smile.

"Yeah. That, too." He stepped closer, wrapped an arm around her shoulders, brought her to his body and held her, feeling as if he should've been around for her sooner, to offer her this from the very beginning. "If you want a show of good faith, Neva, I'll give you this. The money the Bremmer boy shouldn't have had access to? It may belong to a laundering operation."

"The good people of Earnestine? Involved in a crime? Say it isn't so," she mocked, as her head came to rest on his chest. She touched him carefully. She didn't squeeze, didn't linger. And then she stepped back, seeming as reluctant to leave him as he was to let her go. "Speaking of crimes, I need to get Liberty upstairs."

They returned to where the girl paced nervously, chewing her cuticles, her hair a tangled mess of brittle brown strands. Neva gave Liberty a quick reassuring hug before kneeling down to slip her hand into the cubbyhole on the bottom right corner. A loud click sounded as the latch securing that section of the wall released.

She reached around the side and pulled; the partition swiveled open on a hidden base to reveal a small closet, one hiding a steep staircase that angled to the right at the first landing and disappeared between the outside wall of the barn and what Mick surmised to be an inside wall belonging to Candy's apartment.

"Wow," Liberty said as Neva shepherded the girl inside. Mick followed, bloody well impressed with the deceptive setup and layout of Candy's living space. It would take a lot more than a first glance to notice the discrepancy between where the barn ended and her apartment began.

Pushing the cubbyholes back into position, Neva locked the wall into place and used a flashlight she grabbed off the bottom step to illuminate their climb to the top. The door there opened into another small closet; once inside, she entered a numbered code into a keypad on the frame and hung the flashlight's strap on the doorknob.

"Wow," Liberty said again, as the closet wall slid open on similarly concealed tracks to reveal a small sitting room complete with a computer desk and open kitchen area beyond. "Is this where I'm going to live?"

"No, but it's where you'll stay until I can move you out of here safely." Neva flipped one wall switch and the panel closed, flipped another and two table lamps came on. "You need to be sure this is what you want because once I put the ball in motion, that's it. You can't come back. It's too risky to both of us. To Ed and Candy, too."

"I am sure. I want to be able to work and start saving money to go to school. I don't want to be one of five wives doing nothing but changing diapers all my life." Liberty walked farther into the room, ran her fingers over the padded arm of the cushy blue corduroy love seat. "I can't believe that's all my parents want for me."

"Finding this out now is better than finding it out later. You've got your entire life ahead of you and learning now to rely on yourself is going to take you far," Neva said, then glanced at Mick, who was clueless about teenage girls.

He merely nodded and shrugged. Give him a physically menacing threat, he was all over it. And though the idea of hunting down her parents and making them see the light sounded like a damn good one, he had no experience with this. Meaning he wasn't sure he was going to be a whole lot of help. "What do you want me to do?"

She flipped a third switch and an inset section of the wall beside the door and above the desk slid up to reveal a bank of four small screens. Pulling out the keyboard tray, she clicked through several windows on the flat panel monitor, bringing up the feed from the security cameras positioned on the exterior corners of the barn.

"I want to get Liberty settled in her room. Will you watch and let me know if anyone besides Candy or Ed shows up?" she asked, gesturing toward the wall.

"That I can do," he said, feeling much more in his undercover element while his respect for this woman notched upward toward awe. This was one hell of a sophisticated operation she was running.

"Thanks," she said, and smiled, hesitating briefly, as if she had something she wanted to tell him, something she needed to say, before turning and leading Liberty through the kitchen and down the hallway beyond.

Mick crossed the carpeted floor, an obvious soundproofing measure between this apartment and Candy's, and stood in front of the screens, leaning against the love seat where it backed up to the desk. The only movement he saw on any of the feeds came when his dog walked off the patio to sniff around the graveled parking area.

From the far end of the barn's second floor, he heard the murmur of the two female voices, neither loud enough to make out any of what they said. He glanced in that direction, taking in what he could of the utilitarian kitchen. A refrigerator, a microwave, a small stove with a heavy duty vented hood above to keep cooking odors from drifting.

The build-out of this structure had not come cheap. He wondered about the chicken and the egg. Which had come first. The Big Brown Barn's current business success, which he couldn't quite see paying for all of this—or the modifications to the original building, which the business was now supporting. He had a whole lot of questions he wanted to ask Neva Case.

She might be an attorney and an entrepreneur, but there was a hell of a lot more to her than that. Her secrets weren't simple, and he was certain could get her killed. He didn't want to see that happen. He wanted to keep her safe. How the hell he was going to manage that from a state away once he returned to New Mexico was going to require more than pulling a rabbit out of his hat.

He might just have to pull one out of Manhattan.

By the time Neva walked her newest charge through the upstairs rooms of the barn, the girl's exhaustion was evident. Liberty had been sitting on the foot of the bed she'd chosen when Neva left to set out towels and toiletries in the bathroom. Checking back minutes later, she found the events of the past few days had taken their toll. Liberty was fast asleep.

After drawing the chenille coverlet over the teenager's legs, Neva returned to the main room to explain things to

Mick. She didn't want to have to answer his questions. But doing so was a much more palatable alternative than having him leave. He'd said he'd stayed to help, and right now she'd take it—even if she wished he was staying for her.

"Anything going on?" she asked, watching him as he watched the feeds from the cameras.

Pushing up and away from the love seat on which he'd been leaning, he shook his head. "Nothing moving but the dog. Restless mutt."

She crossed her arms, smiled. "He's probably anxious to get back to hunting."

He snorted. "He's bloody useless at it. My fault. I don't know a retriever from a shepherd or a hound."

Her grin widened. He was so cute when he was so honestly clueless. "Could be he's the part of your costume that gave you away."

"And here all this time you've been telling me it was the knife and the gun." When she remained silent, he added, "You do still have my gun, don't you?"

"I do," she said with a nod.

He turned to face her, holding a hand to his ribs. "If you really want me to be any help here, you might think about giving it back."

"I don't need you to shoot anybody," she said, thinking as she did how much safer she felt in the dark with her own gun close by. Thinking, too, how having him here added to that sense of security.

"Then cross your fingers no one comes out of the corner swinging. Because I promise you. That happens?" He patted his damaged midsection. "I'm going down."

"I'll think about it." And she would. He was so stoic in the face of his injuries, she'd forgotten how extensive they were. "But I don't think anyone will be coming after you. If anything, they'll come after me."

He huffed, shook his head. "Women."

"What?"

He stepped closer, hovered, forcing her gaze up to meet his, which glittered dangerously. "Someone comes after me, I'll duck as many punches as I can. They come after you, ducking won't make the same dent as my gun."

Her heart beat so hard she couldn't swallow. She could barely even breathe. She hadn't had anyone on her side in so long that she didn't know what to do but say the first thing that popped into her mind. "Then we hope it doesn't come to that. And if we're careful, there's no reason it should."

"Careful?" His lips narrowed. His eyes, too, the corners crinkling from his time in the sun, from his experience in matters illegal that she was sure far surpassed hers. "You've got five people who know about this already. How many more are going to find out before that girl gets to where you're sending her?"

She blew out a long slow breath and walked around to curl up in the corner of the love seat. She could see the four screens just as well from here as she could from where she'd been standing. And right now, keeping the piece of furniture between her and Mick seemed the smart thing to do. Standing out in the open, she too easily broadcast all of her thoughts. And his antennae were too damn strong.

"Neva?" he demanded in a harsh tone that didn't sound a whole lot like her protector, her hero, her crusader of minutes before.

She looked up and into the eyes of the not very nice man who hunted with a SIG Sauer. "I don't know what to do."

He frowned, then came around to sit beside her, perching on the edge of the love seat's second cushion, leaning forward, elbows on his widespread knees. So much for the barrier between them. She could feel his body's heat, his tension, his instincts kicking in. "What do you mean you don't know what to do? This *is* what you do, isn't it?"

She nodded, brought her knees to her chest, tucked the toes of her boots beneath his cushion. "For five years now."

His frown said it all. "Then I'd think you'd have the system down pat."

"I thought I did." Dear Lord, was she really going to tell him things she hadn't even told Ed and Candy? Her partners in crime? Her hands trembled with the force of her decision, and she tucked them into the folds of her knees. "But I've run into a couple of problems that make me leery to put Liberty into my network."

Moisture welled in her eyes, and she looked away to scan the camera feeds. She would not cry. She didn't have time to cry. Crying in front of Mick Savin was the last thing she wanted to do.

"What sort of problems?" he asked, and when she continued to look away, added, "I can't help if I don't know."

"I'm not sure you can help anyway." She breathed in, breathed out, allowed her stomach to settle, her unshed tears to dry. "I'm not sure anyone can."

"Have you let anyone try?"

She looked over at him then, away from the monitors and to the man staring into her eyes. His piercing expression made it hard for her to speak, to admit that what he was accusing her of was true. She was unnecessarily shouldering this sizable burden alone. It didn't make sense, no, and she knew that. But there were only two others to tell.

Candy had been through one fight for her life already. If this went that far, Neva wanted to spare her friend a repeat of that pain. Ed would ask too many questions, demand answers she didn't have, and then try to take over. And this particular truth was ammunition she didn't want to put like a gift into his hands.

But now she had Mick. Mick who was still waiting, still

patient, still offering to help. "I think there's a leak in my network."

"A leak." He laced his fingers between his spread knees. "Someone's talking?"

She shrugged, feeling stupid for knowing no more than she did. "I don't know if it's talk, or someone not following through, dropping the ball, I don't know. I just know I've lost three of the girls who came to me for help."

His head bobbed as he worked to process what she'd told him. "Lost how?"

"Lost as in vanished. I can't find them anywhere." She moved one hand to the back of the love seat, pinched and played with a fabric seam. "They were with their handler where they should've been, then they were gone. No one has a clue."

Mick glanced over, shifted to face her. "No chance they ended up back in Earnestine and were hidden away?"

She shook her head. "If that had happened, I would've heard. Holden Wagner would never let me live down such a failure."

"Even if he couldn't prove your involvement?"

Smart man. "How fast you're learning the vagaries of our celebrity lawyer."

"Celebrity?"

"Oh, yes." She nodded briskly. "Before he moved here, he was a big First Amendment activist. Upholding freedom of religious expression at all costs."

"What's he doing in small-town West Texas?" Mick asked, his brows drawing together, his forehead furrowed.

"The township apparently made him an offer he couldn't refuse. And yeah," she added, listening to the gears whir in Mick's mind, gears that had whirred in hers for years. "No one I know believes that's the whole story. Problem is, research resources in the area are limited. I've got the only satellite dish for miles. And most people in the area are happy to think of what goes on down the road as gossip. Otherwise they might feel compelled to get involved."

"And you who are involved. You've never wondered?"

"Of course I have." The more she heard, the more she did. "But I've got a business that keeps me hopping eighteen hours a day, not to mention this criminal sideline. Holden Wagner's a back-burner item."

Mick rubbed a hand over the back of his neck. "I'll move him up to the front."

A good start, but not nearly enough. She needed more and told him so. "If you've got those kind of resources available, I'd rather you look into all the places I can't and see what you can dig up on my girls."

"Your girls. Makes it pretty personal, doesn't it?" he asked in that perceptive way he had.

"It is personal. These girls are being abused. They're being raped. They're having anything resembling dignity stripped away." She felt her blood pressure rise, her pulse race, both fueled by her anger, her powerlessness to do more than she was already doing.

She shuddered when she needed to remain calm and focus. "They're not allowed control over their own bodies. Not when it comes to sex or bearing children for men who offer them nothing. No love. No respect. They have no autonomy. They're not allowed to think for themselves, speak for themselves—"

She couldn't go on. It wrung her out to put that much into words. Admitting to Mick anything more . . .

He braced his good arm along the back of the love seat and reached over with his other hand, took hold of hers where she held them twisted together. "I can't promise you anything, but I'll check into it, okay? See what I can do."

She nodded, and this time when her vision blurred, it was too late not to cry. She sobbed softly, drew in shaky, rickety gulps of air. Mick asked her nothing. He simply pulled her into the crook of his shoulder and tucked her close.

He smelled like soap and liniment and fabric dried in the sun. His thigh beneath hers was solid, hard, as was his chest where she rested her head. And when he rubbed his chin against her, the whiskers of his goatee bristled against her hair and she couldn't help but smile.

Funny enough, but being near him was all that she needed. His silence gave her strength. He didn't pry, though she was certain he had questions. He did the only thing she wanted. He supported her and let her be.

It was when she started to move away that she realized she didn't want to. He made her feel so comfortable, as if being in his arms was where she belonged. But since that wasn't the case, it couldn't be, she wouldn't let it, she forced herself to glance back at the four camera feeds, and smiled at seeing Mick's dog nosing around near the edge of the patio.

"What's he doing?"

"How did you know—" was all she got out because once she looked back, once his gaze snagged hers and held it, she couldn't think beyond her need to kiss him.

They were so close; she still sat tucked into his body, her shoulder fitted to the pit of his arm, her bent knees propped on his thigh. His face was inches from hers, his mouth right there. All she had to do was part her lips. Instead, she looked into his eyes.

Oh, dear. Oh, my. So many things he wanted, was thinking, intended to do. She forgot that she needed air to keep from passing out. When it hit her, she sucked in a breath sharply and muttered to herself, "Oh, hell."

And then Mick came toward her, pushing her back into the corner of the love seat so slowly she wasn't sure that their descent wasn't her dragging him down. "I don't like the way you know what I'm thinking," she said, her arms coming up to loop around his neck.

"I know," he answered, bracing a forearm and his weight on the padded armrest beneath her head. His other hand he settled at her waist.

"Then why do you do it?"

"It's who I am. It's what I do."

"I'd rather you do something else."

"Only if you're sure," he said, coming nearer to nuzzle her nose with his.

She caught a whiff of maple syrup from lunch on his breath. "I am," she replied, because nothing else seemed right.

She moved one hand up to cup the back of his head, the fuzz of his hair scratching her palm, and urged him down, his mouth to hers. He was warm and familiar, and she wanted more than his kiss. She wanted his hand on her skin, and reached between them to pull her blouse from her jeans.

His tongue slid into her mouth, his hand beneath the loosened fabric. She moaned at the contact, wished she was naked, and kissed him back. His breath heated her cheek, his beard scraped her chin. The rumble that went through his body tickled her to her toes.

She shifted her legs, straightened them out so she lay beside him, enjoying the press of his body as much as the press of his mouth. And when he opened his hand over her rib cage, spread his fingers and grazed the lace cup of her bra, she rolled toward him, pressed herself into his hand.

He touched her as if he cared, gently, the touch of a lover, not a man notching the posts on his bed. She caught at his lower lip, drew it into her mouth, bathed it with her tongue. He increased the driving pressure, demanding she do the same. As if he knew she was ready. As if he knew she'd been waiting for him to ask.

He'd trapped her one hand between his good shoulder and the cushions. She reached down with the other and tugged up the hem of his T-shirt. The skin of his lower back between his fatigues and the bindings securing his ribs was smooth, resilient, the muscles beneath firm. He chuckled into her mouth as she tickled him there, and then groaned when she took her touch lower and kneaded his very fine and taut backside.

It wasn't enough, this fumbling, groping kiss. His tongue stroked hers, and she imagined the feel of it on the flesh between her legs. She hadn't enjoyed a man's mouth there in so very long. Just the thought of Mick going down and loving her there . . . She sent her tongue deeper into his mouth to find and mate with his, spread her thighs, and whimpered when he pushed a knee between them.

She rocked up against him, unprepared for the urgency of her need. He growled and tore his mouth from hers, buried his face in the crook of her neck, pushed away the cup of her bra, and squeezed the flesh of her breast. What was she doing? What? *What?* Closing her eyes. Reaching between her legs to rub herself with the seam of her zipper. Giving herself up to what Mick did to her body.

He slid lower, shoved her shirt higher, took her nipple into his mouth and tugged. She bit back a cry, feeling her sex swell as if he were sucking her there. It was when he rolled onto her body and settled between her spread legs that she first met the fullness of his erection. The idea of taking him into her body stole away her breath. She wedged both hands between them, cupped him, measured him, then moved her fingers again to his rump, dug in and begged him close.

This was so unfair to him, having him rock against her, arousing him, getting off without being able to truly give back. But then nothing mattered as sensations swept through her body, his hard cock on her clit as she came. There was no ripple, no buildup. It was an explosive burst of pleasure that bordered on pain.

So sudden. So intense. Moisture soaked her panties. She wanted to cry. He tongued her nipple, sucked and bit at the surrounding flesh. She felt so selfish, so relieved. She shuddered as the contractions continued. They consumed her and she let them, giving herself up.

And then it was done. Mick returned her clothing to rights and kissed her. Soft gentle kisses tendered along her cheekbone and jaw as he sat up. Rumpled and disheveled, she did the same, quickly scanning the camera feeds before chastising herself for getting so carried away.

What in the bloody hell was wrong with her—and dear Lord, now she was talking like the man.

Mick cleared his throat, got slowly to his feet, unable to stifle a groan. "Can you point me to the bathroom?"

She flushed to the roots of her hair. "Right past the kitchen. There's aspirin and Advil in the medicine cabinet." She'd probably come close to killing him, as injured as he already was. "Can I do anything?"

"Uh, no." He grunted, winced. "This I'd better take care of on my own."

This time the blush crawled over every inch of exposed skin. She looked down, mortified that she hadn't once thought of his pain. Or his pleasure. And just when she thought to offer, she heard Liberty stir. "I'm usually not this selfish, Mick. I'm really not."

"Neva, don't worry. I'll let you make it up to me later."

A hole, please. In the middle of the floor. Now. "Sure. Okay."

He moved beyond the love seat, stopped, looked back. "When I get back, I'm going to need details on your network."

"My network?" she asked inanely.

"If you want me to see what I can do to help."

She nodded because she had no brain, looked up at the screens in time to see Candy hop from Ed's truck and Spencer drive in behind. She glanced back to tell Mick she'd get the info together.

But he was already gone.

Eleven

Arms hugging her middle, Candy stood next to Neva's truck, watching Ed pull out and Spencer pull in. Dealing with the first man had been emotionally exhausting. She wasn't sure she had it in her now to deal with number two. Especially out here in the open when she had no idea what would come out of her mouth. And so she started walking toward the Barn.

Driving Holden's car earlier, all she'd been able to think about was Spencer's daddy catching her behind the wheel of the stolen BMW. She'd followed near enough to Ed's bumper that anyone blowing past wouldn't have time to examine closely who was hidden by the tinted glass as the sweet ride burned up the road. That didn't mean she hadn't held her breath each time Ed had slowed for a curve or taken an unexpected turn. She'd nearly rear-ended him twice.

They'd left Holden's car sitting in the middle of the property he owned outside of E.T., and left no other tracks behind. No footprints or tread marks from Ed's truck. No fingerprints or other obvious trace evidence. At least nothing the county sheriff would be able to find with the forensic technology he had at his disposal.

If it had been any other time of year, Candy would've

prayed hard for a good rain to wash away any lingering proof of her involvement. She knew she faced prison time should the work she did with Neva be discovered. But Jesus Lord, she did not want to find herself behind bars for being in possession of a stolen vehicle.

If she were caught, that was the future she faced because there was no way she'd rat out Liberty for taking the car. Not when the girl was facing a nasty future with that whack job Holden Wagner in her bed. Candy's stomach had been rolling since hearing that particular news.

And it was thinking about Liberty looking down the barrel of that ugly gun and listening to Ed mouth about Neva getting in trouble with a man like Mick Savin that had Candy's claws sharpened and flexed. Ed knew better. He knew what the Earnestine girls were up against. Yet he didn't seem to give a rat's ass about Liberty. He only wanted to know why Mick was still at the house.

And now here came Spencer when Candy was so not in the mood to deal with men after the good doctor and Holden and yesterday's run-in with the sheriff. Not to mention how the situation in the township had her thinking about all the perverts she'd known in her life. She just knew this wasn't going to go well. Nope. Not today. Not now.

Seeing that she was heading to her place, he followed, teasing her by driving behind instead of giving her a ride or passing her and moving on ahead. She wasn't up for his teasing. She had too much on her mind. Spencer couldn't know that, but that didn't mean she was going to cut the boy so much as an inch of slack.

Taking him down to her place wasn't particularly smart since Neva was still upstairs with Mick and the Mitchell girl, but right now Candy wanted to go home. Her home. Her haven. She needed to surround herself with all the things that made her feel safe, hating—but admitting—that sweet Spencer Munroe was way too big a part of that.

What in the world was she doing loving a white boy who hadn't even yet turned twenty?

She walked past the patio to the back of the Barn and stopped in her apartment's doorway, turning as he braked, parked, and locked up his truck. Looking at him as he climbed down and walked toward her, she wondered why she and Neva trusted their bodies so easily to men after all that they'd witnessed in their lives.

This thing with Mick was the first time since knowing Neva that Candy had seen her girlfriend show enough interest in a man to involve him in her life at a level that had nothing to do with her orgasms. If Mick made Neva happy even before she'd taken him to bed, Candy didn't want to be standing up when that earth moved.

Her own case was just as out of the blue and crazy; she still hadn't figured why it had been so easy to open her heart to Spencer when she'd known from the beginning that their summertime relationship would never last beyond the season.

He was such a beautiful boy. So clean and pure—traits that made it easier to understand the source of her affection, even as she knew she had to let him go. So much in her life had been horribly ugly and dirty. And he deserved better than to have to wash off her stain.

Her hand on the doorknob, she shook her head, knowing this wasn't going to be easy. "I cannot believe you came back out here after last night. You never seemed like a slow learner before."

Spencer took the last four steps to reach her in two stretches of his long and powerful legs. His grin was as wide as the sky. "Feisty this afternoon, aren't you?"

"I'm in a mood, baby. I'm not going to kid you about that."

"Then I should be just the person you're wanting to see." He stopped, shoved his hands in his jeans pockets, and flexed his shoulders, which stretched the cotton of his faded green Pit Stop Pirates T-shirt with all those muscles he had. "I haven't seen a mood of yours yet that has turned me off."

"That's because you're a randy rutting beast." She wanted him to move, to come closer. She wanted to get this over with. Aggravation buzzed around her like a fly. "You have a dick for a brain, boy. You're all about getting turned on."

Spencer winced, then laughed, a nervous, uncomfortable sound. She would've felt sorry for him if she hadn't been busy feeling sorry for herself. She sighed. "This isn't a good time for me, Spencer. Why don't you come back later when I'm feeling more sexy? Let me get over myself."

He obviously didn't think she was serious because he still didn't budge. Just stood there with all that thick dark hair and those broad shoulders, those long sturdy legs and wide chest. He looked like he belonged on the pages of a teen magazine, or in a glossy football program, one pom-pom girls drooled over while they diddled themselves.

She stared off into the distance, blinking back tears. She was so proud of her professional success. She didn't know why it was taking so long to get her personal act together. Or why she had to judge the beautiful Spencer Munroe by the acts of so many others.

And then the mood shifted. She sensed it like a storm on the horizon, swirling and tightening, sucking away the air she was trying to breathe, and it took her a good long time to look over to the source. She wasn't happy with what she saw when she finally got up the guts and did.

"I'm not going anywhere, Candy. In case you haven't noticed, I don't show up only when you're feeling sexy." His dark eyebrows came down to shadow his bright green eyes. "If anyone thinks of me as a dick, it's you. You're willing to spread your legs, but forget about opening your mind."

He paused for a moment, then charged forward, head low, as if he had a ball tucked to his chest. "I might actually be more than a good fuck. But at the rate you're pissing me off, you're never going to know."

And that did it. He wanted to know where they stood? He wanted to know what she thought? She'd show him exactly. "Then we might as well get busy with the one thing we know works between us. Unless this time you didn't bring a condom?"

Scowling, she opened her door and walked inside, leaving it open for him to follow or not. He did, locking the door before walking across the hardwood floor to where she'd stopped in front of her orange chenille sofa, staring when she reached back for the zipper of her skirt and ripped it down.

The garment pooled around the cowboy boots she wore. Her cropped T-shirt went next. She whipped it over her head, slung it toward Spencer's chest, kicked the skirt to land at his feet, and stood there in turquoise lace bikini panties and a matching push-up bra.

Her pussy throbbed with the need to prove him wrong. He wasn't anything but a good fuck. She couldn't let him be anything more. Believing that he was different from all the men who'd wanted her for sex, believing that anything about the way he made her feel cherished was real . . . Believing either one of those meant she wouldn't be able to tell him good-bye, to send him into the arms of the girls his daddy would be proud to have him date.

She didn't want to deal with an empty bed and a broken heart. It was simply easier to believe everything bad than to believe anything good. Especially when bad had been a constant for her first nineteen years, the years she no longer counted, the years before her current life began. The years that would always keep her from having the relationship she wanted.

How could she when that one horrible night would never go away?

Her heart was pounding like a drum in her chest when she walked over to where he stood and dug into his pocket for the knife she knew he carried. She held his troubled and angry gaze as she pulled it out, made sure to drag her fingers along the length of his erection.

And then she took one step back and flipped open the knife. She tested the tip of the blade with one finger before she pressed it to the scar in the hollow of her throat. "Do you want me to tell you about this scar?"

"Don't," he growled, then cleared his throat. "Put the knife away."

She widened her eyes. "You think I'm going to hurt myself? Oh, baby, I've been hurt too many times to even feel this." She dragged the flat of the blade down between her breasts, feeling nothing of the metal, feeling her own arousal, feeling the need to make Spencer understand. "And right now? The only thing I'm feeling is you."

He pulled the brim of his ball cap lower, watched her play the knife over her body. "This isn't funny."

"That's probably why no one is laughing." She drew the knife tip over the slope of one breast then the other. Her nipples were large and hard and visible beneath the sheer mesh cups of her bra—and all she could think about was what had happened to her that night.

About that knife, not this one. The one they'd used on her, the one that had cut her, the one she had feared would end her life, and her hand began to shake. She let the blade fall to the floor, shuddering as she reached for the front clasp of her bra instead.

The moment her breasts spilled free, Spencer's nostrils flared and she reached out to cup him. She licked her lips, stepped close enough to rub herself over his chest. "I want to see you. I want you to take all this good stuff out of your pants."

A desperate groan rolled through his body, but he frowned as she reached for his buckle and zipper. "What are you doing, Candy?"

"I'm going to give you what you've been asking for. I'm going to let you in on all my deep dark secrets." She had to do this, to tell him, to drive him away before she fell in love and he left her. Hurt her. She couldn't take any more hurt.

She reached into his briefs, her wrist tickled by the dark silky hair growing low on his belly, her hand teased by his smoothness and his heat, and lifted him free. He groaned. He hissed. He was rock-hard and oozing already.

She rubbed his tight mushroom head with her palm, stroked it over the skin of her stomach, leaving a trail of sticky moisture, loving the contrast of black against white. Then she tilted her hips forward to hold him against her and used a forearm to cradle her breasts.

"See these tiny nicks? Here around my nipples? They're not easy to see. You probably felt them when you sucked me, thinking they were part of the way I puckered in your mouth. But they're not. They're from the blade of a knife. One a man threatened me with when he raped me."

He gasped. "What? You were raped?"

She nodded, felt him shudder, felt him begin to soften. She didn't want his pity, didn't want him to hate her. Didn't want anything but to have him love her one last time before he went away, unable to look at her any longer without seeing the truth of her past.

She bent at the waist, sucked him into her mouth, took him to the back of her throat. She loved the texture of his cock, the polished head, the root that was thick and veined. With her free hand, she cupped his balls and gently squeezed, sliding a finger deep between his legs to tease him.

Once he was throbbing again, once he moaned like she'd hit the fast forward on his fantasies, she released him. And she stood, smiled, discarded her bra. "Be honest, Spencer. Tell me that I scare you. That I'm not the girl you thought I was. That I'm not the girl you want."

His eyes glittered, the look on his face all grown-up and wild. "I want you in ways I've never wanted you before. I'm not going anywhere. I want to be with you, Candy. I want to be here for you."

He wasn't running away. Instead, he was hooked. She had him. The thought caused her knees to wobble, her hands to vibrate with tremors. "Oh, I'll take what I need, baby. And you'll get yours. But only if you do exactly what I say."

He couldn't agree quickly enough. "Anything."

"Take off your belt." She almost lost her nerve. The words didn't want to come. "Tie my hands behind my back."

She watched the tick of his pulse at his temple, felt sweat blossom in the small of her back. The juice from her pussy ran down her thighs. She couldn't believe how wet she was, how horny, how scared.

But she needed this too much to back out now. It was a cleansing, a purification, an exorcism. And she needed it from Spencer Munroe. She turned around, crossed her wrists and waited . . . It had been so long ago, edges were fuzzy, details hazy, but she remembered the parts that counted.

Things like the fact that no one had used a condom that night. Her soon-to-be stepfather certainly hadn't. He'd bent her over the hood of his car and made her wait while he'd finished his beer. Just left her there, her ass in the air, like a trophy.

The same way Spencer was leaving her now. She pulled in a deep breath and glanced over her shoulder. "What are you waiting for?"

He blinked, shook his head, then backed a step away. "I'm not doing this. No way."

She felt her eyes widen, felt like a wild animal, her nostrils flaring to search out his scent. "You said you'd do anything I told you to do."

"Yeah, but not—"

"Do it," she demanded, her voice quivering. Her nipples tightened as she spun to face him.

He pulled away, looked into her eyes. His battle with arousal and confusion rivaled hers with arousal and fear. After this, she knew he'd never want to see her again.

Except then he reached for her as if he never wanted to let her go. Instead of treating her like the whore she'd been called that night, he slid a hand behind her neck, cupped her cheek with the other, and pulled her close. "I'm not going to tie you up when it's not about pleasure, Candy. You mean too much to me for that."

"Who said it's not about pleasure?" she asked, looking away, looking down, looking anywhere but into his eyes.

"I can see it. You're not even here with me. You're long gone." His throat convulsed as he swallowed. His thumb was unsteady when he stroked her face. "You're back there in the past. With that knife. And I'm not going to be a part of that."

She felt like ice, like fire, freezing and melting all at the same time. "I warned you a hundred times, baby. You wouldn't like finding out about my past."

"No. I didn't." His voice was thick, husky, raw. "I don't want to think of you being hurt. Or going through something as horrible as rape. But it doesn't change anything about how I feel."

No. She wouldn't believe it. It hurt to believe it. To have that hope. "How can you feel anything for me, knowing what happened?"

"This isn't about the past, Candy. It's about here and now," he said, reaching for the hem of his T-shirt and pulling the garment over his head. "This is about you and me.

About you trusting me. Letting me take it all away. About me making love to you."

He reached for the lace edge of her panties then, tugged the garment down her legs, kneeling before her to kiss her thighs that quivered, her knees that quaked, coming back to kiss her sex, her belly, lingering over the scars on her breasts before coming all the way back to her mouth. To kiss her, to press his lips to hers, to slip his tongue inside.

He coaxed her to open, cradled her face in his palms, softly made love to her with nothing more than the touch of his fingertips, the slide of his tongue, the soft nibbling of his lips and his teeth as he claimed her. She held on, her fingers curled into his biceps, and let him have what he wanted, kissing him back until she tasted the waterfall of their tears.

His cock throbbed there where it was trapped between them, bobbing against her insistently. Spencer ended the kiss, his eyes sparkling, and pushed his jeans and briefs to his ankles before he sat back on the couch. She climbed into his lap, her knees sinking into the cushions on either side of his hips, and braced her hands behind her on his thighs.

He sheathed his cock and guided it between the lips of her sex, swirled himself around the knob of her clit. She watched, he watched, and she wept softly with wanting him, with the gentleness he showed her, with the way he took his time to ready her, to make sure the pleasure wasn't all his.

One hand held his cock as he pushed into her, stretching her open around his thick shaft. His other hand came between their bodies to find her clit and play. He pressed up slowly, easing farther inside as she opened to the pressure. She groaned as he filled her, groaned as he stopped.

"Am I hurting you?" he asked tenderly.

Sobs bubbled like lava in her chest, hurting her more than anything he could ever do. *You're supposed to tell me I'm a whore like my mother. You're supposed to shove the handle of your knife inside me and threaten to turn it around and cut me if I talk.* "No. You're not hurting me at all."

"You're so beautiful." His voice broke. "You're so hot and amazing." He moved one hand to her knee, hooking his fingers in the bend, stroking her, squeezing her, such a simple contact, such a sweet, caring touch. "I love being with you, Candy, and making love with you, and this . . ." His voice broke. "It's nothing like I've experienced."

She squeezed her eyes closed. Tear spilled down her cheeks. He wasn't supposed to be so caring; his concern was too hard to take. "You're doing it, baby. You're doing everything right."

He used one hand to finger and play her, one hand to hold onto her knee while he thrust. She contracted around him, squeezed his cock. He grunted and groaned. She did the same. And then it was done. That quickly, she came all over him.

She shook and shuddered as spasms tore through her, as Spencer Munroe, sweet Spencer alone, took away the shame and the terror and every bit of the fear. She milked him, rode him, urged him on, wanting to give him the ride of his life, a memory to keep with him forever.

"God, Candy. I'm gonna come," he said, and even with the layer of protection between them, he warmed her inside when he did, the fingers of both hands digging into her hips and bruising her as he held on.

Once he'd finished, once he'd pulled free of her body, he collapsed back, taking her with him, holding her with one arm wrapped tightly around her back. He toyed with the ends of her hair, with the pooch of flesh beneath the pit of her arm, with the ridge of her spine.

She could've slept in his arms. Could've stayed in that safe circle forever. She wanted to do just that. To feel their heartbeats each race to catch up with the other. But she was

Candy Roman. He was Spencer Munroe. And they could never have more than this between them.

Climbing off the couch, she turned to give him time to adjust his clothing, reached for her skirt and top, slipped into both. Then she bent and picked up the knife, used it to stab the lingerie she would never wear again because doing so would remind her how sweet he'd been.

She pulled them from the blade and shoved the pieces into Spencer's pocket. "You can throw those away for me when you get home," she said, hoping what she saw in his eyes was a twinkle and not a tear.

It took a deep breath for her to say what she needed to say next. What she'd never talked about to anyone outside of court except for Neva. She held out the knife she'd closed, held on when he reached for it, finally letting go. "The last man who tied me up used a knife to rape me."

"What?" Spencer reeled back.

"I'd brought two six-packs outside. My mother sent me. Her boyfriend's posse was partying and raising hell. And she sent me outside." Candy hugged herself tightly, her fingertips digging into her ribs. "Seems I made the perfect party favor. They stripped me, cut me, tied me facedown to the hood of one of their cars, and took turns."

She stared at the toes of her boots, seeing her own reflection from all those years back in the glossy black paint of the car. "The last one was the man my mother was going to marry. He was going to be my stepfather. He was going to be living in my house. When he finished threatening me, I picked up the knife where he'd dropped it. And I killed him."

"What are you talking about?" Spencer croaked out.

"Exactly what I said." She crossed the living area to the corner windows that looked out over the wide expanse of open spaces beyond the Barn. She couldn't look at her beautiful boy anymore. She didn't want her last picture, her final memory, to be disgust in his eyes.

Numb, she went on. "I met Neva when I was in prison. She was my court-appointed attorney."

"How old were you?" His question was a whisper.

"When it happened? Seventeen. When it was over and done and I moved here? Nineteen."

"Younger than me. The same age as Liberty Mitchell."

She couldn't help it. She had to look back. His compassion, his eyes, which were red with emotion, made her wish she hadn't. He looked years older than he'd ever looked before. "She's a cute girl, much more your type. You ought to think about dating her."

"That's not funny."

"I know." She braced her hands on the wall behind her, leaned back against them. "It's just easier to make jokes than to break things off."

"Break things off? Between us? Why?"

"Because of my past. The secrets you've always wondered about. And because of your future." *Because you need a girl with pink apple cheeks and white cotton sweaters who can give you babies to bounce on your knees.* "I'm not a girl your parents are going to want to have sitting down to a family dinner."

His voice was soft, shattered. "What about what I want, Candy? What about what we've got?"

She chewed the inside of her lip, pressed her short nails into her palms, her knuckles into the wall. "Spencer. Trust me. In a year, I'll be nothing but an occasional wet dream to you."

His jaw bulged. "So that's it? I'm just a hick sowing a few wild oats? You really believe that?"

Jesus Lord help her, no. But she let her silence say otherwise until the light died in his eyes. She was so cold. So cold. Her teeth were threatening to chatter. "I hope we can stay friends, Spencer. This doesn't have to turn ugly."

"Turn ugly?" His laugh, a harsh cackling burst of sound, said it all. "It was ugly before I got here."

He turned, slammed the door on his way out. She heard him start up his truck engine, heard his tires spew gravel, heard him drive away.

And then she crumpled onto her sofa, drew her knees to her chest, and cried until she couldn't cry anymore over those lost seventeen years of her life.

By the time Mick got the information he needed from Neva and checked the feeds before leaving the barn, Candy was walking into range of the two front cameras. He headed down the hidden staircase and into the shipping center, hearing the same blowtorch from earlier today firing once he reached the patio door. Candy was back at work.

Neva had told him that she wanted to stay and show Liberty the workings of the apartment. That was fine by Mick. It gave him time to touch base with Rabbit in the SG-5 ops center. Mick's fellow operative might not be thrilled with his plan—Harry never had been happy working in the desert heat. But he wouldn't argue. That was the way the Smithson Group worked. A real bunch of merry musketeers.

FM trotting along at his side and still looking freaky, half the mutt's face missing its fur, Mick headed around the back of Neva's house where he'd moved his Rover before coming in earlier for lunch. Hadn't taken a rocket scientist to figure out Doc Ed wasn't overjoyed at finding another man at Neva's table—though the piece of furniture most on the man's mind had been Neva's bed.

Mick didn't get it. The doc needed to let the woman go and move on. She wasn't interested—a fact Mick had gathered when he was half dead in the bed of her pickup, long before she'd come to life beneath him on that love seat, which was way too short for a man in his condition. And he wasn't talking about the state of his ribs.

He'd only planned to hold her while she got her cry out. And, okay, give her a comforting kiss. Which was bloody fucking stupid when he thought about it. Because comforting and Neva Case didn't fit. She fit with the things they'd done, the groping and getting off. She fit with a whole lot more they hadn't done . . . yet.

And even as he declared it so, he knew it wasn't true. Because being here for her, protecting her, seeing to her safety, and offering the comfort she needed were all part of the same package. A package wrapped around the good stuff he'd eventually get to. As long as he could make this deal with Rabbit and buy himself the time.

He opened the Rover's driver's-side door, flicking the lever that would switch his headlights to bright, were they turned on. Instead, the lever released the lock holding his custom captain's chair in place. He slid his fingers between the seat back and the seat bottom, pulled the latter forward to reveal a compartment beneath.

A pretty damn empty compartment considering the items that would've been stored inside were they not now the property of the clone brothers. He grabbed the text-messaging unit, closed up the Rover, and walked out into the field behind Neva's house. The portable unit made more sense to use than the cargo-hold computer, considering the traffic coming and going through here the last couple of days.

FM lumbered on up ahead as Mick cut beneath the pecan trees, adjusting the sport strap holding his sunglasses in place, brittle fried grass crunching beneath his boots. Neva's place was flatter than the plot of land over the border where he'd taken his tumble and ride. And her view wasn't obscured by rocky arroyos and rolling hills sliced off on one side into sharp abutments.

It was a strange place for this interesting woman to live. A place that just didn't fit. One of these days he would figure out what the hell she was doing all the way out here. What it was she was running from. In the meantime, he needed to work his spy magic.

Far enough away now that no one would be sneaking up while his back was turned, he flipped open the unit's two side wings, turned it on, and extended the antenna. Connection made, he used his thumbs on the miniature keyboard to type his password at the prompt. He doubted Harry would still be monitoring communications this time of day, but he was.

>Rabbit here.
>Savin checking in.
>What's new?
>A name. Holden Wagner.
>Spectra?
>Negative. Lawyer. Big shot.
>What gives?
>Checkered past? Look into it?
>Will do. That it?

Unfortunately, it wasn't. Mick gave Rabbit a brief rundown of Neva's network, the checkpoints, the transfer stations, the safe houses.

>Need to plug a leak.
>I'll find the hole.
>Also need a hack.

This time Mick explained the setup of Neva's satellite dish and Internet connection, along with her system's specs. The rest would be up to Kelly John Beach.

>I'll pass it to K.J.
>Tell him to set up for a possible wipe.
>Will do.
>Thanks, mate. And pack a bag.

Mick could almost hear the other man groan.

>You want me to bring hard copy?
>No. I need you to catch the train.
>When?
>Stand by. I'll check back.
>Right. Rabbit out.

Mick shut down the handheld, tucked it into his pocket. That was about all he could do remotely. He'd have to get with Rabbit in person before going into detail. But the ball was picking up speed, and Mick felt damn good about doing that much at least.

Squinting behind his shades, he looked toward the horizon where the sun was dropping in a big splash of Kool-Aid colors, watched the dog trot a few meters one direction, sniff the ground and the air, trot a few meters in another. Stupid mutt, thinking he was doing anything but blowing in the wind, losing interest in one scent, chasing down another.

If Neva'd been standing here, she would've crossed her arms, raised a brow, and wondered about the rudderless similarities between master and beast. And then he would've reached over and pulled that mass of red hair out of the band she always had it tied back in.

He wanted to ruffle her up, to see that hair fly. To get back to talking about her cause and her life. He didn't want to talk about his family, what he'd done in his thirty-three years, who he'd met along the way, who he'd killed. That shite he'd told her in the kitchen last night? That was nothing. A bit of where he'd been, what he'd seen.

He didn't want her knowing that he had no plan. That he went where Hank Smithson sent him, did what Hank assigned him to do. That when he looked five years down the road there was nothing there to see. His cause had been about taking lives, not saving them. About ruining futures, not salvaging them. And now he had no cause at all.

Which wouldn't have been a problem for the man he'd been last week. The one who pulled on his boxers when he got up in the morning, pulled them off at night, who lay there naked and sweating during the long hours between, wondering when the blood he'd shed would take its toll.

The bloody hell of it was that he'd changed since meeting Neva. He felt more. He wanted more. He wanted *her*, a woman hog-tied to a cause. Go after one and he'd get them both whether or not he was ready. Whether or not he was man enough. He had a feeling he was going to need Neva to help him figure that out.

Twelve

Jeanne wasn't sure if she should've called first. She hated impropriety. Showing up to talk to Neva about Candy and Spencer seemed like the worst sort of gossip. Going behind her son's back, her husband's back. She felt like she couldn't possibly sink any lower.

But when Spencer had come home early this afternoon, she'd known something was seriously wrong. He'd banged through the kitchen without stopping to eat, without saying a word. He'd just thundered up the stairs like his life depended on getting to his room and slamming the door behind him.

He had, and so she'd finished cleaning out from beneath the stovetop, peeled off her rubber gloves, and set about making him a late lunch. He hadn't wanted it. Not a bite. Not even the cookies she'd baked that morning. She'd left the tray on his desk, left him flopped on his bed.

On her way out his door she'd asked him if he was feeling ill. He'd said no. She'd asked if he'd heard bad news about his friend Jase. He'd said no. So she'd asked him if anything had happened to Candy. His reply was a simple two words.

Candy who?

So now here she was, coming to find out what, if anything, Neva might know because making things right for her family, cleaning up after them and for them, was the only way Jeanne knew to survive.

Pulling her ten-year-old Buick Century up to the front of Neva's house, she realized for the first time how late it was. She'd fixed supper at home earlier, then told Yancey she was going to take the pies she'd baked that afternoon to Jonnie Mayer's tonight in case they didn't feel up to visiting at her Sunday evening get-together tomorrow after church.

Yancey had already been settled in front of the television. She didn't think he'd even heard her leave.

The pies were still sitting on her floorboard. She grabbed one and left the car, walking slowly up to Neva's front door and knocking. It was silly, being this anxious, but she couldn't sleep or eat and she wouldn't be surprised if the lemon chess tasted like cardboard. Her mind hadn't been on measuring ingredients but on Spencer while she'd cooked.

The front door opened. Jeanne looked through the screen door into Neva's startled face, smiled, and held up the pie. "Surprise!"

Neva laughed, pushed the screen door out on its hinges and springs. "What's the occasion?"

Jeanne stepped into the small, tidy hallway that divided the front of the house. One side was Neva's office with the living room on the other. "It's Saturday? And I needed to get out of the house?"

Neva shut the door and Jeanne followed her friend to the kitchen. Their footsteps on the hardwood floor echoed against the high ceiling. "Well, I can't think of a better reason for a pie."

"It's not too late, is it? Am I interrupting your supper?" The kitchen was clean. Either Neva had already settled in for the night or she hadn't yet eaten.

"Actually"—Neva gestured toward the appliance—"I

was staring into the refrigerator when you knocked. It hasn't happened yet, but I keep hoping an entire meal will jump out at me if I manage not to blink."

Jeanne set the pie on the kitchen's small square table. Not even a napkin holder or bud vase or salt and pepper shaker. "Spencer does the same thing. Stares until everything inside warms up to room temperature."

"He probably eats more groceries in a week than I buy in two." Neva filled her coffeemaker with tap water, added a filter and beans that looked to be freshly ground, and switched it on. "Pie and coffee sound like the perfect Saturday evening meal."

"Maybe for someone with your figure and your metabolism." Now that she was here, Jeanne wasn't sure what to do. "Neva, why don't I make you a salad at least? Save the pie for dessert?"

But Neva was already digging through her utensils for forks and a pie server. "No groceries, remember? Maybe a half head of lettuce. I've really got to get to town tomorrow. Ed and Candy were here for lunch today, and I made pancakes and bacon. That wiped out all of my meat. Eggs and milk, too, come to think of it."

Jeanne settled slowly into one of the kitchen chairs, laced her fingers on the Formica surface. "Do you and Candy always eat together?"

"Not always, no." Neva set dessert plates and forks on the table, went back to the cabinet for cups. "Breakfast is our only regular meal together. And then it's not even a meal. Just bagels and coffee."

"Now, what kind of way is that to start a day?" Jeanne asked, teasing as she pulled the Tupperware top from the pie carrier. And then she stopped. "Pretend I didn't say that. It sounded horribly like a mother hen."

Leaning back against the counter while the coffee brewed,

Neva laughed. "That's okay. I need to be nagged. Or at least nagged by someone who *is* a mother rather than someone who thinks she is."

"Candy?" Jeanne asked, her fingers still curled around the carrier's top.

"Oh, yeah. She could give a fishwife a run for her money," Neva said, walking over and offering a pie server in exchange for the Tupperware. She had to tug twice before Jeanne let go. "Jeanne?"

"I'm sorry." This was so hard when it shouldn't be. Neva was her friend. Jeanne rubbed at a scar on the handle of the pie server. "I don't know what's wrong with me."

"Well, obviously something you want to talk about or you wouldn't have brought me"—Neva leaned closer to the table to smell the pie—"lemon chess?"

Jeanne smiled, nodded, relaxed. "Coffee smells good."

"You slice and tell me what's on your mind. I'll pour and listen with both ears," Neva said, returning to the counter for the glass carafe. "Black, right?"

"I shouldn't be drinking caffeine this late," Jeanne said, watching the level rise in her cup. "But since I'm not feeling much like church in the morning, I suppose it won't matter how late it keeps me up."

Neva took the seat opposite, cradled her own cup while Jeanne sliced the pie. "Must be something really big going on for you to skip church. And Jonnie's get-together."

"I made the pie to take to Jonnie's tomorrow," Jeanne admitted, feeling a bit of a smirk curl her mouth, feeling a bit of a laugh she wasn't going to be able to keep down. She let it out, chuckling, a huge sense of freedom sweeping through her as she did. "Oh, Neva. If I have to go to one more of Jonnie Mayer's Sunday suppers, I'm going to pull out the rest of my hair."

Neva sputtered her coffee, grabbed a roll of paper towels from the counter behind her. "Why, Jeanne Munroe. Here all this time I thought you were the cloned offspring of Martha Stewart and Emily Post."

"You're missing a chromosome in there, if I remember my biology correctly." Jeanne cut off the biggest bite of pie she could put into her mouth. But the laughter faded and she found she couldn't eat. She shook her head slowly, sorrowfully. "It's that chromosome giving me trouble, Neva."

"Yancey?"

A deep breath and a long exhalation didn't blow away any of the pain. "Spencer."

Neva's fork hovered unsteadily above her plate. "Is he all right? Is he hurt? I doubt if he was you'd be here bringing me pie . . ."

Jeanne found herself smiling, shaking her head, toying with the dessert she no longer wanted. "He's fine. Physically healthy, anyway. I'm beginning to wonder if he's mentally sound. He's threatening to give up his scholarship."

"What?" Neva's eyes widened before she frowned. "You're kidding. Why?"

"I'm not kidding, no. And because he wants to be a good person. Not just a good football player." Such a noble-sounding reason. Such a complicated truth. "He wants to stay and help out on the Bremmer ranch, what with Jase missing and calving season being right around the corner."

"Wow." Neva sipped her coffee thoughtfully. "That's some sacrifice. I'll bet his father's proud."

If only that were the case. "Not proud. Furious."

"Really." Neva cocked her head to the side. "Huh. Though I guess I shouldn't be surprised. I've heard rumor that Yancey is adamant about Spencer playing ball."

"It's not so much the football as it is the education. We could never afford to send him to a school like Texas Tech." Jeanne thought of the pennies she'd pinched, the magazine subscriptions she'd canceled, their vehicles, which often seemed held together with crossed fingers and baling wire.

"Neither one of us wants him to give that up whether it's for a good cause or because of a girl."

For a long moment the room was silent, Neva drinking her coffee, Jeanne wondering if she'd said the wrong thing, if she'd gone too far. If she wouldn't have done better to come right out first thing and admit why she was here.

But she and Yancey had always kept their private life private, and talking about this now, even with a friend, seemed like a betrayal of the promises she'd made with her husband.

Finally, Neva exchanged her cup for her fork and sliced into her pie. "By girl, I'm assuming you mean Candy?"

Jeanne nodded, dropping her gaze to her own plate, her own wedge of perfectly browned pie, the tiny flecks of silver and gold in the Formica tabletop. "I hate to pry, but does she talk to you about Spencer at all? Her feelings for him? What goes on between them?"

"Not really, no," Neva replied once she'd swallowed. She cut off another bite. "I know she's very fond of him."

"Fond," Jeanne repeated. Such a superficial word. She was quite fond of the lotion she used on her dry elbows. Yancey was fond of pouring ketchup on his eggs. "I know she's older than he is . . ."

"I don't think that has anything to do with it," Neva responded, pinching the corner of fluted crust from her pie and popping it into her mouth. "I think it's that she knows Yancey doesn't approve of her."

"Yancey doesn't approve of Spencer seeing any girl," Jeanne admitted rather harshly, aiming the sentiment at her husband's unyielding insistence that their son would have a better life were he not tied to Pit Stop. Implying that their own lives weren't all that they could be.

That she was at fault for choosing to leave Dallas and make their home at the end of the road. She looked back across the table at her friend. "He doesn't want Spencer to have any reason to come back once he leaves."

Neva shifted in her chair, tucked one leg up beneath her and huffed. "As long as you're living here, he'd damn well better have reason."

Jeanne smiled at her friend's indignation. "Besides coming back to see me."

"What if he wants to stay here?" Neva asked, waving an encompassing arm. "I know it's not Houston or Dallas, but you have to admit it's got its own quirky charm."

Oh, yes. Weren't they all here for the charm? "Is that why you moved here? The charming appeal of a single country grocery store that doesn't know a shitake mushroom from a cow patty?"

Neva laughed. "That, and your lemon chess pie. Oh, and ew. I'll never eat a shitake again."

"But at least you know what one is," Jeanne said, and sat back.

Neva did the same, ran an index finger along the table's ribbed aluminum flashing. "It's going to be hard to have him go, isn't it? When does he leave?"

"He has to be at football camp in just a few weeks," Jeanne answered, glancing toward the window over Neva's sink, the sun that was setting, another day stolen away. "I didn't think it would get here so soon."

A nod of agreement. "The summer's going by fast."

"I don't mean his leaving for school. I mean his being grown up and out on his own." Jeanne felt her chest and throat tighten, felt like she wouldn't be able to squeeze out another breath. "It seems like he was ten only yesterday. Five the day before that. But next summer he'll be twenty. How the hell did I get to be so old?"

Leaning forward, Neva reached out a hand. "The same way we all do, sweetie. One day at a time."

Jeanne wrapped her fingers around her friend's and squeezed. "Well, I don't like it one bit," she said with a halting laugh. "I'll tell you that right now." She also didn't like the way so many of her emotions were bubbling up.

"You know what we should do? Take a girls' day away. Maybe one day next week? Go to El Paso and play. I'm desperate for a break," Neva said, a twist to her mouth. "Not to mention a couple of bras that have all of their hooks."

"How sad is it that we consider taking care of the basic necessities to be pampering?" Jeanne asked, uncertain whether to laugh or to cry. "If Spencer or Yancey need anything, I don't hesitate to pick it up."

"I guess it's our plight as the female caretakers of the species," Neva said, adding a small private laugh. "Though I have no excuse for the state of my underwear. I'm not taking care of anyone but myself."

Jeanne couldn't help a stab of uncharitable envy. But only a small stab. She did, after all, love her husband and son very much. Possibly more than she loved herself. "Well, you do have a business. And you have Candy."

"Candy takes care of herself. And takes care of half the business. Then there's that nagging thing." Neva smiled, reached for the carafe and refilled her own cup when Jeanne declined. "And for some reason she manages to have a Victoria's Secret wardrobe to die for."

"I suppose Spencer enjoys that," Jeanne said wryly.

"Yeah. Men are like that." Neva grew silent, toyed with the edge of her plate. "I guess it's hard to think of your son as a man. At least when it comes to the sex thing."

Jeanne shrugged. What was she going to say? Deny that Spencer was any different than Yancey had been at that age? Any different than any male was? "I don't dwell on it, but I'm hardly blind. I've been sitting in the bleachers watching him play ball for years. I've seen the way girls react. I've heard them talk. And Spencer being young and healthy, well . . ."

"He's sowed a wild oat or two?"

"Or two." Candy no doubt being the wildest, Jeanne mused. "It's to be expected, I suppose."

"Sure." Neva shrugged. "He's a good-looking kid. Takes after his father," she added with a wink.

A simple comment. One Jeanne had heard more than a few times in her life. One to which she'd responded with a smile, with a thank-you, with a nod of proud agreement. But this time she felt a rush of words she couldn't hold back.

And so she let them go, tears coming from nowhere to fill her eyes. "I wouldn't know."

"Jeanne?"

All she could do was stare at the blurry mess of crumbs and lemon zest on her plate and shake her head. "Yancey isn't Spencer's father. He is, of course. He's been the only father Spencer has known."

"But he's not his biological parent," Neva said softly, reaching across the table with both hands.

Jeanne kept her trembling fingers laced tightly in her lap, catching all she could of her tears. And then she couldn't breathe. Her chest squeezed the air from her lungs as it tried to hold in the pieces of her breaking heart. She shook all over, shivered. Her entire body turned into a quivering mess of frightened nerves.

"Jeanne?" Neva prodded gently.

She blurted it out, her voice breaking. "I was raped. Oh, Neva. It's been twenty years and I've never told anyone."

Neva gasped. "No one? Not the police? What about Yancey?"

"Yancey knows. Yes. Of course, he knows. But, no. I didn't go to the police. I didn't tell my parents. I couldn't. It happened at a party the night we graduated." She tore a paper towel from the roll on the table, folded it, and dabbed it beneath her eyes. "We were going to get married later that summer. Yancey was a criminal justice major. I studied elementary education at North Texas State. When I found out I was pregnant . . ."

Talking about this now, talking about this here when for so many years she'd stayed silent . . . She shuddered, hugged herself tightly. Neva's chair legs scraped across the floor as she got up and came over, dropping to her knees, offering her arms and her shoulder.

Jeanne leaned against her friend and cried, talking through her tears. "I was drinking, everyone was. I don't even know what happened or who it was. We'd gone with one of Yancey's friends back to his frat house. And it was wild." She sniffed, dabbed at her nose with the towel. "I woke up in the middle of the night and realized my panties were gone. And that I was sore and the sticky mess between my legs wasn't all me."

"Oh, Jeanne," Neva crooned, stroking a hand over her friend's hair. "I'm so sorry. So, so sorry. That's such a horrible violation to live with. I'm so glad Yancey was there for you."

Jeanne nodded briskly. "He was. He always has been. When I realized I was pregnant, he told me the choice of what to do was mine, but that he'd be there no matter what. Whether I wanted to end the pregnancy, give the baby up for adoption, or raise Spencer as ours."

"Spencer doesn't know, does he?"

"Oh, no. No. And I shouldn't have told you." Jeanne sat up straight, shredded the towel with shaking fingers. "Yancey and I swore to never tell anyone for fear he'd find out."

"He won't find out from me, sweetie," Neva said, returning to her chair. "I promise you that."

"And you won't tell Candy?" She felt like a hypocrite of

the highest order for even having to ask when she'd been the one to put the truth out there.

"Jeanne, I promise. I won't tell anyone." Neva's eyes glittered with tears. "It's not my place to tell."

"You know, I don't think I ever thought but once about not having him," Jeanne said, tucking her feet together beneath her chair and sitting forward. "I didn't know what had happened that night. To this day, I can't remember. I could've been a willing participant. It seemed so wrong to punish a baby for that."

"Are you sure you weren't punishing yourself?"

A friend who was both understanding and perceptive. Jeanne felt the return of her smile. "I very well might have been. I can hardly remember back that far," she said with a sigh. "And of course I have a wonderful son who makes it easy to forget." A wonderful son who was hurting.

She pushed her hair from her forehead then braced an elbow on the table and propped her chin in her palm. "I think he and Candy may have broken up."

Neva's face came alive when she smiled. "So you brought me a pie to bribe me only to find out I don't know a thing."

"I'm so transparent. And such a nosy busybody. Just what Spencer doesn't need," Jeanne added with a laugh.

"No, Jeanne. You're a mother who cares," Neva said sagely. "And that's exactly what all children need."

"Yancey wanted more children. He brought it up once or twice, asked me how I felt. But he never insisted." She swayed back and forth on her elbow, unconsciously mimicking her inner distress. "He thought it would be good for our son to have a sibling. He thought Spencer would be lonely. But I just couldn't do it. I'm a terrible, terrible person."

"No. You're human. You were probably afraid he'd love his biological child more. That's a natural assumption," Neva said in a calming voice.

Sighing, Jeanne sat back, crossed her arms, shook her head. "I couldn't stand the idea of being pregnant again. It was too much a part of the rape that I couldn't remember."

The same familiar sensations tingled now in the pit of her stomach, dread and panic and nervous clawing fingers. "I used to wake up in the middle of the night scared to death that I would give birth to a hideous monster. Silly, I know, but I've never been able to explain that to Yancey. Especially when it seems so simple to explain it to you."

Neva waved a dismissive hand. "It's not silly at all. You can tell me because you know I won't be hurt. You've been carrying this tremendous load of guilt for years. It had to come out sometime." She cocked her head and considered her friend thoughtfully. "How do you feel now?"

How *did* she feel? "Like I've just shit a bowling ball," Jeanne admitted, relief sweeping through her, cleaning away years of emotional detritus.

Neva sputtered into giggles, Jeanne joining her, until both women were laughing so hard they blew pie crumbs from the table to the floor—a fact that wouldn't have been so funny had both not reached for the same paper towel at the same time and knocked Jeanne's coffee cup into Neva's lap.

Neva gasped, jumped back, then continued to laugh while Jeanne sat horrified. "Oh, God, Neva. Is it still hot?" She rushed around the table, dropped down to a crouch and started wiping at the stains. A useless endeavor. She was doing nothing but leaving paper towel balls on the denim. "Let's get you out of your pants and get you some ice."

She was fumbling to tug the jeans down Neva's legs when she heard the squeak of the kitchen's screen door, and then a deep male voice saying, "Uh, I can come back later. Or I can come back right now with a video camera."

A silent second ticked by, and then Neva laughed so hard Jeanne lost her balance and fell back to the floor. She sat there, staring at the big man who'd walked in wearing camouflage gear over a very hard body and a tattoo almost as sexy as his shaved head and goatee.

His bright gray eyes twinkled with glee, as did his smile, completing a picture that left her unable to find her dignity or her voice. She had no trouble finding her appreciation.

And Neva wasn't hindered at all. Jeans around her knees, she made the introductions. "Mick, this is my good friend Jeanne Munroe. Jeanne, another good friend of mine, Mick Savin. We were just cleaning up a spill, Mick."

He reached into the refrigerator for a quart carton of orange juice, considered them for a moment before heading back outside, leaving them with a wink and a cryptic, "Don't let me get in your way. But if you need any help . . ."

"Wow," Jeanne said once the door slammed shut behind him, because it was the only word she could find. "Who is *he*?"

Neva sighed wistfully. "To tell you the truth? I really don't know."

Neva had lied to her friend earlier. When Jeanne had knocked on the door at seven-thirty, Neva hadn't been staring into the fridge waiting for a meal to jump out. She'd been staring into the fridge and trying to decide what to do about wanting Mick Savin.

The sustenance he offered was the only thing on her mind. She was so very hungry for him, so wary of taking her fill. The battle between her appetites had been raging since she'd looked into his glazed eyes that day on the side of the road. Yet she still wasn't able to make up her mind.

Should she send him away before it was too late to do so? Or keep him around forever since it already was? She was falling for him. Stupid, stupid, stupid to fall for a man about whom she knew so little. And what a silly heart she had, thinking the things she did know were enough to make the risky tumble worth taking.

She paused in front of the guest room door, standing where she knew the floor wouldn't creak with any nervous shift of her body weight. The only light shining was the one she always left on over the sink in the kitchen. It reached this far, reflecting off the room's brass doorknob. She wouldn't have to fumble for it. She wouldn't miss it when she reached.

What a joke. If she went in, she wouldn't miss or fumble. Her body knew what it wanted. She just needed to make up her mind if this was the right thing. Or, if not, the degree of wrongness she was facing. And if she could live with herself when all was said and done. That was the biggest hurdle. The aftermath of her soul.

She reached out her hand, flexed her fingers, clenched them before taking hold of the knob. It turned easily in her palm, which was sweating, and she pushed open the door. She blinked, but she had no need. The guest room was no darker than the hallway. It was brighter, in fact. Mick had opened the shutters and tied up the shades on all four of the eight-paned windows.

The hardwood floor gleamed, as did the glossy pine furnishings. The white comforter embroidered with sprigs of blue flowers reflected the ghostly light, washing the entire room with a glow the same color as the pale blue walls. The atmosphere was eerily unreal and perfect. She could blame anything that happened on the light from the moon.

Mick stood staring out one of the windows, at what she had no idea. That side of the house faced nothing but wide open spaces. Maybe the emptiness was what he was looking at. Maybe he was feeling cooped up, wanting to fly. It was a good thing she'd never thought seriously about tying him down.

All she wanted was the relief he could give her body, a fulfillment more intense than anything she could give herself, more complete than what he'd shown her this afternoon.

That was all she wanted. She certainly didn't want the emotional sensations tugging at the strings of her heart.

He never turned when she closed the door and started across the room. He didn't say a word. He didn't move. The same light that brightened the room caressed his body; she saw details she'd never before seen. The dimpled skin on his side beneath his bandaged rib cage. A gouge of flesh missing from the bulge of his calf muscle. More damage from the life she didn't want him to tell her about.

She didn't want to know. She didn't want to care. She didn't want the involvement she knew she was walking into. All she wanted was to touch him. Her socks shushed over the floor, the sound barely louder than an indrawn breath as she moved to stand at his back. He hadn't looked at her once, yet she knew he was aware of her presence. The tension in his body rolled off in waves.

She settled her hands at his hips, her fingers curling into the waistband of the gray sweat shorts that matched hers. Though the air in the room was cool, his skin was toasty warm. He wasn't feverish, his temperature not enough to cause concern, simply enough to tempt her.

And so she slid her arms around him, her hands up his torso, her fingers through the fine dusting of hair covering his belly and chest on either side of his bound ribs. She was gentle with her touch, remembering his bruises, feeling the rough scabs covering his healing scrapes.

He was taller than she was, and she couldn't see beyond his body to follow his gaze through the window. So she pressed her cheek to the center of his back, nuzzled against him, and breathed him in.

He shuddered as she held him, and she eased away a bit, not wanting to hurt him more than she had if that was the cause of his response. He assured her it wasn't when he moved his hands from the window frame, found both her wrists, and pulled her close again. She smiled against his skin, turned to kiss the indentation of his spine.

His gooseflesh tickled her; she was so pleased that he wanted her near, and that once he had her where he wanted her, he loosened his hold, threaded their fingers together, and pressed their one big fist to the center of his chest where his heart pounded more fiercely than hers.

He made this so easy, made it so hard. Made her want to open more than her body—a feat no man before him had ever accomplished. Past experiences, previous men had been nothing more than physical encounters. Those, she'd closed her mind and summarily enjoyed.

What Mick offered her that no one had before was as complicated as it was simple. She couldn't stop to break it down. She only knew she felt safe. Safe and secure and protected. Trusted. Believed. He hadn't laughed over her paranoia. He'd asked for facts so he could clear away her worries and fears.

She pulled her hands from his and slid her fingers to his shoulders, massaging tiny circles there, walking her fingertips along the slope to his neck, rubbing her knuckles softly against the base of his skull. She loved touching him. Didn't think she'd ever get enough.

With one index finger, she outlined the tribal decoration cupping his neck. "Tell me about your tattoo."

He shook his head and pulled her around in front of him. His eyes sparkled like silver coins in the moonlight. "I don't want to talk. Not about my tattoo, or your barn, or which one of us has been living a lie longer than the other and owes the biggest round of apologies."

"Then what *do* you want?" she asked coyly.

He answered with a pirate's plundering grin and a growled, "Everything that's mine."

Thirteen

"Does that include me?" she asked, thinking she liked the idea of being claimed as a pirate's booty. Especially with this man doing the plundering. "Or are you still worried I'm not going to give you back your gun?"

"Screw the bloody gun. I've got a half dozen others." He hooked an elbow around her neck, pulled her flush to his body. "But you, Nevada Case, are one of a kind."

The way he looked into her eyes as he said it, the way it rolled off his tongue, as if he didn't know an endearment more precious, had never seen her in a light that revealed what this one did, she didn't even mind him using her full name. In fact, she kind of liked it. Liked, too, the idea of him owning that part of her, if nothing more.

She reached up and ran her fingertips over the patch of hair beneath his lower lip. "I think you're pretty special, too."

He pulled the elastic band from her hair. "Which is it, then? Pretty or special?"

She grinned. "A whole lot of both."

"Hmm. I'm not sure I've ever been called pretty," he said, spreading her hair out across her shoulders and admiring his handiwork. "Why don't you wear your hair down?"

"Because it gets in the way of everything," she said, loving the way he played with the strands, combing his fingers through the thick unruly waves. She closed her eyes, leaned back her head. "Do you know how good that feels?"

"Tell me," he nearly grunted.

"Well, my nipples are hard, if that says anything," she said, and felt herself blushing. Like she was some virginal schoolgirl. Please.

He dipped his head, drew one peak into his mouth—tank top and all—swirled his tongue around and around until the cotton covering her breast was as wet as that covering her sex. She dug her fingertips into his biceps to hold on.

And then he released her, moved his mouth to her ear. "It tells me that I'm going to love getting you out of your clothes."

"Oh, feel free," she said, and he laughed, nipping at her earlobe, her neck, the soft skin beneath her jaw. "I'll be glad to help."

"I can manage, thanks," he replied, working his way lower, to the scoop of her neckline where he drew his tongue along the edge of the fabric and over the slope of both breasts. His fingers followed, dipping beneath to tease the tightly puckered edges of her areolas.

"Okay." She panted, whimpered. "If you're sure. It's just that you're really taking way too long."

His chuckle was more of a roar than a laugh. One that was deep and throaty and tickled her in places already aching to be scratched. "You in a hurry to get somewhere?"

Only into your bed, she thought to herself as she curled her toes in her socks. "Uh, no."

"Good." He was back to licking her now, her neck, the dip in her throat, her collarbone. His hands at her waist held her where he wanted her, where he could get to her the best. "Because I'm not going anywhere. And there's a whole night ahead."

Oh, dear. Oh, my. She wasn't going to last that long. She didn't *want* to last that long. She wanted to come dozens of times. She wanted to smell him and taste him and feel the hair on his belly and between his legs.

"Oh, hell." She heard herself murmur, heard Mick laugh, heard the way his breathing was already as labored as hers. And then she wondered why he was having all the fun. Who said she had to wait?

She moved her hands from his biceps to his shoulders then down to his chest, threading tufts of the silky hair in the center through her fingers, pressing the balls of her palms into his pecs until he groaned. The sound echoed in the spartan room, rumbled in the pit of her belly. She leaned forward, drawing the flat of her tongue over one of his nipples, swirling the tiny bud with the tip.

He set her away, his jaw taut, his grin equally so as he stared into her eyes. "Following my lead, eh?"

Still using her fingers to play, she shrugged with all the innocence she could manage—not an easy feat with the tension throbbing between them and the room just waiting for the shedding of their clothes. "What's good for the goose . . ."

"Okay, then," he said, and laughed, his teeth white in his dangerously beautiful smile. He captured her hand and held it. "Let's see if you can keep up."

Gulp. She might have been living a life of crime for five years, but she wasn't sure she was cut out to be a pirate. At least not the brigand she'd need to be to pillage at this one's pace. His hand was already settling in the small of her back, his fingers digging for booty beneath the elastic waistband of her shorts.

Chin lifted, brows, too, she met his gaze squarely, boldly, and slipped her hands to the skin of his back exposed beneath his bandaged ribs. He was warm there, warm everywhere, muscled and healthy and resiliently taut. She couldn't get enough of touching him and didn't hesitate, didn't wait, but breeched the fabric barrier.

His grin widened. All he needed was a parrot on his shoulder and a hoop in his ear, a cutlass between his teeth. Or so she had time to think before his hands made their way into her pants. Then she couldn't think of anything but spreading her legs.

"Have I mentioned how much I like fast women?"

She pinched his ass and glared. "For a man who didn't want to talk, you're doing a lot of it."

He was taller, his arms longer, his reach much deeper than hers. His fingers found their way beneath the curve of her cheeks to all those places she wanted to give him. She pushed up to her tiptoes so he wouldn't have to work quite so hard.

"Have I mentioned how much I like it when you wet your pants?"

"Shh!" she hissed and spanked him. "If you want to talk, do it with your hands. If you must use your mouth, do it from your knees."

Laughing, he rubbed a finger around her back entrance before finding his way to the front. He circled her there, making her weep and shudder and clench long-unused muscles, then pushed inside. Oh . . . dear . . . Lord, but his finger was thick and long. She moaned, the sound starting in the pit of her belly and rolling out of her throat.

"You like?"

Why was he still talking? "You have to ask?"

He pushed in farther, pulled all the way out, found her clitoris and rubbed. "Only because you're not doing a very good job of keeping up."

"I'm selfish that way," she admitted, shivering anew. "Besides, my arms aren't as long."

He lowered his head, returned to nuzzle her ear. "Feel free to go in from the front."

The thought of touching him, fondling him, feeling all his different textures, his thickness and weight . . . Her imagination held no candle to the reality. He was so hot, felt so good. She breathed him in and slid her hands from his buttocks to his thighs, sensing his muscles seize beneath her hands, feeling the indentation at his hip where he flexed.

She also felt the edges of a bandage on his thigh. "I'm afraid I'm going to hurt you."

"If you don't hurt me, then we're not doing this right," he said, his voice a low growl, his fingers kneading the lower curves of her ass. "Please, Neva. Hurry up and hurt me."

She smiled to herself, her lashes fluttering as she looked down at the contrast between skin and bandages and cotton jersey, at that between his body, which was so very big, and hers, which suddenly seemed small. And then she brought both hands around to his front. Right where he wanted them.

She knew that because of the words he bit off that were sharp and raw and filled with more feeling than any soft seduction or whispered pillow talk, the words of a pirate, not a very nice man. His shaft was thick. And long. Just as she'd known it would be.

What she hadn't known was that her fingers would barely meet around him. Nor had she any idea how tight his skin would have to stretch to accommodate the blood filling the head of his cock. The slit in the tip opened. She thumbed it. He groaned, a sound he repeated, one she didn't think would fade because she had no intention of letting him go.

She reached back then, cupped his heavy balls, which tightened as she rolled them in her palm. She waited for a shudder to course through him before she released him and asked, "Am I hurting you yet?"

"You're getting there," he answered, and then he moved his hands back to her waistband, slipped his fingers beneath it, and slowly pulled down her pants. "But you'll do a lot better job of it naked."

Cool air hit the moist heat between her legs and she shivered. "And I suppose now I'm supposed to do the same for you."

"You'd bloody well better," he ground out, this time reaching for the hem of her tank top and pulling it over her head and off. "God, Neva. You're so fucking beautiful. I can't decide where I want to start."

Her chest was aching, her voice shaking, her eyes blurring with all that the break in his voice made her feel. "Maybe by getting into bed?"

He shook his head. "I was thinking about getting to my knees."

"Probably not such a good idea in your condition. Especially since the come-along's outside in the truck."

He laughed, but then her hands were at his waist and there was nothing he found funny about that. He sobered, tensed, waiting for her to strip him. She took her time, not so much because she didn't want to hurt him but because she wanted this to last, this anticipation, this moment of decision, this taut sense of change.

She eased the fabric down his buttocks then stretched the waistband to accommodate the bulge of his erection. He wasn't wearing boxers or briefs, and so when released from confinement, his cock thrust upward, seeking her attention and not too proud to beg. He moved his hands to her shoulders; she bent to slide his shorts down his legs to the floor. And while she was down there, she decided to stay.

She used their discarded clothing to pillow her knees and knelt in front of him. He was beautiful, thick and full and turgid, a ripe plum tempting her palate, full to bursting in a deep purple hue. Or so he appeared in the moonlight. She placed her palm beneath his shaft, stroked her thumb over his bulbous glans, loving his texture and heat and all the sounds he made when she adjusted the pressure of her touch.

His thighs tensed, as if those muscles were the only ones keeping him on his feet. The last thing she wanted was for him to fall, and so she scooted back toward the window. This time he was the one who followed her lead, stepping out of his shorts, bracing his hands on the window frame, leaning his weight into his arms and looking down.

She locked her gaze with his, parted her lips, and took him into her mouth. His heat was the first thing she noticed as she cupped the head of his cock with her tongue, licked her way along the sensitive underside. He widened his stance, thrust forward. She took him to the back of her throat, her lips pressed tight to the base of his shaft.

And then she sucked him, pulling away slowly until she held nothing in her mouth but his tight mushroom head. She teased him, the slit in the tip, the ridge where sensation centered, the flat surface of skin stretched taut, the divisions on either side of the rigid seam. Licking away the salty bead of moisture he released, she wrapped the fingers of one hand around his shaft, used the other on his balls.

She held his weight, cupped one side then the other, rolled his testicles with her fingers, sliding one between to separate his sac. Boldly, she explored, finding the hard extension of his erection that ran behind and pressing against it.

Vulgar words spilled from his mouth. Sticky liquid spilled from the slit she toyed with her tongue. He clenched against her probing finger, thrust forward, eased back, setting a slow steady rhythm in and out of her mouth.

It was a rhythm she wanted to feel between her legs, and slid one hand to her sex, pressing a finger to the side of her clit as it throbbed. She wanted to come. She wanted to come now. The wait was testing her patience. But Mick wasn't having any of it. He pulled free of her mouth, hooked his hands beneath her arms, and set her back on her feet.

"My turn," he said, his jaw tight, his voice grating as he turned her and backed her into the bed. She sat, scooted into the center of the mattress. On his hands and knees, he followed her, crawled over her, loomed above. Bracing her upper body on her elbows, she drew her knees close, her heels to her hips, the thrill of the chase burning a trail down her spine.

Mick grinned, his teeth a slash of white in his wickedly gorgeous face, and shook his head. In response, her belly tightened, tightened further when his large hands covered her knees. She opened; he leaned forward, his palms flat on the sheet right above her hips. Flutters replaced her heartbeat; she could hardly breathe.

He wet his lower lip, captured her gaze and held it as he descended. He kissed her low on her belly, dipped his tongue in and out of her navel, caught the loose skin beneath and sucked it until he left a sexy red bruise. She couldn't remember the last time a man had given her a hickey. This one she would never forget.

And then he moved lower, his coarse whiskers tickling her clit as he made his way down. She wanted to close her eyes, to lie back and enjoy, to do nothing but experience his lips and his tongue, his fingers and his teeth. But he was devilishly compelling, the way he teased her with that brigand's grin, and there was nothing she could do. She had to watch.

Chin tucked to her chest, she did, scooching her feet farther out to the side, her knees falling all the way open. Mick drew in a deep breath and shook his head as if her wanton ways amazed him. She wanted to laugh, to tell him that was nothing, but he closed his lips around her clit, leaving her capable of only a moan.

He sucked her, licked her, dug the tip of his tongue beneath the bud and pushed up, catching her with his teeth. Her hips surged off the bed as he bit her. Her head fell back and she cried her way through the sting of pleasure, shuddered, shivered, shook. Releasing her, he moved lower, nipping at her flesh, drawing on her lips, pressing the flat of his tongue through her folds.

She'd been dying for this orgasm, *dying*. Yet it was too soon. She wasn't ready. She wanted more of what he was doing. She wanted to teeter on that edge for as long as he'd let her, to hold on and make this night last. When she looked back, it was as if he'd been waiting, wanting her to watch.

He held her gaze, slid his thumbs to her entrance and opened her, then pushed into her with his tongue. Her chest rose and fell rapidly with her effort to hold still, hold on, but her blood was running heavy and hot. Desire pooled in her belly; he found the spot and licked, lapping her up, drinking all that she gave him.

She tried so hard not to come, but her will was no match for her body. Or for his insistence, his lips, which returned to suck her clit, his fingers spreading her moisture as they slid deep, his thumb settling over her puckered rear entrance and pushing.

It was all too much—he was everywhere at once, taking her apart, turning her inside out. She burst, a fantastic pot-of-gold-at-the-end-of-the-rainbow sensation that went on forever. He stayed with her all the way. His fingers, his tongue, his lips.

He never left her, but eased her back to a place where, when she opened her eyes, she was afraid she would find out she'd died. Dear Lord. What *else* had she been missing? And how soon could he show her?

Stretching out her legs and the kinks from her hips, she groaned. "Can we do that again? Or do I need to change the sheets first?"

He sat back on his knees, his palms on his thighs. She

tucked her chin to her chest and stared. At the pulse jumping in his temple. At the tic hammering in his jaw. At the head of his penis bobbing and straining toward his belly. At the lines of pain etched in his face about which he hadn't—and wouldn't—complain.

Finally, he found enough of his voice to speak. It was gravelly and thick when he did. "No need. Unless you plan to spend half the night doing laundry."

She felt the spirit of Blackbeard descend. "No, mate. I plan to spend all night doing you."

He didn't think he'd ever hurt in his life the way he was hurting now. A wrong move of his torso left his ribs protesting. A wrong move elsewhere and tape pulled, scabs tore, bruises ached as if they were as blue as his balls. Not to mention his cock, which he swore was about to split its skin. And the woman expected him to keep pace with her all night.

Good thing it took more than pain to keep him down. He crawled up over her, loving the way she tried not to shiver but couldn't stop the aftershocks. She giggled, a nervous, manic twitter.

He wanted to laugh because she tickled him so, but he didn't. Laughing hurt, and the reminder of his condition pissed him off. She had the most amazing tits and he couldn't even straddle her chest and fuck them.

Instead, he rolled onto his back and patted his abs. "Get up here and ride me like a pony."

She turned to her side, propped herself up on her elbow, reached down and wrapped her fingers around the base of his cock. "I take it back. You deserved to be treated in the large animal suite. You are hung like no pony I know."

He grew what felt like another three inches. And then he growled, "Do I need to remind you of the fact that I'm not a very nice man?"

"You don't scare me, Mick Savin." She said it, and then she was the one hovering above him, the one crawling around the bed on her hands and knees with her gorgeous ass in the air. "You or your big bad gun. In fact"—she was kneeling between his legs now, her hands underneath his thighs, pushing up—"I think you're the nicest man I know."

She leaned forward, flicked her tongue over the head of his cock. He thrust upward, filled her mouth. It was like she'd taken lessons, the way she sucked him, the way she knew where he wanted her thumb as she held him, where he wanted her lips and her tongue.

He opened his legs wider. Smart woman that she was, she took the hint, licking her way down his rod to his nuts, which were ready to crack. And then her fingertips found their way to his back door and knocked.

He couldn't take any more. He hooked his heels around her thighs and pulled her up his body. Canary feathers fluttering when she smiled. She climbed over him and leaned forward. He grabbed her tits and buried his face between them, breathing her in, loving the way she smelled. Like clean skin and sunshine and summer in the wind.

All the things missing in his life were right here. She was everything he wanted and never thought he'd find. The jolting realization would have easily brought him to his knees had he not been flat on his back already. And if she hadn't been nibbling her way across his collarbone, nipping him beneath the chin, nuzzling up against his cheek.

He reached down between their bodies, took his dick in his hand, and guided himself into place. She felt him there and opened, sitting back, sliding down, swallowing him whole. He throbbed as she stilled, throbbed harder as she stirred.

And then because he feared he was just about to blow it, he ordered her, "Stop. Don't move. Just . . . don't move."

"Am I hurting you?" she asked softly.

"Only in all the right ways." His balls felt like they'd

been tethered to the end of a paddle and slammed back up into his gut.

Jaw clenched, he glanced down to where the base of his shaft spread her wide. He didn't think he'd ever seen a more beautiful sight, his cock stretching her open, her folds exposed and glistening.

And then she milked him. Without moving a visible muscle, she clenched him, held him, her smile telling him she knew how close he was to coming. He wondered if she'd take it in her mouth if he asked. He wondered if she'd lift that ass in the air and let him have her from behind.

He wondered why the bloody hell he was painting mental pictures of the ways he wanted to spend the rest of the night instead of making her come again now.

Reaching down, he thumbed her clit where the hard nub stood at attention. She wrapped her arms around his uplifted knees and rotated her hips, grinding down hard against him. Eyes closed, she bit at her lower lip and rode him up and down until he began to pump.

He watched the slide of his shaft in and out, watched her breasts bounce, her hair swing free. He'd always been so strong; she reduced him to rubble. A tingling, tickling surge of heat coiled at the base of his spine and sparked. That was it. He was bloody well done.

He held her by the hips and drove upward, groaning as he came. She cried out as she followed, falling forward and bracing her hands above his shoulders on the bed. She continued to crush their bodies together, continued to belly dance, to rub her clit against his shaft, to squeeze him, grip him, wring him dry.

"Mick," she panted. "Oh my god." And then she pulled free and slid onto the mattress at his side. "That's one hell of a pony."

He chuckled, smiled; it was all he could do. Sweat coated his body. His pulse thundered. His fingers and toes tingled as the blood that had been elsewhere flowed back. Still, his dick stood at half-mast. Five minutes, he'd be ready to go again. To spend the night with Neva riding him like she'd promised, working him and wearing him out until both of them went blind. She was worth it.

She was worth everything. Even the sharp stabbing pain to his heart. And when she curled up against him, tucked her head beneath his chin, her hair smelling like wildflowers and feeling like strands of Indian silk, he wondered how he was going to tell her that he had to leave.

The sun waved streamers of red, orange, and yellow through the Munroes' kitchen window, sparkling off the faucet and stove front and countertops, which Jeanne always kept spotlessly clean. Yancey should've been at the office by now instead of sitting around thinking about his family. But they were all he had on his mind.

He'd had a hell of a short weekend, a hell of a messy weekend. Ever since Friday he'd been waiting for Monday to roll around. Start over. New beginning. Make it all up to Spencer and Jeanne. Prove that he really wasn't a big bad ogre. More like a teddy bear with a couple of tears.

But he'd been dragging the trash from the cans at the back of the house out to the burning bin before daylight when his eye had been caught by a shimmering piece of turquoise lace. It wasn't anything he remembered ever seeing his wife wear and, well, curiosity killed the cat.

Bikini panties and a push-up bra. At least what was left of the lingerie. Not Jeanne's style, and he was pretty damn sure neither piece was her size. Which meant he was going to have to have a come-to-Jesus meeting over breakfast with his son—not the foot on which he wanted to start off the day or the week. Especially since the last time he'd seen the boy he'd been dodging Spencer's fist.

When Jeanne had finally come home from Jonnie's on

Saturday night, she'd climbed into bed beside him and told him about Spencer slamming through the house earlier in the day and holing up in his room ever since. Yancey hadn't been much interested in Spencer, only in getting his wife's nightgown unbuttoned, but he'd promised he'd talk to the boy.

On Sunday, by the time he'd come downstairs to find Jeanne making eggs with biscuits and red-eye gravy, it had been too late for church and the boy had been gone. Telling his mother earlier he and his friends would be out at the Bremmer place most of the day.

That was okay with Yancey. The boy was helping out a man in need and that was as good as going to church in his book. But then this morning, Monday morning, and the trash, and there wasn't much good at all in what Yancey had found.

He wasn't trained in forensics but he knew enough to differentiate between a slice and a rip or a tear. The garments had been stabbed or slit, and that brought to mind too much of what had happened to Jeanne almost twenty years ago.

He wasn't going to sit back and have Spencer disrespecting, mistreating, or harming any woman. He wanted to date Candy Roman, the boy would damn well be a gentleman about what they did together. Rough play was one thing. The blade of a knife was another.

At the sound of Spencer's heavy boots pounding down the stairs, Yancey palmed his coffee mug and looked up. "Your mother's still sleeping. You might want to keep the noise down."

"Sorry." Spencer trudged toward the refrigerator, grabbed milk and orange juice in one arm, then raided the pantry for the Raisin Bran and the Rice Krispies. He dropped the lot on the table where the night before his mother had set out his glass, spoon, and bowl.

"What's on your calendar for today?" Yancey asked. The boy had been working odd jobs since graduation, picking up spending money here and there, enough to keep his truck running good enough to get him to Lubbock next month.

"I'm doing the yard around the post office this morning. It's grown up pretty high in the back. Then I'm checking in with Doc Hill. He has some cleanup he needs done around the clinic. Trash to burn. Stuff like that."

Yancey watched as Spencer poured the two cereals into the same bowl and flooded the mixture with milk. "Look, about Friday night—"

"It's done. It's over. I don't want to talk about it." And now he couldn't because he'd shoveled his mouth full of food.

Talking wasn't exactly on Yancey's list of fun things to do either, but they needed to get this out of the way. "It had been a long day. I'm sorry it went sour. I took a lot of crap out on you that I shouldn't have."

Spencer nodded, shrugged, and filled his glass with orange juice, keeping his gaze averted, avoiding the situation, the subject matter, everything but that noisy cereal blabbering away in his bowl.

Yancey felt his frustration rise. Yeah, he'd screwed up. But he wasn't the bad guy here. He was just a father doing his job, raising his son to be a responsible man. "Here's the thing, Spencer—"

Spencer groaned. "Do we have to do this now? I'm already running late."

"You're goddamn tooting we have to do this now." Yancey reached into the seat of the chair behind the table and grabbed up the trashed lingerie. He slammed the pieces down on the table so hard milk sloshed out of Spencer's bowl.

"We have to do this now because I want to know what the hell you think you're doing taking a knife to a woman's clothes."

Fourteen

Spoon in hand, Spencer stared down. "Where did you get those?"

"Right where you left them. In the trash."

Seconds clicked by, and then he dug back into his cereal. A petulant child blindsided by the error of his ways. "Did you think maybe they were there for a reason? Like I didn't want to see them again?"

"Well, you're seeing them now, aren't you, boy?" Yancey barked back. "And you're going to tell me what happened, because I'm not going to sit around on my thumb and let a son of mine hurt any woman."

"I thought you didn't like Candy," Spencer said with a sneer that didn't quite reach its full potential when he shoved a spoon in his mouth.

Yancey took a deep breath. "What I don't like is your smart mouth, for one thing. For another . . ." Shit. He didn't even know what to say to the boy. He didn't know how to get through. "Talk to me, Spencer. Tell me what went on here so I don't have to drive out to the Barn and check on Candy myself."

At that, Spencer's shoulders drooped as did both corners of his mouth. "Leave Candy alone. I'm not going to be seeing her again, okay? She's fine. I'm fine. The whole fucking world is fine, so drop it."

In the past, Yancey *had* dropped it. Each and every time. He dealt with enough conflict on the job that he didn't want to deal with it at home. A big mistake which might have a whole lot to do with the bond he and Spencer now seemed to be missing. How they couldn't talk about anything. How they each walked out of their way to avoid the other.

That wasn't the relationship he'd envisioned sharing with his adult son. "No, son. Nothing's fine. Not when we can't talk like two grown men."

The kitchen clock ticked its way loudly toward eight o'-clock—the only sound in a silent room with Yancey letting Spencer stew, Spencer stewing, swirling his spoon through the milky mush he no longer seemed to want, keeping his head down as he did. "Since when did you start thinking of me as a grown man anyway? I'm pretty sure three days ago that you were treating me like a no-good kid."

Sighing, Yancey sat back in his chair, spread his knees, and crossed his arms over his middle, which he hated to admit was beginning to bulge. "If I treated you like a kid, it was because you were acting like one. But I've never once treated you like you were no good."

"Seemed that way the other night. Running me off the road like you did."

"And I apologized for that. If it helps, I'll apologize again." Funny how it wasn't quite as hard to say it this time, he mused before pressing on. "I let my temper get the best of me. In my line of work, that should never happen, but it especially shouldn't happen with you."

Slumped back in his chair now, Spencer reached up, pushed his ball cap back from his face, then changed his mind and pulled the brim lower as if he wanted to hide. "I'm not going to be seeing Candy anymore."

"Why not?" Yancey asked calmly when what he was feeling was a reviving blast of cold fresh air.

His son looked up, frowning and confused. "Why not? That's all you have to say? No 'I told you so,' or 'It's about damn time'?"

Here was where he needed to tread lightly. To keep this conversation from heading south. "I'm concerned about you being distracted. You've got a lot coming up this next year. I've told you that. That your head needs to be on school, not on girls."

Spencer snorted. "Not *in* girls. Wasn't that what you said Friday?"

Yancey's teeth clicked together as he held back the words his temper was raring to speak. "I know about being your age, Spencer. I was dating your mother and only a few years older when you were born. But I knew how important it was to get my degree. And the opportunity you're getting from Tech isn't one that comes along every day. I don't want you to blow it off or waste it."

"I don't see what the big deal is," Spencer said and shrugged, getting back to the distraction of his breakfast. "Your degree didn't keep you from ending up out here in Podunksville."

What a big fat cluster fuck this was. Yancey could tell his son the real truth, alienating him forever. Or he could tell the alternative truth, that Jeanne's pregnancy had taken them away from the life they'd planned together and brought them out here instead.

It was a twisted version of the point he was trying to make. But he would not betray the woman he loved more than he loved anything. "Your mother and I *chose* to live here. We wanted a simpler life after growing up in the city. This is all you know, son. Get a taste of something else before you come back here. And then if you do, so be it."

Spencer got to his feet, carried his dishes to the sink, rinsed and stacked them, returned the cereal to the pantry, the milk and juice to the fridge. Then he pushed his chair up beneath the table and stared down. "What if I come back for Candy?"

Toying with a rip in the tablecloth, Yancey took a deep breath. "If you do, you do. If you want to come back here and ranch, or even join the department, that's fine. I just don't want you to settle if there's more that you want. And these are the years you need to take to figure that out."

Spencer's head bobbed, which Yancey took as thoughtful agreement. Or at least he took it as thought. And then the boy pushed away, gestured toward the back door. "I'd, uh, better get going."

"Okay, then. I'm late myself so I'll follow you out." Yancey crossed to the sink, emptied the cup of coffee he'd never finished and rinsed it out.

"Uh, Dad?"

Yancey turned to find Spencer pressing a finger to the broken glass in the door. "Yeah?"

"About Candy and the . . . clothes." Color rose and darkened his face. "Seriously, nothing bad went on. The knife was, uh, her idea. It was a game. That was all."

Not any sort of game Yancey had interest in hearing about. Still, he appreciated the boon. "Then we won't talk about it again." He paused, swallowed, found his own gaze averted, found himself speaking from the heart when he said, "And if things aren't working out with you two, I am sorry."

"Yeah, me, too. I'm, uh, gonna head out now," Spencer said, and Yancey let him go, watching through the kitchen window as the boy who was as tall as he was, who had the same dark hair his mother once had, who would never know the truth of how much he was loved, drove away.

It was several minutes later before Yancey managed to

pull himself together in order to face the rest of the day. But then the eight-minute drive, which took him from the edge of town to the county offices smack-dab in the center, left him calmer than he'd been all morning.

The talk with Spencer probably could have gone better, but things that needed to be said had been. And Yancey couldn't feel bad about that. What he *could* feel bad about was letting something at home keep him from getting to the office when he was due in.

In all his years of working for the department, there was only once he could remember that happening. The day a six-year-old Spencer had decided to drive himself to school and had bashed Jeanne's car into the edge of the carport, requiring stitches across the bridge of his nose. Kids. He chuckled to himself. Hard to live with 'em, couldn't imagine living a life without.

Pulling his car into the small asphalt lot and parking in his assigned space, Yancey gathered up his belongings and headed inside. The boy had been the same blessing and curse he figured all children were. He was just damn proud to have had a part in this one's upbringing—a truth that nothing would change, he mused, pulling open the glass door emblazoned with the department's logo.

"Oh, Sheriff Munroe?" his secretary Kate called from the cart where she stood making fresh coffee. "You've got a visitor waiting—"

But Yancey was already walking into his office and discovering that for himself. He came to a stop just inside the doorway where a hand slapped what he knew to be an official court document against his chest.

"Wagner. I see you're still not shy about shoving your way in and making yourself at home." Yancey grabbed the paperwork and circled around his desk, finally looking up to meet the other man's gaze—and to be taken aback when he did. His visitor looked like shit.

Holden's pupils were dilated, his nostrils quivering, his hair standing up on his head like a porcupine's quills. He ran his hand through it again, advancing, his dress shirt wrinkled like he'd slept in it for days. "The Mitchell girl has disappeared again."

"Oh, really?" Yancey couldn't say he was going to mind watching this one go down, though the attorney's appearance suddenly made a hell of a lot more sense. "Is her family coming after you for legal malpractice?"

"Her parents are reporting her as officially missing. You have all the information in front of you along with a warrant signed by Judge Ahearn." Holden jabbed a finger into the papers Yancey had dropped on his desk blotter. "The warrant authorizes a full search of the Big Brown Barn and the residence of Nevada Case."

"And what am I looking for?"

"Evidence relating to Liberty's disappearance or the whereabouts of any of the girls who have vanished from the township."

"That so." Yancey settled back in his chair and unfolded the creased and rumpled pages. The warrant was real enough, and had him wondering again how far the judge's nose was stuck up Wagner's ass. "Well, let me take a look and make sure everything's in order—"

Holden snatched the papers out of Yancey's hands, slammed the wadded sheets down on the desk in his fist. "I wouldn't come here if everything wasn't in order. The girl is gone. My car is gone—"

"Did you file a stolen car report?" Yancey interrupted the interruption to ask.

"No. I did not." Wagner shoved one hand to his waist, rubbed the back of his neck with the other. "Liberty took my car. She was seen by your own postmistress driving it onto the Case property. I don't plan to file charges. I want both found and returned to me."

Well, now. Wasn't *this* interesting? Yancey spread the documents out on his desk. "Returned to you? Not to her parents? When I released her into your custody on Friday, it was because you said you were taking her home. To her home, Wagner. To her parents." He brought his head up, cut the other man with his sharpest gaze. "Doesn't sound to me like that's what happened at all."

The attorney paced the room. His answer chilled the room. "What happened after we left the Barn is between me and my fiancée."

Yancey wasn't sure whether to choke or to sputter or to vomit now before he ate lunch and the mess was worse. "Your fiancée? Liberty Mitchell? What the fucking hell are you talking about, Wagner? The girl's young enough to be your daughter."

"Whom I choose to marry is none of your business, Sheriff."

"It is if you're marrying her without parental consent. She's underage, you prick."

"I'm an attorney, Munroe. I know the law." Holden stopped pacing, stood behind the visitor's chair. "All of our documents are in order."

Yeah. And how many of them were forged? Yancey folded the warrant that was unfortunately not and got to his feet. "Too bad you don't know how to keep your *fiancée* around until after the ceremony. Or maybe it's that she's not as anxious to share your bed as you are to crawl into hers."

Holden lunged across the desk. Yancey dodged. The pencil mug fell to the floor and shattered. The desk blotter slid, carrying Wagner over. The attorney sailed headfirst into the chair, grunted, crumpled, caught his breath, and rolled up to lean against the back wall.

Yancey didn't even look down. He was afraid if he did he'd piss himself laughing. What a fruitcake. What a fucking moron. Marrying a seventeen-year-old girl? The man deserved to look like the ridiculous fool that he was.

Picking up the warrant, the sheriff left his office and headed for the building's exit. Stopping in the open doorway to settle his sunglasses into place, he called back to his secretary, "Kate, radio Jason and Levi. Have them meet me out at the Big Brown Barn. And check with Wagner in there. See if he needs a Band-Aid."

Mick was packing his Rover, having just shoved a chunk of antibiotic-laced coffeecake down FM's throat, when he heard the cars pull into Neva's drive. Cars plural. Lights flashing, sirens off. All three county vehicles belonging to the sheriff's department.

Jesus bloody hell. What now? Sunglasses in place, he reached up to smooth the sport strap around his head, reached down to ostensibly tie his boots. While he was there, he checked the accessibility of both his knife and his gun. This bunch of cowboys was working his very last nerve and he was in a Boy Scout preparing state of mind.

He'd spent a large part of the morning just this side of the New Mexico border, working out logistics with Rabbit for the other man to pick up that half of the Spectra assignment. Mick would do what he could on this end to find Jase Bremmer's connection to the money train while Harry would see about finding the clone brothers and the rest of their kind.

Mick had also arranged his own networking system to keep tabs on Liberty's movements, one he'd decided not to share with Neva quite yet. What she didn't know couldn't hurt her. What he didn't tell her, she couldn't unintentionally spill when the bad guys shoved bamboo shoots under her nails.

Besides, he couldn't tell her what he'd done without telling her about the Smithson Group. He wasn't ready to do that. His number one priority, however, was to make sure no one got to his woman.

Because she was his woman. And she had been since she'd hefted his half-dead backside off the side of the road. He'd been working on figuring it out when she'd cut off his clothes in the clinic. But that night she'd spent in his bed it had all come together.

She was everything he wanted, all that he needed. He was getting damn close to loving her, or getting as close as he could, considering he'd never had a taste of love anywhere but in a woman's bed. Until now. Until Neva. Until she'd doctored him and teased him and fed him from her box of Patsy Cline's fudge.

But he couldn't dwell on any of that now. He and his SG-5 partner had a hell of a lot of work ahead. And it was a damn good thing they'd taken care of business this morning, because now here came the law.

Hearing the screen on Neva's front door bang shut, he glanced over and felt a hitch in his heart like he'd never felt before. She was wearing boots and jeans like she always did, with a sleeveless and collarless shirt tucked in. The shirt today was a soft buttery yellow, and she'd left her hair down so that it blew around her shoulders as she squinted, bringing up a hand to shade her eyes.

She was a proud woman, not skittish or easily cowed, meeting everything head-on that came her way. He admired her, he liked her, he appreciated her for who she was. And he lusted over what she made him feel as much as he did her body. That was a new one for him. Caring for a woman's well-being, bearing the weight of that responsibility wasn't anything he understood. Neither was being cared for.

He wouldn't trade either for the way he'd traveled so long between assignments, wearing blinders so he wouldn't have to see how deeply the pain he caused ran. She'd taught him the value of life with the way she worried herself over his needs as well as the needs of others.

These boondock goons were going to have to go through him before they even thought about getting to her. He slammed the Rover's cargo door, ordered FM to stay put, and took up his position at the base of her front porch steps.

"This can't be good," she said, crossing her arms over her chest. "Yancey and both of his deputies? They've got to know about Liberty."

When a fourth car pulled into the drive as the other three parked, Mick was inclined to agree. He glanced from the black sedan as it slowed to Sheriff Munroe climbing from the first car and slamming the door. Two of his lackeys parked behind and followed, keeping their distance as he walked up to the porch where Mick stood.

"Neva." The lawman looked beyond Mick to the porch where Neva still stood silent, and pulled a document from his shirt pocket. "I've got a warrant to search your residence and the barn."

"What?" she gasped, moving closer and placing a hand on Mick's shoulder. "What are you looking for?"

"We now have probable cause to believe you're harboring a runaway. A missing person's report has been filed in the case of Liberty Mitchell." He held out the warrant as Holden Wagner stepped from the last car to arrive.

The lawyer looked like he'd tumbled through a washing machine and been hung out to dry. Mick ignored him and took the warrant from Munroe's hand. "I think you've already been through this with Ms. Case, Sheriff."

"The situation has changed Mr. . . ."

Mick didn't respond to the lawyer's comment. He didn't even acknowledge the presence of the other man. He simply held the officer's gaze and passed the paperwork over his shoulder to Neva. Seconds later he heard her curse sharply under her breath.

"Neva, I need you to step on out here with Jason." Munroe waved one of his deputies forward. "Let me and Levi take a look through your place here before we head down to the barn."

Feeling Neva at his side, Mick stepped to his left, grabbing her hand and not letting her pass. Keeping her there. Keeping her with him. "Go ahead, Sheriff. We'll wait right here."

Wagner pushed his way past the deputy. "Interfering with a police investigation. Sheriff, I hope you're going to arrest this man."

"Shut up, Wagner," Munroe snapped, turning back to Mick and pointing a finger. "She waits at the car with Jason. You can stay. What you can't do is impede the search or our questioning."

"No worries, mate." Draping his arm over her shoulder, Mick guided her toward the deputy's car and away from the house, from Holden Wagner, and out of earshot of anyone around. The deputy, Jason, opened the car's back door.

Neva sat, and Mick stood in the opening, one hand on the roof of the car, one gripping the frame of the door. The deputy gave them privacy. Wagner returned to his own car, hovering like a watchdog until Mick was ready to pounce.

A sharp tug on the fabric of his fatigues stopped him. He glanced down into Neva's face, felt a similar tug in the pit of his stomach. "I'm not worried about the house. There's nothing there." Her voice was barely audible when she next spoke. "But if they find the safe room in the barn . . ."

He dropped down, crouched in the wedge of space between the car and the open door, feeling helpless to do more than stand by. He was only just back from meeting with Rabbit. He'd had no time to process the smaller safeguarding measures they'd outlined. Only the priorities had been handled.

He bloody well hoped that was enough. That and the fact that K.J. had come through with a command for a remote system wipe. Doing little beyond mouthing the words, Mick asked, "There's no reason they should, is there? That place took me by surprise."

"I know," she said, and shivered as if she were cold. "But then you weren't looking for it. And they are. If they take a measuring tape to the attic, I'm so screwed."

He placed one hand in her lap, squeezed her thigh. "Can you trust me on this? And not worry?"

"Yes. And no," she admitted softly and with a touch of wryness to her voice. "I'm trying not to worry. But I am, of course. And I do want to trust you—"

"But you don't."

She placed her palm over his hand on her lap, stroked him, rubbed him. "No. I do. I think," she said, and gave him a tender grin.

"It's hard to explain, Mick. You're here, and I love that you are. But I've always known I'd be the one to bear the brunt of our discovery. No matter what you *can* do, that's one thing you can't change. This is my crime to pay for. My failure to live with."

About that much, she was right. If he'd gotten here sooner, been here longer, had a body in better working condition and a mind not on the fritz . . . yeah.

He was doing a lot of good here, wasn't he? A bloody fucking lot of useless good. Jaw taut, he dropped his gaze to the ground, then looked off into the distance, the view marred by Holden Wagner leaning against the grill of his car looking rumpled and smug.

Mick indicated the other man with a lift of his chin. "There's got to be more of a story with him."

"Holden? He's tried repeatedly the last year to get inside. It's been like an obsession with him. My house. The barn."

Mick looked over. "Your bed?"

She shook her head, caught his gaze briefly before glancing toward Wagner. "I don't think so. Our relationship has been either reserved or antagonistic. There has definitely never been any heat. In fact, this bizarre plan of his to marry Liberty makes no sense. He's the most asexual man I've ever met." Lips compressed, she shrugged. "A shame considering his looks."

That last comment was one Mick preferred to ignore. "So he's not marrying her for sex."

"From the gossip I've heard, he's not involved in Pastor Straight's church except in a legal capacity." She collapsed back against the seat, exhaling her frustration. "I don't see him buying his salvation with numerous wives."

"Then he's buying something else." Mick shifted his weight to his other leg, his nape tingling. "Like a ticket out of town."

"Or out of trouble." Neva's eyes narrowed. "What could a seventeen-year-old girl like Liberty Mitchell possibly offer a man like Holden Wagner?"

Mick turned to study the other man. "Or what could she be holding over his head? You've told me about him, but what exactly do you know about *her*?"

She didn't have a chance to answer. At the sound of approaching footsteps on the gravel drive, she looked beyond Mick's shoulder. He pushed to his feet, stifling a groan as he did. Neva climbed out of the backseat of the car, crossing her arms as Sheriff Munroe came toward them.

Hands at his hips, his calculated gaze taking in more of Mick than of Neva and paying no attention to Wagner at all, the lawman cocked his head to the side and spoke. "We're going to take a look at the barn now. You can walk down with us, but you'll both have to wait outside. Or you can stay here. It's your choice."

"I'd just as soon be there," Neva said, lacing her fingers through Mick's when he offered.

Munroe hesitated as if he had more he wanted to say, then turned away with nothing but a nod. He and his deputies started up their cars and drove the short distance to the barn. Holden slid behind the wheel of his own vehicle and followed. Still holding Mick's hand, Neva started forward on foot, tucking herself behind his arm.

They hadn't gone but ten steps when she said, "According to Liberty, her family's lived in Earnestine less than a year. Her parents moved there for their children's souls, or so she claims they say. She hates it and wants more than anything to go back to California. She was dating Jase Bremmer, and you know the rest. So I don't know much at all."

Mick's ears pricked. Rabbit's digging had produced intel connecting Wagner to California. His parents had been missionaries and had died there. It was a stretch, but Mick had worked stranger and iffier connections all the way to the ground. He'd work this one, too. But first he had something pressing he needed to do.

The conditions were finally right. He had time, space, and no hovering goons in the way. He pulled his hand from Neva's, reached into his pocket for the transmitter Rabbit had delivered earlier from K.J.

"Hang back a second," he said, and she slowed her steps. "Don't look at me. Keep looking down the road."

"Okay." She even brought up a hand to her forehead to shield her eyes from the midday sun. "Are you going to tell me what you're doing?"

"Later," he said, palming the transmitter, extending the antennae with his index finger and thumb. He kept walking, kept his chin and head up, kept watching as the other men parked and bailed out of their cars.

Only his eyes cut down to his hand. The transmitter's red light blinked steadily. Mick put his thumb to the button and pushed. The blinking stopped. The red light glowed, darkened, then started pulsing again.

That done, he whistled for his dog. FM looked up, lumbered out of the field where he'd been sniffing every inch of ground, and trotted out to meet them on the road. Mick ruffled the fur of the mutt's back with one hand, used the other to slip the transmitter into one of the slits in the leather collar, then started walking again.

At his side, Neva reached for his arm and held on. "Now are you going to tell me what you were doing? And what that business with the dog was all about?"

"No can do."

She jerked at him lightly. "Why not?

He covered her fingers where they gripped him. "There are some tricks of the trade mule deer hunters like to keep to themselves."

Fifteen

They reached the barn in time to see the sheriff and one of his deputies disappear through the side door into the studio. The second deputy, having finished his search of the showroom, walked out a few minutes later and followed.

A few minutes after that, Candy flounced through the same door onto the patio and growled, "Why are these people back?" she asked, shoving her goggles to the top of her head. "Did they *not* get what they came for the other day?"

At Mick's side, Neva started to speak before Holden Wagner walked up and cut her off. "Things have changed since then, Ms. Roman. This is now an official police investigation. The sheriff has a warrant to search the premises. I'd suggest you not interfere unless you want to face charges."

"Neva, what's going on?" Candy waved her hand in front of Wagner's face. "There's a pesky fly bothering me, and I didn't hear what you were trying to say."

Mick chuckled under his breath and glanced at Neva, who had to fight back a grin before she answered. "It seems Liberty never made it home. And someone in an official capacity managed to convince Judge Ahearn that even though we weren't hiding her last time, this time there is probable cause that we are."

"Jesus Lord, why can't those pesky buzzing flies leave a body minding its own business alone," Candy said with a huff and a pointed glance in Wagner's direction. "Makes a girl just want to swat 'em flat to the ground."

Holden didn't budge. He didn't say a word. Simply stood still and stared until Candy pulled her goggles from her head and turned back to Neva. "If you need me, I'll be at home watching *Oprah*. The sheriff and that cute Deputy Jason said they shouldn't be long. They're working their way through the studio and shipping center."

"Where's the other deputy?" Mick asked. The more cursory the search and the quicker the three finished, the less likely any of them would stumble across the safe room.

She pointed overhead. "He's in the attic. Digging through five years of files and other accumulated crap."

Mick heard Neva's alarmed hiss of breath before she quickly recovered from the surprise to complain, "That place is a mess unless you know what you're looking for. He'll be up there forever."

"Not to mention he'll come out smelling like a mothball." Candy shrugged—consummate actress that she was—then headed for the back of the barn and the door to her apartment, calling, "Wake me up when they're done so I can get back to work. I've got orders going on three weeks and I'm not happy about it."

Neva walked away from the patio and began to pace, leaving Mick alone on the covered porch with the attorney. He used the advantage of his sunglasses, staring until the other man backed up a step, stopping him from moving farther by saying, "I understand congratulations are in order, mate."

"Excuse me?"

"I hear you'll be tying the knot with the missing girl. If you can find her. And manage to keep her from running off again."

"My intentions toward Ms. Mitchell are none of your business, Mr. . . ." He waited expectantly for Mick to fill in the blank.

Mick didn't. He boosted himself up to sit on the nearest table, braced his boots on the seat, leaned into his knees. "No worries. Just thinking you two are getting a good start, both of you coming from San Francisco, sharing that background and all."

Holden bristled. Or tried to. He looked more like a leaf shaking in the wind. "You don't know a thing about our backgrounds."

Mick glanced off into the distance, glanced back. "I know you both were raised by religious zealots. And you both ran away. Liberty figured it out a lot sooner. You stuck around long enough to see your parents killed."

This time it wasn't just a leaf that was shaking. It was the whole bloody tree. "I don't know who you are—"

"But I know who *you* are." Mick pulled off his sunglasses, met the other man's gaze directly, and yanked him up by the roots. "And I know what you're doing. Give me another few hours, and I'll know what you did."

Wagner tumbled. A redwood felled by a mightier wind. He stepped back, unspeaking, expressionless, then turned and walked off the patio toward his car. He didn't run. He didn't rush. He just left, defeated, flattened, done in by the destruction of Mick's promise.

Neva returned to the patio, approached Mick where he sat, placed her hands on his knees. "Please tell me how you managed to run him off. I'll take notes."

"Trade secret," he said, looping the sport strap of his glasses over her wrists, binding her to him. "I'd tell you, but then—"

"Stop." She pressed fingertips to his lips. "You're already killing me here. You and all this private non-profit business making you not a very nice man who I don't know what I would do without."

He started to tell her everything, to assure her men didn't

come nicer, that she'd never find a good guy wearing a whiter hat. But the door from the studio opened, and the sheriff walked through, his deputy on his tail. The duo never said a word. They just headed toward the back of the barn.

"Candy's place," Neva said, and Mick pushed off the table to follow. He heard Wagner's car door slam but didn't give the man any satisfaction by looking back. Instead, he slowed enough that he caused the other man to do the same. Point made, point taken, and he'd never uttered a word.

When they caught up with the sheriff, it was to find Candy blocking her doorway, one hand at her hip, the other handing the warrant back to the deputy. "This is not Neva's residence. Nor is it part of the Big Brown Barn. This is my home, and it's not included in your warrant."

The sheriff looked from Candy to his deputy and back to the warrant, folding it and slapping it against his palm. "She's right. We're done here."

"No, Sheriff. You are *not* done here," Wagner boomed from behind them.

Munroe turned, pointed a finger, stopped inches from jabbing it into the other man's chest. "This is my search, Wagner. Not yours. I'm allowing you here as a professional courtesy only. Don't think that means I won't cuff you if you get in my way."

"Uh, Sheriff?"

At the question from his second deputy, the one who'd been searching through the attic and was just now catching up, Munroe turned. The younger man dusted dirt from his shoulders and cobwebs from his hair before shoving his hat on his head.

"What is it, Levi?"

Levi jerked a thumb back toward the direction from which he'd come. "The back wall on the second floor? It's not the back wall. I mean, it is. But there's an inconsistency in the construction. It doesn't quite fit."

"Bloody fucking hell," Mick muttered, hearing Neva catch her breath.

Munroe frowned. "Fit? What're you saying?"

The young deputy nodded, adjusted his glasses on the bridge of his nose. "The age, the materials. The rest of the attic is original. The back wall is more consistent with the newer construction downstairs."

Mick had to give the sheriff credit. Munroe ignored Wagner's gloating chuckle and turned. "Neva? You want to tell me what Levi here is talking about?"

She shrugged, shook her head. "I had different contractors in and out during the original remodeling of the barn. One of them replaced rotting wood in several places. I'm assuming that's it."

"Uh-huh." Yancey turned back to Levi. "Find a way through the wall. Take out a board if you have to. I want to know what's behind it."

"Sheriff, please." Neva stepped forward, her hands clenched and held to her chest. "Searching is one thing. Destroying is another. This is my place of business. My livelihood."

"Which is why I'm keeping it to one board," he emphasized, holding up one finger. "I won't make it two unless I have to. And I won't have to take out the one if you can prove that wall is just a wall."

Neva cut her gaze toward Mick. He heard what she was asking, gave her an imperceptible shake of his head. No reason to volunteer ammunition. Let them find what they might find on their own. He hated to have her place turned upside down. But cleaning up later made for a much better option than rolling over now and playing dead.

Neva sighed, crossed her arms, and said, "Do what you have to do, Sheriff."

"I'll take that as your consent," he said, and she nodded, though it hardly appeared a willing concession.

Ignoring Mick as had been the case since arriving, Munroe

held her gaze for several more seconds, seeming to deflate as he gave a go-ahead nod to his deputy and followed the younger man back toward the studio door. The second deputy and Holden hurried to catch up.

Mick looked over to where Neva stood hugging herself tightly and staring into the distance. Hands at his waist, he let his gaze fall to the ground, bit off words he never said aloud. He'd been upstairs in the safe room. The wall Sheriff Munroe was on his way to tear down opened into the rear of the dormitory.

Neva was aware of the same thing and obviously making a mental run-through of the room as she'd left it. She had no way of knowing nothing was the same. That he'd been there since she had. That the arrangements he'd made with Rabbit meant the sheriff wouldn't find a thing. And that much, at least, she deserved to know.

He crossed to where she was standing, took hold of her hands, waited until she looked into his eyes, then whispered his demand. "Trust me. They're not going to find a thing tying you to Liberty or any of the girls."

She huffed, a laughing sort of exhalation that he wasn't sure whether to take as a yes or a no. "They'll find the room. And that's enough. That's all they'll need. I'm done here," she said before she turned and headed back to the patio, not even waiting for him to catch up.

He did, and they entered the studio, took a left instead of a right, and made their way beyond Candy's work area to the main staircase rising to the barn's second floor. The steps and railing here were new, matching the build-out of the rest of the structure, the ascent less steep than that of the flight hidden behind the shipping center.

Once in the attic, however, the newness quickly wore off and old took over. As they picked their way in and out and around a half decade of storage, the clutter of boxes and shelving and bins, Mick realized how an addition to the main structure could easily stand out. And when they reached it, how much it did.

"I can't believe this," Neva muttered at his side, standing back and watching the young deputy take a crowbar to a vertical two-by-eight in the center of the wall. "I was looking for an old order of Candy's, digging through boxes. I didn't even think about putting them all back."

"Boxes wouldn't make any difference." The wall was aged, yes, but not to the degree of the rest of the attic. "It's obviously not original."

Neva looked caught between anger and exhaustion, her skin pale, her freckles in high color, bright enough to stand out in the overhead light that was dim and slanting in through the walls, spotlighting dust motes. "Why didn't I paint it or stain it or something?"

The woman amazed him, the way she never gave herself a break. The way she had to take all the blame, carry all the burden. The way she leaned on him one minute, seemed to forget in the next that he was there to help.

"That's not a hard one, Neva. You were more concerned with what was going on on the other side." A *what*, Mick realized straight away, that everyone and their daddy was another two-by-eight from finding out.

The deputy handed the first board to the sheriff, who authorized a second to be pried away. A third followed, the gap wide enough now for even Munroe to wedge through once his underling used the crowbar to pull back the layers of cotton candy insulation.

Or it would've been wide enough. Except then Levi ran into the back side of the Sheetrock. The sheriff shook his head, turned to look at Neva. "You still telling me this is nothing but a wall?"

"Looks like a wall to me," she said and shrugged.

He glared, glanced at Levi, and held out a hand for the crowbar. The deputy passed it over. Munroe took a step back and swung. Powdery white dust sprayed and settled as he swung again and again. Chunks of wall tumbled. The sound echoed off the rafters overhead.

Mick stood at Neva's shoulder and watched the dorm room come into view. "I cannot believe this," she whispered as the hole grew larger, wider. Then she growled harshly as Wagner peeked through and made a noise that sounded like an admonishing cluck of his tongue. "I swear, if I had my gun? I'd shoot that man right out of his ego."

"The cleanest kill's right between the eyes," Mick said without thinking, catching himself in time to shrug and add, "Or so they tell me."

"They being your fellow mule deer hunters?" she asked, not waiting for a response but turning back to watch Wagner follow the three officers into the room. "I guess this is it. The end of my road. I can't believe it. I wanted to take down Earnestine Township and go out in a blaze of glory—not through a stupid hole in the wall."

She started forward but he stopped her, pulling her around and crushing her with his kiss. She gasped, and he bruised her, but she quickly caught up, pressing herself to him and pouring him full of her fear. Her body trembled, as did her mouth. He even felt the shudders in her tongue.

He took it all, there in that musty, dirty, cobwebbed room, took her dread and her panic until he felt her strength rise, until he sensed her apprehension fade. When he pulled away, there were tears in her eyes. Soft ones that dug in and cut out his heart. She owned him, body and soul, and it wasn't what he'd expected.

It was nice. Damn nice. And it only got better when she took his face in her hands and told him, "I love you, Mick Savin."

He didn't have a chance to respond. She slipped away and into the safe room. He followed, pulling up the rear. Once inside where they joined the others, Munroe glanced back. The sheriff ordered them to wait with Wagner by the room's newly made entrance and not to touch a thing.

Mick didn't take orders well and touched Neva, wrapping his arm around her shoulders and keeping her close, telling her physically what he couldn't say in the middle of this crowd. He felt strangely impotent anyway, as if holding her was nothing compared to what she'd given him. But it was the best nothing at the moment he could manage to do.

They watched the three lawmen make their way through all three rooms, searching beneath furniture, through cabinets, behind appliances, above, underneath, and inside every nook and cranny in the place. It didn't take long. The rooms were fairly spartan. There wasn't much that couldn't be seen by just standing and looking around.

"There's nothing here, boss," Jason was the first to admit, coming back from the sitting room through the kitchen and into the dormitory where Mick and Neva waited. Where Wagner had pushed away from the same wall where they leaned, as if drawn toward Liberty's bed.

"Don't be so quick to give up, Deputy," the attorney advised, staring down to where a thin gold chain lay half-hidden beneath the pillow. Holden lifted it away, lovingly retrieved the necklace, and dangled it over his palm. "I gave this gift to my fiancée three days ago. On Friday night. After we left the barn."

Sheriff Munroe was halfway across the room when Levi called out, "Hey, Sheriff! I think you'd better see this." Munroe stopped, looked at the necklace Holden held, ordered Jason to collect the evidence, and returned to the sitting room as if all hell was breaking loose in there.

Neva followed, and Mick was right behind, arriving to find the sheriff standing and staring at the sliding panel above the desk and the wall beside it. Both had been opened. The lawman glanced toward Neva and asked, "What's at the bottom of the staircase?"

She brought the backs of her fingers up to scratch beneath her chin. "It goes into the shop. This is an apartment, Sheriff. Like Candy's. The cameras let me keep an eye on the house if I work up here during the day. I just don't like everyone knowing it exists."

Munroe didn't bite at the bait of her explanation. He pointed at both deputies. "Search Ms. Roman's place. Now. And go through the barn again. If the Mitchell girl was hiding up here, she could be anywhere."

"Sheriff, please—"

"And confiscate the computer equipment," he said, cutting her off, glancing over, lifting his handcuffs from his belt. Then, as she gasped, he said, "Neva, I'm afraid you're going to have to come with me. I'm placing you under arrest."

Neva stood facing Mick, the bars of her county jail cell between them, the smell of wet concrete and pine cleaner hanging in the air. Being here did not make her happy, but at least she had the place to herself. One of the only advantages to being arrested in a county with very little crime because of so few able to pay.

Right now, the crime on her mind was her own, involving Liberty Mitchell. Moving closer to her visitor, who Yancey had allowed in out of consideration to his wife's good friend, Neva curled her fingers around the cold hard metal and whispered, "Please tell me she's safe."

Mick blinked. That was all. No verbal assurance. No nod. She didn't need anything more. She blew out a heavy breath, dropped her forehead to her hands, relief rushing like rain from her pores. Dear Lord, how had he anticipated what she hadn't seen coming?

Why hadn't *she* thought to move Liberty out of the Barn instead of leaving the girl there like a sitting duck? If Mick hadn't had the foresight . . . Her head came up. "What are they going to find on my computer?"

He cocked a brow. "Not a bloody thing."

This time she couldn't take the deep breath she wanted. Her throat and chest constricted. Tears filled her eyes. "You did that, right? Blew it up somehow while we were walking to the Barn?"

Folding his fingers over hers, he nodded, his eyes glittering in the dim light from the bulb overhead.

Air whooshed from her lungs. "How did you manage—"

He cut her off. "It's what I do."

"Have I ever told you how much I like what you do?" she asked, wishing the light was brighter, wishing they were in some other place so that telling him again that she loved him didn't seem like a desperate claim.

He was too distracted; she was well aware of his clipped answers, concise replies. But she was able to catch a glimpse of the smile that flashed quickly over his face. "I seem to remember hearing something about what you liked when you were talking in your sleep."

"I do *not* talk in my sleep," she said, trying to tease, failing miserably, ending with a sigh. "How long do you think this will take?"

"Until they figure out they don't have squat on you? Till about now," he answered, his confidence comforting. He reached back, rubbed his hand over his nape. "How long till they let you out of here? You're the lawyer. You know what they can do legally."

"Legally, yeah." She released the bars, tucked her hands behind her, and turned to lean against the institutional-yellow cinderblock wall. "It's what they might do illegally that I'm not too happy about."

"I missed the necklace. I'm sorry."

Surely not . . . She frowned. "You don't think that's the only reason I'm here, do you?"

He wasn't ready to forgive himself. She saw it in the harsh set of his mouth. "It's the only thing connecting you to this case."

She pushed off the wall, schooled her expression carefully, gestured as she paced. "Ladies and gentlemen of the jury. The fact that I employed Ms. Mitchell for a week guaranteed her full access to my property. It requires no stretch of the imagination to then conclude that she returned of her own accord to where she felt safe and hid in my private apartment without my knowledge."

"Nice," Mick said, nodding and applauding softly.

"Don't worry." She closed the distance between them. "Once I'm out, nothing's going to stick."

His gaze softened. "I have to worry."

"I know, Mick." She wanted to break through the bars and hold him, to feel his arms, his chest, his heat. "It's part of what you do."

This time he had a harder time meeting her eyes. "I also have to go."

That one took a bit longer to swallow. But she did. "I know that, too." Her breathing steady, she smiled. "You have mule deer calling your name."

He grunted. "I've also got a rabbit."

She frowned. "What?"

"Never mind. I'll explain later." He stepped back, his stance wide, his arms crossed over his chest. "I won't be gone any longer than I have to. I'll swing by when I get back and spring you if you're still here."

She wanted to ask where he was going to go, how he was healing, but she didn't ask him a thing. "Candy or Ed can pick me up. I'd ask Jeanne but I'd rather not put her in the hot seat between her husband and his prisoner. Besides, you might be gone longer than you think. I figure you have a girl in every port."

"Just one down the road a bit," he admitted with a wink. "I'm going to talk her into keeping my dog for a day or so."

Liberty. It had to be. Thank God. "Okay then. Be safe."

He lifted a hand and waved, and then he was gone.

Sixteen

It was the next morning when Yancey released her. He wasn't pleased to find her hard drive wiped. Neither did he like admitting to the fact that by itself, especially lacking proof she'd hidden away Liberty or any other girls, the safe room wasn't evidence enough with which to charge her. But it wasn't until she made her argument about the necklace, the same one she'd made to Mick, that he finally let her go.

First, she called Candy, who hadn't answered, requiring Neva to leave a message telling the other woman she'd go ahead and call Ed. He was closer, she didn't want to wait, and she could probably get him to stop at the grocery store before bringing her home.

Turned out Ed was just coming out of surgery; he rang her back while Yancey was asking one of the deputies to drive her home. Candy had called right after to complete the game of phone tag. Of course, the day would've started out a lot nicer if it had been Mick instead of the doctor picking her up. She missed her Mr. Savin already.

Climbing up into the crew cab's front seat, she sighed and flopped back. "Thanks. I really appreciate it."

"Not a problem," Ed said, putting the truck into gear. "Yesterday must've been a hell of a day. You should've called me when the sheriff got there. You didn't need to go through that alone."

She wanted to roll her eyes but didn't. "There wasn't time. And truly, there wasn't anything you could have done. Besides, I wasn't alone." She took a deep breath. "Mick was there."

Ed pulled up to Pit Stop's one red light and they sat and idled in silence. A silence that was tense and uncomfortable, but one with which she could deal. After all, she'd just spent the night in a jail cell. There wasn't much that could get to her today.

The light changed and Ed accelerated. "I guess that was it then, wasn't it? The end of the Big Brown Barn."

"In its current incarnation?" She shrugged, laced her fingers, propped her hands in her lap. "Maybe. We've always known it could happen. But no. We're not done. At least not permanently."

"Ah, now that's better," he said, reaching for the AC's temperature control and notching it up. "More like the woman with a cause that I know."

Please don't say it. Please don't say it. She couldn't take it if he added "love." "Listen, do you mind taking me by the market?" she asked. "I never did get my groceries bought yesterday."

He glanced over. "What? You couldn't find time for shopping between all your criminal activities?"

"Something like that," she answered, humoring him when he wasn't very funny at all.

"Sure. But are you in a big hurry?" he asked. "I wanted to show you something. It's a bit of a drive."

She was dying to spend about an hour in the shower. But she wasn't the least bit anxious to see what sort of mess she'd be returning to clean up. And Mick wasn't there, so indulging Ed now would be more palatable than putting him off later. "I guess there's no rush. What is it?"

"A piece of property I'm considering buying," he said, making the turn onto the state road that led out of town.

Interesting. She wondered where that had come from. "And you just decided this today?"

He shook his head. "I've been thinking about it for awhile. But I thought with the Barn being compromised, this might be the perfect time to jump. I could eventually move the clinic. We could build another shelter."

It was something to consider, getting right back to work. On the other hand, if she told Ed she was taking a break, putting some time between this incident and what she decided to do in the future, she might find a way to weed him out of the operation.

Giving up the work she and Candy had come here to do wasn't an option. The hiatus, however, was. The reorganization was. They could make their way further underground. Tighten the network. Get rid of the control freak at her side.

She stared out the window as Ed drove, realizing what an opportunity she'd just been presented. And if she and Candy weren't the mothers of all invention when it came to turning bad into good . . .

Several minutes later, Neva found herself frowning as Ed put on his blinker, felt a strange rush of adrenaline as he slowed and made the turn. "Ed. This is Holden Wagner's property."

"I know." Ed chuckled beneath his breath. "He's thinking of selling it. Seemed like poetic justice to be the one to snap it up."

He'd heard Holden was selling? Since when? "That's strange. I'd heard he was thinking of building on it. He had huge plans for a house."

"He thought he'd be marrying Liberty." The truck bounced over the property's cattle guard. "A man's plans change when he doesn't get what he wants."

Something wasn't right here. Obviously Ed knew about Liberty's disappearance. That was the reason Neva had been in jail.

She brought her fingers up to rub beneath her chin. A frisson of unpleasant anticipation buzzed along her skin. "I didn't know his plans to marry Liberty had changed. I'm sure she'll be found soon enough."

"Maybe," he said, his tone indifferent, flat, then distracted. "But it will still be too late for Wagner."

Neva grabbed for the armrest as the truck bumped along the rutted drive, her pulse pounding from more than the shock of the ride. "Ed, what's going on here?"

"Tell me something, Nevada." He swerved off the dirt road and into the rocky pasture, sending her sprawling into the door. "What do you see in Mick Savin that you don't see in me?"

Okay. Now she *knew* something wasn't right here. In fact, it was very, very wrong. She pushed up slowly, one hand hovering near the door handle, the other settling on the button of her seat belt release.

"What are you talking about?" she asked, her heart bouncing between her chest and her throat. "What does Mick have to do with anything?"

"Nothing, really. I'm just curious." He adjusted the AC's temperature again. She saw the sheen of sweat on his forearm and the back of his hand. "I've been working for over a year to figure out why you stopped sleeping with me. And then he shows up out of nowhere. He sticks around for no obvious reason. It's got to be about getting in your pants."

She'd had enough. This was getting weird and scary, and she didn't like weird and scary when she didn't have her gun. "Ed, take me home. I've seen Holden's property. And I'll pick up my groceries later. I've just spent the night in jail, for God's sake. I need sleep. I need food. I need a shower. I don't have time for your games."

"You have time, Nevada. Your boyfriend left town yesterday and your girlfriend knows you're safe with me. You don't have anywhere you need to be. Besides, there's more to the property than what you can see from here."

What did he mean, she didn't have anywhere to be? And how did he know about Mick and Candy? He was so perfectly stoic, so strangely calm . . . "Ed, what are you—"

"Goddamn, Nevada. Would you shut the hell up?" he erupted then, reaching beneath his seat and pulling out a handgun he brandished in her direction. "I don't know why you have such a hard time letting someone else call the shots. I have something to show you. And I'm taking you to see it whether you like it or not."

Don't panic. Breathe in. Breathe out. Breathe in. Breathe out. God, what was happening here? "You're kidnapping me because I broke off our relationship?"

He laughed, a flat, cool sound. "Oh, no. This isn't a kidnapping. It's retribution, and it's been a year in the making."

Now she was panicked. Her gaze darted from the gun to the door handle to the rocky terrain ahead. "Ed. What have you done?"

"It's the oldest cliché in the book, Nevada." He spun the wheel, brought the truck to a stop. "I've made sure since I can't have you, no man can."

He shut off the engine and ordered her out. Since he had a gun, she didn't argue. She shaded her eyes and crossed the rocky ground he indicated, climbing up a small incline, stumbling, catching herself on her knees and both hands, damning herself for not paying more attention to where she was going. And for getting in the truck with him at all.

It was on the downside of the rise that she saw the opening in the ground. A small limestone cave, not at all uncommon in this area, carved out over time by the trickle of water through the cap rock above. One she was quite sure she wasn't going to like being forced into.

Because that's exactly what happened. Ed took hold of her arm and urged her inside. She ducked her head, straightened once they'd made their way around the curve of the entrance tunnel. The main chamber was dry and dark.

Ed pulled a flashlight from his back pocket, switched it on, and tossed an arc of light over the room. Neva cried out. Lying bloodied and beaten on the other side was Holden Wagner.

And behind him, in the corner, three sets of human remains.

Holden Wagner looked like hell. He sat leaning against the opposite wall, his wrists and ankles tied together, as were hers, his body bound with ropes to a rocky outcropping, as was hers. His eyes were bloodshot, his cheek bruised, his mouth crusted with dried blood.

The face of his expensive watch had cracked in a starburst pattern. His shirt and pants had both been ripped in more than one place. But it was the expression on his face, the eerie acceptance of his fate at Ed's hands, that frightened her the most. He was beaten. He'd given up. He'd lost his fight and his will. He was just as numb as she was.

And how could she be anything else after listening earlier to Ed tell his story? How the first time she'd blown him off, he'd taken it in stride. How the second time was a bigger knock to his ego. How the third time left him crushed, the fourth fumbling for answers.

Then came the fifth time, the last time, the one that set him on a path to settle what he thought was an uneven score. She shouldn't have been surprised to find that a man would think of sex as a scale for weighing a friendship. Not when she'd known men who'd used it as a weapon, others who'd thought of it as a game.

But Ed *had* surprised her. His bitterness, his rage. His ridiculously misdirected sense of entitlement, which she'd thought all this time was simply Ed the control freak demanding his right to be in charge. Instead, she'd been seeing hints of Ed the psychopath.

She couldn't believe the lengths he'd reached to get back at her. He was the one who had whisked away the three missing girls. They were pawns, disposable, the first step in his plan. He'd known she would worry—over what had happened to them, over the possible leak in her network.

He'd counted on that worry. He'd wanted her on edge. Her emotional state guaranteed she'd be suspicious of Holden when the attorney came snooping around. Ed had been responsible for that, too. Dredging up enough of Holden's past to shake him. Sending him in her direction, looking for clues. Making sure their paths crossed repeatedly.

It was all a setup. A simple case of a man scorned. He had used her cause to ruin her life, claiming her focus on her cause had been the ruin of his. It was a revenge he found fitting but a full circle she found made little sense. She had tired herself out and failed miserably trying to get from there to here as he had.

She leaned against the rubble where he'd tied the ropes that bound her midsection, pulled her knees to her chest, and wondered when she'd quit crying, only realizing it now because she had no more tears. She had never in her life been this exhausted, and wondered if she looked as beaten up, beaten down as Holden.

On the opposite wall, he stirred. "You thought it was me, didn't you? That I'd discovered your network. That I'd taken back the girls."

She did not want to have this conversation. She did not want to think about Ed killing the girls, dumping their bodies, planning all this time to blame her and implicate Holden.

What type of wool had he pulled over her eyes to blind her? God, but she'd been such a fool!

She answered Holden's question with a question. "What network?"

"The one Dr. Hill told me about," Holden said, and tried to sit straighter, groaning, grimacing, drawing a breath in sharply. "I knew you had one. That you were taking the girls out of Earnestine. I just never could figure out how you got in, or how they knew to find you."

Tears welling again, Neva glanced toward the mouth of the cave through which Edward Bronson Hill, a man she'd called friend, a man who'd been an associate, a man whose bed she'd once shared, had left. He had an afternoon house call to make, he'd told them. No doubt part of his elaborate alibi before he returned to do them in. At least his absence gave her time to think, to figure a way out.

Or it would if Holden would stop talking. "I don't know why you thought I would kill those girls," he said. "I've never tried to do anything but give them the best lives they could have. That's what I was brought to Earnestine to do."

She rolled her eyes at that. "I never thought you had anything to do with the leak. If you'd found proof of what I was doing, you would have rubbed it in my face."

He smiled weakly. "You're right. I would have."

She looked over, studied the man slumped across from her, seeing his vulnerability for the very first time and aching. Whatever he'd done, he didn't deserve this. Neither of them did. "I know why Ed hates me," she said. "What I don't get is what he has over you."

He squirmed to get comfortable, his face twisting. "It's a long story."

"We all have them, Holden," she said softly. "Why don't you tell me about it? Maybe talking will keep your mind off things."

"There's really not much to tell," he said, settling back as much as was possible. "I feared my past had come back to consume me. But it hadn't. It was Dr. Hill exploiting what he'd found out."

Neva glanced over and frowned. "I don't understand."

"My parents were missionaries. Did you know that?" He tilted his head to one side and considered her. "Did your boyfriend tell you?"

"Mick?" God, where was Mick? Why hadn't she told him again that she loved him? "He hasn't said anything to me about your family."

"He knew." Holden closed his eyes. "Not that it would be hard to discover. The newspaper clippings are archived. It was quite the sensational case. Two of the Lord's flock snuffed out on his altar. Their bodies discovered by their son."

"You?" she asked, stretching her legs, her shoulders aching from holding her arms behind her, her nose itching from breathing in the dry dust.

"Yes. Though that wasn't exactly the truth. I didn't discover them." He paused; she watched his chest rise and fall, watched him struggle to breathe, to cough without causing himself pain. "I was there when they were killed."

Time stopped. Her eyes widened. "You witnessed their murder?"

He shook his head, the heels of his Italian leather shoes scraping over the hard-packed ground as he shoved his lower body up against the wall. "I caused their murder. In fact, I helped plan their murder."

Her gasp echoed in the small dim cavern. "What?"

"It was a difficult way to grow up, trying to meet their expectations. I needed a chart. A to-do and a to-don't list." Holden's tone was wry. "Especially since what was right and what was wrong seemed to depend on what they'd discovered during a particular day's studies."

"That must have been frustrating."

"Frustrating I could have lived with. This was worse. Waking up each day afraid to step foot out of bed. More afraid not to. Uncertain whether the clothes I put on were plain enough, whether I should have added a tie. Whether a T-shirt and jeans were appropriate or vulgar. Not knowing if I should eat breakfast or fast."

"This was their idea of faith?"

He nodded. "Faith that an outsider would have seen right through. But I didn't know anything else. I was educated in the mission's school and only allowed to socialize with other members of the congregation. Which I did. At least until I was older and they hired me out to work as a stock boy for one of the elders. He ran a small grocery."

"And you finally saw the light."

"In a matter of speaking," he admitted. "Most of my coworkers were also part of the flock. It just so happened that I became fast friends with the one who wasn't. Ronnie was Mr. Robinson's nephew. His parents had been killed and the Robinsons took him in. Our favorite pastime quickly became plotting the downfall of the church."

He tried to laugh but coughed, a racking sound that made Neva wonder about damage to his ribs and his lungs. "Holden, if it hurts to breathe, don't talk. It's not that important that I know. I'd rather you be comfortable," she said, offering what little bit of solace she could.

"It doesn't matter," he said, a verbal dismissal of her concern before going on. "Nothing matters any longer. In fact, nothing has mattered for a very long time. Not since the night Ronnie decided to kill two birds with one stone. You see, if my parents were out of the way, there would be little holding the mission together. And I would be free."

A chill pierced her at the base of her throat and slid like ice through her body. "He killed them."

"He slit their throats while they were kneeling in prayer in front of the altar. The blood . . . It was everywhere. I don't think I screamed. Or cried. I couldn't." He coughed again, groaned again, unable to work into a comfortable position. "I'd hated them both for years. I'd dreamed of killing them. It was like watching my fantasy."

He paused then, stayed silent so long Neva heard the cave echo with his raspy breath. But then he shuddered, as if brought back to the present by his own thoughts. "I could've saved them. If I'd opened my mouth. If I'd warned them. I didn't. I wanted them to die. And I was an accessory because I'd stood by and watched and done nothing. Nothing."

What he'd lived with was a horror as bad as what she carried with her. What Candy tried to forget. What Jeanne never would. Yet this was different. Candy and Jeanne and all the girls Neva had known were the innocents, the victims, the prey of this sort of evil.

Holden *was* the evil. A choking ball of emotion—fear? revulsion?—rose in Neva's throat. She wanted out of here, to wash her hands, to breathe fresh air. To never again see this man's face. "What I don't get is why you would work for Earnestine Township. Why you would marry Liberty. Why you wouldn't put anything to do with religion behind you. With your history?" She shook her head. "It doesn't make any sense that you would be a First Amendment advocate."

"A penance, perhaps? A making of amends?" He rocked his head back and forth, closed his eyes. "I don't know. What I do know is that for over a year now, I've been threatened with exposure. I let the killer get away. I told the police I didn't know what happened. I didn't want anyone to know that I'd sat back and let Ronnie do what he'd done. That I didn't lift a finger to stop him. That I'd been a part of it."

He faltered, struggled to breathe. "Liberty's parents lived

in San Francisco when my parents died. I thought the notes were from them."

"Notes?"

"The threats. To expose me."

"So if you married Liberty—"

"They'd have to leave me alone. Harming me would be harming their daughter."

God, she was so confused! "But if they were members of Straight's church, why would they want to hurt you?"

"They didn't." At the sound of Ed's voice, Neva turned. He met her gaze and moved toward her, loosening the bindings securing her. "The notes were from me."

And she'd thought she couldn't hate him any more. "Why would you do that?"

"Because I needed a fall guy for the murders of the girls. I made Wagner nervous and he came after you." Ed bent, untied her feet, leaving only her hands bound at her back. Next he moved to release Holden. "The evidence will make it obvious that he bungled his attempt to put a stop to your efforts. You came after him. The two of you tangled and fought. To the death, of course."

It was like listening to a bumbling cartoon character. She couldn't even believe this was the same man she'd worked with and respected, whose advice she'd so often sought. God, but she had to get away.

What was it Mick had said? *The cleanest kill is right between the eyes.* Simple and direct. Just like the only option it looked like she was going to have.

She struggled to her feet and took it. "You know, Ed, I never figured you for an idiot. But you're the biggest one I've ever known. Another deep leveling breath, then, "I'm leaving."

Slowly, he stood where he'd finished untying Holden's ropes. "You're not going anywhere, Nevada."

"Oh, but I am. You're not going to get away with this, Ed. You're not accomplishing a thing." Bile rose like lava to boil in her stomach. "Holden's hurt. Since you're not helping him, I'm going for a real doctor. And for the last time," she added, "*don't* call me Nevada."

She turned her back on him, choking, her stomach heaving, smelling her fear in her sweat. She took her first step, took her second, took a third that seemed like the longest she'd taken in her life.

"Nevada! I'm warning you. I will shoot."

Then shoot! she wanted to scream. But she kept walking. And walking. Even when she heard the unmistakable sound of his gun's slide being cocked, she kept walking, and walking, feeling the warmth of the sunshine now, smelling air that was free of mold and dust, walking, walking . . .

He shot. She ducked, hurled herself to the ground.

She waited, felt nothing, no pain. No pain. Rolling to her side, she looked back. Ed stood staring at his gun, Holden lying at his feet, blood pooling on the ground from the gaping hole in his chest.

Dear Lord! Oh God! "You shot him! Ed! My God! What are you doing?"

Ed didn't move. He continued to stare, finally raising his glazed eyes to meet hers. "The bullet was meant for you, Nevada. I told you. I'm not going to let you go. And now you can add Wagner's blood to all of that already on your hands. I don't know why he thought he could save you."

He raised the gun. She tucked her body into a ball. Ed took a step toward her. She heard his footsteps. She couldn't move. Couldn't get up. She was going to die and she couldn't even swallow. And then she heard a thudding sort of ping.

Ed stopped, startled, a red circle appearing between his eyes, blood dripping down his face. He staggered a step in reverse then fell back. She screamed, scrambling backwards, sobbing as she got to her feet. And then she turned because she knew what had happened. She knew Mick was there.

She only had to wait a few minutes before she saw him in the distance, walking toward her, a monster of a sniper rifle held in his hand. His steps were long and sure, and he rolled from his hips as he moved. A fluid motion, graceful and lithe. She wanted to run toward him, but stayed where she was in the mouth of the cave, watching, waiting.

It took him forever, but she couldn't even mind. All she could do was watch his body in action. His broad shoulders, his chest, his powerful arms and legs. The sun glinted off his glasses. When he drew closer, she saw that his mouth was grim. And then he was there, holding her, hugging her, letting her sob against his chest as she asked, "How did you find me?"

He spun her around, cut the ropes from her wrists. "I called to make sure you got home. Candy told me Ed had picked you up hours ago. That you were supposed to stop by the market. She called there. No one had seen you."

His hands shook as he pulled her free and pocketed his knife, turning her and drawing her near. "The sheriff's secretary told her you left with Ed. Then Ed showed up for his afternoon house call. I caught him while he was there. And followed him here."

What? Followed Ed? "From New Mexico?"

He shook his head. "I choppered in. Picked up my Rover from the house my partner rented. It's got a lot of yard for that fucking mutt of mine to roam."

She cried. She couldn't help it. "And Liberty's there?"

"She is. So's Jase."

"What? Oh, Mick. Oh my god! You found him?"

"Not me. My partner, Rabbit. Harry van Zandt. He took over my assignment in New Mexico. Ran into a bit of a hassle from a guy with a patois and dreadlocks."

Neva gasped. "The guy Liberty mentioned. One of the ones you were hunting?"

"He is. And he's not." Mick reached up, brushed strands of hair from her face, the corner of her mouth. "He and Harry made an exchange. The boy for some information that will get Ezra closer to getting out of the situation he's in."

She couldn't process any of it. All that mattered was that he was here. "Oh, Mick. You're making my head spin."

A brow came up over eyes that brimmed with moisture and were as red as hers. "In a good way, I hope."

God, but she loved this man. "In every possible way."

He hooked an elbow around her neck and brought her with him out of the cave. "Let's get out of here and call the sheriff. You can tell me all about it while we wait."

Seventeen

Five days later

She was the only person Candy knew in Pit Stop who refused to drive a truck. Except for Jeanne Munroe. And unless she was driving Neva's. Which she admitted to doing a lot because she liked parking her own car in the building behind the Barn. It was half garage and half storage shed, where they kept the riding lawn mower and power tools—the sorts of things most people's barns were used for.

Today, Saturday, seemed like a Jaguar kind of day.

The drive from home to town took about twenty minutes. She didn't mind—not that she could've done a thing about it anyway—because it gave her time to think about where she was going and what she'd say when she got there.

Of course, she'd been working on putting the words together for more than a few days, talking them through until they made some sort of sense, wondering if they still would when she finally managed to get them out. Apologies had never come easy. And it was obvious from her debacle with Spencer that she lacked a Toastmasters' communications skills.

Now that she was here, however, pulling into the Munroe's

driveway, it was equally obvious that she should've scribbled crib notes in her palm. She parked nearer the front of the house than the back.

Her door opened onto the sidewalk cut from the drive in an *L* to the front steps. The house reminded her a lot of Neva's. Two-story, white frame, heather blue shutters around taupe window casings.

The biggest exterior difference was the porch. The Munroe's was little more than a cozy welcoming alcove, too small for a swing or a railing. She smoothed her palms down her skirt, this one knee-length and black linen, fluffed her bangs with her fingertips, checked the bow ties on the vamps of her Bruno Magli pumps.

And then she knocked. And waited. Making sure the hem of her sleeveless white menswear-styled shirt hadn't come untucked. She was squirreled around, looking over her shoulder at her waistband, when the door opened. She whirled back and swallowed hard. "Hello, Sheriff."

Yancey Munroe nodded. "Ms. Roman."

"I was wondering if Spencer was home and if I could see him. If he was. Is." Whatever, gah! She knew he was home. His truck was here. And she'd called his line earlier and hung up when he answered.

The sheriff pushed the door open and invited her in. "He's in his room. It's up the stairs"—he pointed toward the staircase next to the kitchen entrance—"to the left. The second door."

"Thank you," she murmured, holding tight to the shoulder strap of her bag. "I won't be long."

He shook his head, seemingly pleasant. Strangely affable. Maybe even . . . cheerful. "Take your time. I'm just watching a ball game. Jeanne's out picking up a few things."

Candy simply smiled and nodded as she crossed the room with its sofa and matching recliners, its entertainment armoire and dried floral arrangements, all done in oak and heathery shades of peacock and sage. It was a nice home, a comfortable home, exactly the All-American sort that fit Spencer.

Climbing the stairs, she glanced briefly at the framed family portraits, mostly of Spencer, and the athletic team portraits, all including Spencer, and thought again of how their backgrounds hadn't kept them from finding one another and connecting as tightly as they had.

It was that connection she'd come here for. It was one she wanted to test without making promises. Life offered no guarantees; she knew that. But she couldn't let Spencer leave until she'd fixed what she'd broken so badly. If she wasn't so tense, she'd laugh. How could it take her so many times to get this right?

She knocked on his door, took a deep breath when he answered, "Yeah. Come in," and did, pushing the door open into what her idea had always been of a jock's bedroom. Trophies and ribbons, posters and photos. And Spencer on his back on the bed, tossing a football into the air and catching it. Toss, catch, toss, catch—until he looked over and saw her.

Then he didn't toss anymore. He just stared, took her in from head to toe, finally cleared his throat and asked, "Whaddaya want?"

A better reception, for one thing. She closed the door, crossed toward the desk next to the bed, set her purse beside his computer keyboard, swiveled the chair around and sat. Demurely. Knees together. Feet together. Jesus Lord, she even kept her hands laced together in her lap.

"I wanted to see you."

He started tossing the ball again. "Look your fill. I'm not going anywhere."

Or so he thought now. "Good. I like a captive audience."

"I thought you wanted to see me. Not talk to me."

She clucked her tongue. "Now, when have you known me to do anything without talking?"

Ball in his hand, he glanced over, snorted. "That would be never."

"Exactly." And then she paused because as she'd suspected, everything she'd planned to say was gone. "Here's the thing, Spencer. I'm a mess. I mean, I was already a mess when you met me, but the other day . . . in my apartment"—she gestured with one hand—"that sorta made everything worse."

Spencer sat up then, swung his legs over the side of the bed and faced her, his big hands gripping the ball, his elbows on his knees. "I think I asked you about that. About dredging up all that shit not being the best way to get it out of your head."

"Oh, no, baby. I don't mean what we did." Eyes closed, she pressed her fingertips to her temples, smiled to get her bearings, and tried again. "I mean I messed things up with you. And me."

"I didn't think there was a you and me," he said, his voice pitched deep and low.

"I didn't think there could be." She opened her eyes and looked at him then. At his irises, which almost matched the green in the living room color scheme. At his lips, which she knew so well and wanted to feel again, to taste again, to see smile. At his hands, which appeared to belong to the football he held.

He had such a huge future in front of him. She wondered what she'd been thinking coming here. "I'm still not sure there can be."

He shook his head, stared at the ball. "I don't get you, Candy. I really don't."

"Then I guess I'm doing a damn fine job with the mysterious older woman thing," she said and winked.

"You're doing a damn fine job screwing with my head." He pushed to his feet, walked around her to the room's window. "If that's what you wanted to hear . . ."

She got up and followed, standing behind him and hesitating only a few seconds before she slid her arms around his waist and pressed her body to his back. "You're such a beautiful boy, Spencer Munroe. I never wanted to hurt you. Why would I when everything about you is good?"

He snorted, and he didn't touch her. But neither did he push her away.

"I'm serious," she said, slipping around to stand in front of him. "You're honest and kind and loving. You're fun. A talented athlete. You're also sexy as hell."

Another snort, but his face colored, and she knew the sound was more about being embarrassed than mad. She brought up her fingers, gently cupped his face.

"Hurting you makes no sense, baby. Not when being with you makes me happy." She stopped to swallow the knot of insecurity balled up in her throat. "And makes me think there might be more to me than the ability to string beads on a wire."

This time, before he frowned down, before he placed his palms on her shoulders, he tossed the football to the bed. Candy heard it bounce on the bedspread, but most of all she heard the hitch in Spencer's breathing. Unless what she had heard was the hitch in her own.

"I know you don't want to hear this, Candy—"

Please don't say it. Please say it. Please say it. Please don't.

"—but I love you." His Adam's apple dipped up and down as he swallowed. His expressive eyes darkened like a forest of pine. "I've never said that to any girl. Ever. And I didn't plan to say it to you." His voice softened and shook. "Not when you were always blowing off talking about yourself. I didn't want to love a girl I didn't know."

And now she couldn't see him at all because of her own silly tears. "Why would you want to love me now when you know everything?"

He slid his arms around her, pulled her to his chest. His heart beat beneath her ear like it was trying to hip and hop right out of his chest and into hers to dance. "You trusted me enough to tell me what you've never told anyone but Neva. I may be a hick and I may be young, but I'm not stupid. I know what that means."

"Then maybe you could tell me?" She laughed, she sobbed. She was ruining the makeup she'd spent so much time on.

She'd wanted to come here looking her best, to come here being her best. To show her beautiful boy that what he'd learned about her wasn't all of who she was. That it didn't change anything about the things he made her feel. That driving him away just seemed easier to bear than watching him run when he discovered her past.

"It means that I'm more to you than a good fuck," he said, chuckling a little bit. "And I think that means you're going to miss me."

"Oh, baby. I am. I so am." She pulled away then, looked up and smiled. "But I'm thrilled that you're going. School's going to be the best decision you've ever made. Well, besides dating me."

He gave a one-shouldered shrug. "I'm not sure it wasn't made for me. I play football. It's what I do. What I've always done. Just like you string beads."

She slapped at his shoulder. "I do a lot more than string beads, and you know it."

"God, Candy." A shudder ran through his body, and he hooked an elbow around her neck and pulled her close. "School may be the best decision, but leaving you is going to be the hardest."

"You have to promise me something, Spencer," she said, breathing him in, memorizing everything about the way they fit, knowing she'd remember forever his tenderness. "You can't think about me. Not about hurting me, or about how I'd feel about what you're doing. Once you leave, you're free."

"And if I come back?"

"To visit? Or for good?"

"Either. Both."

"Well, we'll see." It was all she'd let herself promise. She was young, but he was younger. Neither of them needed a heavy commitment when they both had so much growing up to do. But something less binding would be nice. "Spencer?"

"Candy?"

She smiled to herself. "Would you go out with me tonight?"

Canting his upper body away from hers, he frowned down. "Out? Like on a date?"

Teasingly wide-eyed, she looked up and nodded. "Dinner and dancing."

"Around here? You've got to be kidding."

"Not around here, no. I thought we could drive to El Paso. I brought my car." She stepped back, gave him a full once-over. Not bad for a white boy. "You'd need to bring a change of clothes. And pajamas. If you wear them."

He shoved both hands back through his hair, laced them on top of his head. "You want me to spend the night. With you. In El Paso."

She nodded, braced her hands on the window ledge and sat back. "Does that scare you?"

"Are you kidding? After last weekend? I don't think there's anything you can do to scare me."

Or so he thought. "Even telling your father I'm taking you away?"

That caused him to gulp, but then a wicked light lit up his eyes, and he grinned in that way he had. The way that reminded her exactly why she adored him as much as she did.

"You know," he began, "it'll go down easier if you let me drive your car."

"Is that so?" she asked with a laugh, thinking it might actually be worth crossing her fingers if doing so would bring this one back to her for good.

"Was that Spencer I just saw driving that Jaguar?" Jeanne asked, walking into the kitchen from the mudroom carrying groceries.

"It was." Yancey pushed back from the table where he'd been waiting and took the load from her arms. "You have more bags in the car?"

"Just this one," she said, shaking her head, frowning as he set the bag on the countertop, set the milk in the fridge. "Was that Candy he was with?"

"Yep."

"That's *her* car?"

"Uh-huh." He didn't mean to be abrupt. He just didn't want to talk about Candy or Spencer. Right now, the only person he wanted to spend the evening with was his wife—which would work to his favor if she wasn't worrying about the boy, he finally admitted, and took a deep breath. "She's taking him to El Paso for a night of dinner and dancing. I think she mentioned having reservations at Billy Crews."

Jeanne's hands went to her hips. Her eyebrows lifted. "And you let him go?"

"Sure." Damn but it was hard to keep a straight face when he knew what he knew. Or what he thought he knew. More secrets discovered when hauling the trash to the burn bin. And this was a secret he couldn't wait to share. "It'll do him good. He's been moping around way too much lately."

"Why shouldn't he mope?" his wife asked, carrying rice and vegetable oil to the pantry. "He's missed her."

Yancey dismissed the idea with a snort, stacking a block of cheddar and a block of mozzarella on a shelf in the fridge. "It hasn't even been a week."

Jeanne came behind him and moved the cheese to the lower drawer. "A week he's spent thinking he wouldn't be seeing her again."

"Which is damn stupid when you take into consideration the size of this town. Everybody sees everybody sometime." He folded the grocery bag, slid it into the narrow cabinet where Jeanne kept them. And then he took her by the hand and wouldn't let her go.

"Yancey!" she exclaimed, chuckling as he led her down the first-floor hallway to their bedroom. "What are you doing? It's the middle of the afternoon!"

It was, and he couldn't have cared less. Especially since he'd been waiting forever for her to get back from her errands. He never had been much good at holding in a surprise. He was amazed she had held in this one. Being married to the woman this long, he was usually much better at reading her.

He stopped at their bedroom doorway, turned and leaned his forearm on the doorjamb while he waited. Her expectant gaze raised to meet his; she was frowning even as she smiled. "Yancey? What's going on?"

He indicated the doorknob with a twitch of his chin. "Go on in."

"I'm almost afraid to," she said with a bit of a laugh, but she did. She turned the knob, gave the door the shove she knew it needed. And then she gasped, both hands flying up to cover her mouth. "Oh, Yancey!"

He'd never been the romantic sort. One of those shortcomings that he just never seemed to be able to overcome. He loved his wife dearly. He couldn't imagine having lived his life without her around. But showing it in the way women wanted had never come naturally. He was a lug and he knew it. Which sure as hell didn't explain the way watching her now had him choking up like some old cow.

Jeanne walked to the foot of the bed and stopped. On her dresser, candles burned from the holiday candlesticks, the only ones he'd been able to find. The rose petals on the bed weren't as plentiful as he'd wanted.

But stripping all the flowers in the arbor behind the house hadn't seemed fair. She put so much work into tending the bushes. The same work she put into tending to their son, to their house, and to him.

He couldn't have been easy to live with, the job he had to do, the worries she had to have brooded about, whether her life would've been better in Dallas, whether he would keep his promise to love their son.

"Oh, Yancey. I love you, but this makes me want to ask you who died." She laughed nervously, walking over and placing her palms on his chest. "I love this. It's a wonderful surprise. But now you've got to tell me what's going on before I start imagining all manner of things."

So much for his attempts at romance, he mused with no small amount of self-deprecation. He took hold of his wife's hands, so small in his own, so cool until he touched her, as if she needed him for warmth the same way he needed her to live.

"I thought maybe you had something you wanted to tell me?" he prompted, keeping her close while he rubbed her fingers, watching as she blinked away her frown of confusion and realization dawned.

She gasped. "You know? How could you know?"

He watched her face color, a soft pink that matched the petals on the bed. The fact that she could still blush, that she was still shy with him years later left him feeling like he would take on the world for her all over again. "You'd be surprised what tumbles into the burn bin from the trash."

She closed her eyes, shook her head, moved her hands up

and looped them around his neck. "I haven't gone to the doctor yet. I wanted to tell you after I was positive."

"That pink line looked pretty positive to me." He wrapped his arms around her waist and held her. "How're you feeling? Have you been sick?"

"Not really." She brushed the fringe of bangs from her eyes, one hand toying with the hair at his nape, the other with his shirt's top button. "Maybe a little queasy, but I've been blaming that on nerves."

"What've you had to be nervous about? Telling me?" His breath caught in his throat as he asked, "Deciding what you want to do?"

Both of her hands stilled. "There was no decision to make. You've wanted this for so long."

"Don't make this be about me." He wouldn't have it, wouldn't stand for it. Couldn't live with it any other way; it choked him up to think she'd make any sacrifice for him. "It can't be. Everything's always been about us. What's best for you *and* me."

"I have to admit I've been thrown off by the idea of being sixty-three when this child is twenty," she said in a soft whisper as she slid his top button through its buttonhole and moved to the next. "And it's not easy to picture a forty-year-old Spencer with his twenty-year-old sibling."

He looked down. Her fingers had reached the last visible button. She unbuckled his belt, unfastened his pants, pulled his shirttail free, and finished what she'd started. Once she had, she slid her arms around his bare waist, rested her cheek against his bare chest.

It wasn't easy to know what to do. He'd meant what he'd said. Their life together had always been about being together. Decisions made as a couple. Sharing the burdens as well as the joy. Parenting their son. He didn't want her thinking of this unplanned pregnancy as a debt she owed him.

"Yancey?" Her breath tickled the hair on his chest. "You're awfully quiet."

"Why now?" The question burst out before he could stop it. "We've talked about this. About finances and my job, needing a bigger place, another college fund, downsizing Christmas. The way athletics for one child, the games on the road, the booster club and barbeques, ended up replacing family time—"

"Yes. We've talked about all of those reasons. In doing so we also talked around the truth." She stepped back far enough to look up into his eyes. Hers were misty, and her mouth quivered.

His wasn't so steady itself. "You mean whether or not I would love another child more than I love Spencer."

Her fingers stroking his back trembled. "No, Yancey. Not that. Never that. I've always known how much you love Spencer. And I know you. Another child would never replace him in your heart. But what we didn't talk about was me not wanting to be pregnant again. That I couldn't face the memories it brought back. The guilt of what I'd done. To you. To us."

"What do you mean, what you'd done?" He used his hands on her shoulders to set her away, and crossed the room to the window. He braced a forearm overhead on the frame and stared out through the blinds at the street where they'd lived for so long. "You were a victim. One in the wrong place at the wrong time. And I'm the one who took you there. That's eaten at me for twenty years. I've wanted to turn back the clock more times than I can tell you."

He heard the squeak of springs as she climbed up onto the bed, heard her inhale the scent of the roses, heard her sigh. "I want you to know something, Yancey Munroe. I have never ever *ever* blamed you for what happened to me that night. We went to that party together. As a couple. If anything, I blame myself. Drinking as much as I did was a foolish, foolish thing."

Yancey turned, looked at the woman he'd loved for more than half of his life sitting in the middle of the bed they'd shared for almost as long, rose petals surrounding her, candlelight in her hair. He didn't think she had ever seemed as beautiful to him as she did now.

His chest drew up so tightly, he wasn't sure he could speak. "I don't want being pregnant to cause you to relive any of that. I have Spencer and I have you, and my life couldn't be any more perfect. I love you, Jeanne. I don't want you to be hurt all over again."

Her face softened. She patted the bed, and he pushed away from the window and joined her, cocking one hip up onto the edge of the mattress. "I've suspected that I might be pregnant for almost a month now. I've done nothing but think about what it makes me feel. I haven't thought about the hurt or the past at all. Only about the present. And the future. And you know what? I feel absolute joy."

He waited several seconds for her to change her mind. To add what she'd left out, but she didn't. She only met his gaze as she always did once she'd spoken her mind. He closed his eyes for a long moment, opened them slowly. She was still there, still his wife, still his love.

And she was carrying his child. He thought he would die from the flooding rush of emotions. "That's it? Are you sure?"

She nodded, grinned. "Well, there is the absolute terror of having to keep up with a toddler at my age."

"You're the youngest forty-two-year-old I know," he said as a smile spread over his face like daybreak on the horizon. "Except maybe for me."

"Trust me. You'll be feeling your age in your bones soon enough. You'll be running and jumping and swinging and climbing and sliding—"

"Okay, okay," he said with a laugh. He was going to be a father again. They were going to have another baby. It was a gift he'd never expected, and what a lucky man he was. "I'm aching already, if it makes you feel any better."

"I'll tell you what will make me feel better," she said, one of her brows going up and saying thousands of words she didn't need to say.

He understood her perfectly. With both his body and his heart. He undressed her slowly and laid her back, shucking out of his own clothes before covering her and kissing her and, several long minutes later, sliding into her.

And as had been the case for all of his life, loving her more today than he had yesterday, but not as much as he would tomorrow.

Epilogue

Two days later

Neva stood in the field behind her house, loving the sweeping sense of the wide open spaces, the beauty of the horizon and Guadalupe Peak, the feel of Mick's arms around her. She could breathe. She could think. She could lean back against the man to whom her heart belonged and draw on his strength.

He'd been gone for a week the second time, after finding her, putting an end to Ed's madness, bringing Jase and Liberty home. That day . . . It was hard to believe it had happened, though not as hard as it was to have experienced those grisly moments. To have turned around there in the mouth of that cave and found that Holden Wagner, whom she'd so long despised, had given his life to save hers.

To have been an unwitting victim of Ed Hill's obsession, one to which three innocent girls would never know they had sacrificed their lives. To have witnessed Mick putting an end to it all with one shot. So much unnecessary bloodshed in order that she might go on living. She would never forget. She would carry the weight of that debt forever.

Yet the hardest thing she'd ever faced was waiting alone

for Mick to return—strange, when she'd been on her own forever and had never been lonely before.

She'd known he had a job to finish that had nothing to do with her. Not with saving her life. Not with being with her. Not with loving her. It was about doing the things that made him who he was, the things he hadn't yet told her, the ones that he claimed defined him as not a very nice man.

She didn't think he could be any nicer. Especially after today. She'd been in the kitchen washing up from lunch—Candy having returned to work already—when she heard car wheels on the gravel road and looked up. Breathless, anxious, hopeful. The sight of his Range Rover pulling to a stop beside her pickup had done her in.

Sobbing, she'd slammed through the back door, knocking the screen off its hinges, and ran around the side of the house, launching herself into his arms just as FM had clambered over him and Mick had climbed from his seat. He'd whooshed out a breath and grunted; she'd apologized with kisses for knocking him senseless, then burst into tears.

She'd tried to stop and couldn't. He'd walked her out here and held her while she cried, as if knowing how much she had to tell him about who she was, how many things she had to say about where she'd come from before she would ever be able to ask him to stay.

She took a deep breath now and started. "The first time I saw this place, I fell in love. All this room to roam. No dark alleys or shadowed streets. I knew I'd never have to fear turning a corner. Or fight my way out of tight spots. If anyone wanted me, I could see them coming for miles."

A shudder ran through her when she paused, and Mick rocked her side to side, his voice low and gruff, his breath warm against her ear. "You can tell me about it, you know. I'm not going to leave because you've been through something ugly. And I'm sure as hell not going to judge you."

She knew that. Knew that she could trust him. With her

present, her past. With her secrets, her life. "My mother died when I was a toddler. My father raised me. I was an only child and he never remarried."

Hissing out a sharp breath, Mick tightened his arms around her middle, drew her back into his body until it seemed their hearts beat with the same rhythm and they wore the same clothes. "He abused you."

"No." She shook her head, then turned her face into his cheek and closed her eyes. "He was the perfect father to raise a daughter alone. But we did live in an area that wasn't all sweetness and light. And I went to school with a lot of kids who weren't as lucky as I was. I also went to school with boys who'd grown up being taught by example that girls were no better than possessions."

Mick stopped her then. Brought his fingers to her lips and shook his head. "And treated them as such. Or worse."

"Worse is an understatement." She thought back to the abuse she'd seen inflicted on her friends. The bruises. The breaks. The tears. How even though she hadn't suffered she'd still been afraid of the dark, where she knew so much of the damage happened. "That was where it all started for me. Too many girls I knew thought they deserved what they got. That it was their lot in life. I knew better. It wasn't. My father taught me that."

"And you set out to save the world," he said, swaying with her from side to side, rock-a-bying his baby's worries away.

"Not really. Not until Candy. I'd forgotten so much until she reminded me." Neva sighed, held tight to his arms, losing herself in all that he offered, everything he made her feel. Safe and secure and protected, and above all else loved. "And I knew then what I had to do. Even if I only helped a few girls. I had to do what I could to get them out of situations that might escalate, and away from their abusers."

"You did a good thing."

She breathed deeply of the fresh air representing her freedom. "I wish I could do more."

She fell silent then and Mick followed suit, doing nothing but holding her. It was all that she wanted. All that she needed. Being here with him forever . . . And then she felt it. A shift in the wind. A murmur of discontent. He stopped rocking her. And he began to talk.

"I've killed men for doing less than abusing women, Neva. I've killed men because they knew something they weren't supposed to know. Because there was the possibility they might talk. Because they opened a door into a room and saw a handshake they shouldn't have seen."

She wasn't sure which of their pulses she felt thundering in her veins. "Do you do that now?"

He shook his head. "Only in self-defense. Or to save an innocent life. If I take a life, there's a reason bigger than being assigned the hit. I work for a man who rights wrongs. I stopped causing them when he took me in."

They stood quietly together for several minutes, her arms holding his where he'd stacked them around her waist. Her head rested on his shoulder. His chin rested on her cheek. She couldn't believe it was the dog bounding through the field in front of them who had brought this man into her life. What he had done was in the past. This was their future. She couldn't wait to wake up to him every morning.

"Did I tell you Liberty's going to be living here and working with Candy? At least until she gets things together enough to go to school."

She felt him shake his head. "Her parents agreed?"

"She gave them a choice. Either they let her leave or she would file for emancipation. There was no way she'd lose a case once we presented the facts of her case to a judge."

"At least a judge not in Holden Wagner's pocket."

"Oh, Mick. I can't believe Holden saved my life." Even now, knowing she was safe, fear boiled in her stomach like a cauldron. "He gave his life for me. I don't know which is harder to live with. That or knowing what Ed did, and why."

"You don't have to live with either of them." He continued to rock her, to soothe her. "None of what happened was your fault. Both men acted on their own."

"Logically, I know that. But having Ed turn on me . . . He was bright, intelligent. Hell, he was brilliant. Yet because I didn't love him, innocent girls died."

"No. Innocent girls died because he was a twisted man. You did your part. You helped the girls. You got them away. They knew the risks."

"They didn't know this risk."

"No one knew this one. No one could." He released her, turned her around, cupped her face in his hands. "Listen to me, Neva. You can't protect anyone from a danger you don't see coming. Life just doesn't work that way."

His eyes were beautiful, a soft dove gray. "And to think I didn't see you coming at all. Yet every time I turn around and need you, you're here."

"I love you. I'm supposed to be here."

She shook her head even as her heart blossomed. "No one comes to Pit Stop unless they're running away from something or have nowhere else to go. Which is it with you?"

"That one's easy," he said, and smiled. "I'm running toward the only place I want to be."

They spent the night upstairs in her bed instead of in the first-floor guest room, because this time he wasn't a guest. He was her lover, her love. He was the man she wanted to walk at her side as she went through the rest of her life.

She'd thought it would be strange to bring him here, to show him as they climbed the stairs which ones creaked and would give him away should he try to sneak up and surprise her. She'd also showed him where she kept her big bad Dirty Harry Colt .45 just in case he did. He'd laughed and added a Browning and a Ruger to her collection, keeping the SIG for himself.

Once she'd promised she felt safer with him than she had at any time in her life—a feeling that had very little to do with their arsenal and everything to do with their love—he'd undressed her and taken a slow journey over her body, tender as he explored the skin he uncovered, erotic as he left her wet and wanting more.

He barely fit in her bed. Her full-size didn't have the length of the guest room's queen. She liked the cozy dimensions when sleeping alone. He told her she wouldn't be sleeping alone again anytime in the near future, and the beds would be switched out first thing. She'd smiled and nodded. It was hard to argue with a pirate.

And then he'd told her the story of his tattoo. Of a woman in Barbados who'd wanted his babies as payment. He'd told her no can do and given her cash. She'd laughed at the idea of him being a father. But only until she'd sobered and thought about being a mother to his child.

They had time for that. Weeks, months, years. Right now was all about each other. Learning and loving. Sharing truths and trust. He wanted to take her to Manhattan, he said, sliding a palm over her belly, his fingers stroking the line of her softly trimmed hair. He wanted her to get to know more of Rabbit, to introduce her to Hank Smithson and the rest of his partners, whose names he'd rattled off and she couldn't for the life of her remember.

She pushed him onto his back and told him she'd like that. But not half as much as she'd like seeing him wearing something other than combat boots, T-shirts, and fatigues. He'd argued that she'd seen him in gray sweat shorts, and that she'd seen him in skin.

It wasn't enough. She wanted to see him in Hugo Boss or

Armani. His broad shoulders filling out a custom-fitted suit coat. His eyes covered by Oakleys sans strap. His shaved head, goatee, mustache, and tattoo against the backdrop of St. Patrick's Cathedral. He told her no can do, changed it to might can do when she told him she was going to sleep.

Her cool cotton sheets absorbed his body heat like they did that from the sun when hung out to dry. She told him it seemed like she'd known him forever, not the less than two weeks that she had. He'd told her the *Rocky Horror Picture Show* claimed that time was fleeting, so she'd best stop counting and take advantage of his wood.

She'd slapped his ass, but then he'd tumbled her to her back and filled her in one never-ending motion. She'd taken him in, caught breathless by the sensation of loving him, his length and hardness and gentle touch, and always, always his warmth.

He'd stroked slowly; she'd pleaded for more, sweating beneath him, aching and needing and taut. He wouldn't let her come. And that was okay. She had more than all night. She had the rest of her days.

And she had the man above her, her own larger than life hero, to love.

Get ready for a long, hot summer—
and mayhem, mystery, and hot men.
WHO'S BEEN SLEEPING IN MY BED?
by Gemma Bruce is
coming in July 2005 from Brava . . .

Delia and Ben stepped out of the gallery to a gust of March night wind that lifted the ends of her cape and whipped right up her silk dress to bare skin. Delia shivered.

Ben pulled her close. "You should have worn a longer coat. We wouldn't want anything getting cold." He smiled meaningfully. "I'll get a cab."

Delia waited in the shelter of the canopied entrance and watched a woman trying to light a cigarette against the wind. She looked vaguely familiar; obviously one of the gallery attendees. Delia must have seen her inside. Oh yes, talking to Ben when Delia first arrived.

A cab pulled up to the curb.

"You're not waiting for a cab, are you?" asked Delia.

The woman shook her head and lifted her cigarette. "I'll take one when I finish this. Thanks." She smiled and Delia and Ben got into the cab.

Delia wasn't surprised when the cab stopped in front of a luxury complex that overlooked Central Park. Ben had several pied-à-terres around Manhattan. She had learned that from the real estate records at the courthouse downtown. She also knew that he took women to all of them, except the brownstone in the village. She had surmised that from reading several years of the tabloids and the *Post*.

She did remember to look suitably impressed when Ben took out a plastic card to feed into the penthouse slot in the elevator.

To judge from the lighthearted smile Ben gave her when they stepped into an opulent, spacious apartment, he was pleased to have surprised her. And she felt a pang of guilt at leading him on this way.

Guilt isn't your style, she reminded herself. Not anymore. And this was an investigation, not an affair.

She let him take her cape and pour her a brandy, though she was having trouble appearing to drink without really drinking enough to lose her edge. For a brief moment, she wished she could just enjoy her time with Ben and forget the real reason she was here.

But that didn't work. Men came and went. Even if they took six years to do it. This had no better chance of lasting than any of her former liaisons or her marriage. And proving Ben was a murderer would definitely put a damper on things.

She hardly had time to take in the heavy, dark furnishings before she found herself on the couch, drink put aside, and Ben's arms around her. A more experienced detective would be able to case the joint while making passionate love with its owner, but Delia was more experienced in love—well, at least sex—than she was at investigation. So when Ben's hand slid up her inside thigh and found its mark, she closed her eyes and gave herself up to the pleasure of the moment.

The way her libido was crescendoing beneath his touch, it would only take a minute or two before she zinged through space. Once she settled to earth again, she'd get back to work. But until then, oh yes, there. . . .

Delia opened her knees a little wider as his finger circled

her bull's-eye, each pass sending her closer and closer to the edge. She curved her pelvis to me his finger as it glided into her, and she circled her hips against it and against his palm.

She opened her eyes when he slid off the couch to the floor, knelt between her legs and withdrew his fingers to push her skirt up to her waist. He caressed her thighs and pushed her knees apart.

He looked up at her then, his expression smoldering with more than desire—with need. She tried to pull him up to her, but he trapped her hands and, holding them to her sides, he leaned toward her, slowly, slowly, until Delia wanted to scream.

Just when she thought she'd have to break his grip and grab his head, his tongue slid through the wet curls of hair between her legs and she shuddered uncontrollably. Now he moved, circling, licking, sucking until she was bucking like a snared animal.

He paused long enough to look up at her, his mouth still attached to her skin, then with a final exhilarating sweep of his tongue, Delia soared.

Wave after wave drove her upward. She was free. And still his tongue didn't stop. It was almost painful, but when she would have pushed him away, another intense wave pushed her even higher. She gave in, as she spiraled into a place where there were no confinements, no rules, no soul-numbing propriety.

"Worth the wait?" Ben's voice sounded far away and Delia realized she had closed her eyes again.

She smiled. "Worth the wait. Take your clothes off."

He stood up and shrugged out of his jacket, pulled his sweater over his head, unbuttoned his shirt and let it drop onto the floor. Delia stretched her legs until her feet rested on the coffee table and he was penned between her knees. Then she leaned back to watch the rest of his striptease.

His hands moved to his belt, his gaze fastened on her

open crotch. His fingers fumbled, then his belt opened. The zipper lowered.

Delia ran her tongue across her bottom lip and laughed to herself when Ben's cock jumped at her when he pushed underwear and trousers down his legs.

When he was standing before her totally nude, she hooked her ankles around the back of his knees and pulled him into her.

"You're—you're—" Ben sounded like he was choking or suffocating.

"I am, aren't I." She leaned forward to take his ass in her hands and his dick in her mouth.

Ben immediately fell forward until his knees were braced against the front of the cushions. He caressed her hair as she captured him with her tongue. She'd once been really good at giving head, and she got a thrill knowing that she hadn't lost her prowess. You had to really love dicks to give good head. And she loved dicks. Almost as much as she loved donuts.

Ben's hands tightened on her head. "God." Delia smiled to herself, but kept at him. His hands were kneading her scalp and he began to rock back and forth. She hung on, moving faster, sucking harder, clutching the taut muscles of his ass with her hands, her knees gripping his thighs.

The cry that wrenched from him when he came bounced around the room. Delia drank him up as he shuddered and jerked against her, and it wasn't until he was collapsed against her, his head on her bare lap, that she realized that his cry was more than one of climax, but held a note of desperation. And she was hit by a feeling of compassion that sat uneasy on her heart.

She wanted freedom and wild, abandoned sex. She didn't want involvement. Especially with a possible murderer. But she stroked his hair until his breath evened out and she thought he must have fallen asleep.

Just like a man, she thought. She eased out from under him. She'd find a cab on the street and go home. Some things didn't change.

She managed to take one step before an arm caught her around the waist. Ben pulled her down on the couch and sprang on top of her.

"Round two," he said and wrestled her dress over her head.

And don't miss Amy J. Fetzer's
sizzling thriller
NAKED TRUTH,
an August 2005 Brava release.
Here's a sneak peek . . .

For the first time in his life, Killian was breathless. The anticipation of kissing her riddled through his blood like a burning fuse on its way to detonation.

"I don't trust you one bit," she said and her words breezed across his lips.

"Who said trust had anything to do with this?"

"Like danger and death, two different things?"

Oh, yeah, he thought. A double-edged sword, sharp and dangerous—and poised between them. One of them would get cut. Killian had a feeling it'd be him. So he lived in the moment, breathing her in, absorbing every nuance. The heated fragrance of her bare skin beneath his palms, her lush naked contours pressing to him and making him so hard he thought he'd come right now. Jesus.

"Killian."

"Huh?"

"Kiss me before I die."

He did; like an animal devouring its prey, he took her mouth like he owned it. Like she was there for him alone. And the fire between them instantly raged.

There were no games, no sweet, tender desire. Only irrepressible power. Seething with hunger, boiling over with passion. He'd never known any woman who could do this to him. Make him lose control. Lose everything. Even his ethical boundaries.

He didn't give a damn either, and pushed his tongue between her lips. His own deep groan shocked him. Inflamed her. And she took back, battling like they had since first contact. The same struggle he'd felt in her before she unleashed the first blow.

His hands slid around her, molding the curves of her spine. The simplicity of the move heightened everything inside him, and his erection throbbed and flexed. Eager to be free, to be pushing inside her. God, the thought made him tremble. She wasn't being still, either—or quiet. Her eager whimpers drove into his bones with the power of a mallet, each little begging sound he had to hear. Needed.

His hand swept lower to cup her smooth behind, pull her tighter, and she moaned and thrust, then latched onto his belt, throwing it open.

"Alexa." He couldn't believe the question in his own voice. *Shut up and take,* his body screamed.

Then she said it. "Come on Moore, this is what you wanted, right? To fuck me."

Hearing that from her was just too damn ugly. "No, not exactly." Another shock.

She stilled, looked up, frowning. "Make love? Oh, you've got to be kidding. No one does that anymore. No one cares that much."

"I do."

Her eyes went thin and she pushed back. "I don't want that. It's a complication I can't afford. Not now, not ever." She snatched the sheet, wrapping herself, then started rummaging through the drawers for clothes.

Killian felt like a man tottering on the brink of insanity and scowled. "So you want to be screwed like a whore?"

"No, well . . . oh, forget it." She snapped a skirt out of the drawer. "You've lost the moment."

He reached, gripped her arms, dragged her back against him. "We can get it back." Slowly, as if waiting for a blow, she met his gaze, and he saw something he never expected.

Fear.

Of him, and whatever was going on between them. In a flash, he got a rare bit of insight. Exposing herself—the real woman, not the operative—terrified her. He didn't know why that excited the hell out of him, but it did. Nothing seemed to faze this woman. Running for her life, missiles, knowing she was on a hit list from hell. But a couple kisses left her this shaken?

He passed his hand over her hair, tipping her head back. "Let me try."

"Are you always this confident?" Her voice trembled, and she caught her lip under her teeth.

"In some things."

Before she could say anything more, deny herself this, he kissed her. Like mad. Hot and passionate and blowing any control she had right out of the water.

He overcame her, slaughtered her with sensations and Alexa's legs softened like warm putty as he trapped her against him with one hand, the other exploring her body with ruthless intent. She groaned as he enfolded her breast, and wildly thumbed her nipple, sending a pulse of heat through her veins, stirring every cell and making it scream.

Oh, God, oh, *God.* It had been so long since any man had touched her. Her. Not Jade, or whatever persona she'd had to wear, but Alexa. Part of her wondered if he was just horny and she was available, yet her body had other plans. Dark, lonely spots ached to be handled, touched, smothered with a powerful, sexy man, making her feel like she existed, and not floating between identities and missions.

"I'm losing you," he murmured as his hand slid heavily over her hip.

Between heated kisses, she met his gaze. "You started this. Try harder."

He ducked and closed his lips around her nipple, flicking and tugging and there was no time to think, no thoughts allowed to manifest. His hand was heavy as it rode over her hip, pausing to squeeze, then slide between her thighs.

Suddenly her world sparkled. Her legs gave out. He parted her and pushed deep inside, stroking her toward a climax.

"That better?"

"Oh, yes."

She breathed his name over and over and he watched her writhe in his arms, his gaze glancing down to watch her hips following his moves. "Christ, you're hot."

"What gave you a clue?" She peeled his T-shirt off over his head. The ropy muscle and wide chest were a playground for her mouth and hands and she licked and teased, kissed.

"I want you on fire."

"Then get these off!" She yanked his jeans open.

His fingers plunged into her softness, then retreated, over and over, never giving her a chance to catch her breath. Alexa gave in, and leaned back over his arms, spreading wider, then hooked her leg around his calf and unbalanced him. They fell to the bed in a tangle of arms and legs, and she went crazy on his clothes, pushing his jeans down and diving her hand inside.

Killian flinched when she enfolded him and flexed her palm. "Jesus, wildcat."

For a moment, he closed his eyes, savoring her touch, and Alexa felt the power of being a woman, sliding her fingers over the slick tip of him, feeling him lengthen in her hand. She wanted him on the edge, as helpless as she was, and showed him no mercy. She spread her thighs, urging him between, and guided him a little into her.

He trembled, pushing without control. "Condoms," he moaned as if it were a personal offense.

"This place is littered with them, oh, Killian, hurry."

He reached, slapping the end table and bringing back a handful. Alexa grabbed one, tore it open, rolled it down and made it worth the wait.

He quaked down to his heels. "Oh, God, woman."

"I want this." She guided him. "Inside me," she whispered in his ear. "Deeply."